Always Want More

Diane,
I celebrate you and
all that you do for students.
God bless!

Barb Apt Mc...

Always Want More

Banke Awopetu McCullough

Concrete
Rose
Publications

For Rochester

1

*"I gotta make a way. I gotta do this now.
If they don't know your dreams, then
they can't shoot 'em down."*

J. Cole

"Two Deep for the Intro"

TRACY'S FIRST DREAMS HAD been set in Harlem. When she was a child, February was the most enchanting month of the year. There was African drumming and dance and pot lucks with steaming bowls of greens and gospel concerts where mass choirs in sharp robes sang so sweet that you could just about see Jesus. The best of it was when black and white picture books were taken out and the Great writers were discussed. Langston Hughes smiled up at her in a tuxedo, his eyes twinkled with the dreams that he so eloquently wrote about. These dreams gripped Tracy's heart and would not let go. Tears welled in her eyes as she recited him at her first poetry reading. "Hold fast to dreams, for if dreams die life is a broken-winged bird that cannot fly." As she grew older she moved on to James Baldwin and Zora Neale Hurston and Alice Walker and Countee Cullen. The truth they spoke of stirred her in the deepest of places. When she closed her eyes, Harlem loomed.

So on her first night as a Harlem resident, she allowed herself the luxury of rambling around the streets taking in the Apollo Theatre and the old Cotton Club and the Lincoln Theatre. She was on her grind her first day there; she dropped in on unwelcoming receptionists and left her portfolio, and then sent thank you cards, and then she called to verify that they had read her work. After three weeks she crossed off the thirty-seventh name on her list and fought back tears. No one had even bitten. Harlem was not cheap and dreams did not pay bills.

After seven weeks and half a dozen rushed through phone calls with her parents, she no longer could stop the tears. She was reduced to lying on the floor in that room, stretching and pulling her body in an attempt to center herself. After another week, she ended up curled up in a ball calling out to Jesus. This had to work.

Two days later she landed an interview with *The Real*. She shook the feature editor's hand and managed to suppress her cries until she made it to the street. She jumped up and down. "Thank You God!"

In college, she had read *The Real* religiously. It was in its pages that she learned of the shocking lengths Republicans had gone to block Black voters, the effects of the Supreme Court's repeal of affirmative action. Her hands shook when she read the feature on Michelle Alexander, who simply and poetically explained how mass incarceration was *The New Jim Crow*. Sandwiched between liquor and fashion ads and features of hip-hops talented elite, *The Real* exposed the hidden truths that were plaguing her people. It was the perfect platform for all that she wanted to say.

At first she was a glorified intern, answering phones, keeping schedules, only occasionally writing small articles. Outside of the office, she pounded the pavement. Tracy plugged *The Real* at every event. She rubbed every shoulder, kissed every cheek, tweeted and instagrammed everything.

There was a celebrity basketball tournament at the Rucker. Tracy, and hundreds of other people, watched from against a metal fence. She spanned her camera around the crowd and panned back to the court. Cam'ron caught a fast break, cut to the basket and dunked the ball. The crowd roared. Tracy turned the phone towards herself. "The Rucker is just as live as I imagined it would be. Can you say New York City?" She uploaded the video to instragram and tagged *The Real* and Cam'ron to it.

It took forever to make it out. Warm greetings were shouted out as men slapped each other up, the crowd moved and swayed to accommodate them. She bumped into Lindsay, a burgeoning fashion stylist. "Hey girl, what you doing tonight?"

Tracy shrugged. "Can't call it. Why, what's up?"

"Roll with me to Perfections."

"What's that?"

"Damn, how long you've lived here? It's a strip club." She waved her hand. "All of these niggas will be there."

"Ok cool."

Lindsay met her at her place around 1 am. She made a disapproving face at Tracy's outfit. "Girl uh unhh."

Tracy looked down at herself. She thought she looked sexy, but classy in an electric blue tube skirt and white wife beater. "What?"

"I know you're Miss Writer and all, but you look like somebody's secretary. She made Tracy swamp out the wife beater for a turquoise camisole and step into gold stilettos. She finished the look with a chunky gold necklace. "Now you look like someone a nigga would want to interview him." Tracy couldn't help but agree. And after the shots of tequila that they slammed back, she was ready to make it a night. Lindsay had arranged for some dudes that she knew to pick them up. They raced towards Queens and passed around a 5th of Hennessey.

It was dark inside. Beautiful women who ranged from Serena Williams thick to Eva Pigford model sexy roamed around like gazelles. On stage, a Puerto Rican dancer with an ass that would put Jennifer Lopez to shame, bent over and made it clap. A familiar stirring rose in Tracy's loins. Men in the crowd crumpled up bills and threw them at her. The dudes they rode with promptly ditched them and Lindsay began acting out her stripper fantasies. She twerked alongside the bar and laughed in the face of every guy who paid her attention. It worked for Tracy. Every time a man offered Lindsay a drink she insisted on one for her and before long Tracy was zoned out and screaming along to the music. "You say no to ratchet pussy/Juicy J can't!"

The lights came up at four. Tracy and Lindsay linked arms in an attempt to sober and steady themselves. They made it to the door before they remembered that they didn't drive. They had no idea where their ride was.

"Let me call them." Lindsay frowned into her phone. "It keeps going to voice mail."

Tracy laughed. "How do you know them anyway?"

"Well I used to fuck with the real tall one, but he always comes too quick. He's chill though. We kick it from time to time."

Tracy spotted Cam'ron walking towards the exit. Her heart quickened a bit. What if she got a story tonight? She laughed to herself. Six months in the city and she would be drunk and in a strip club when she lucked upon her first feature. That would be an interesting context though. "Fuck it, let's get a ride with him." She walked over and tapped him on the shoulder. "Cam, can me and my girl get a ride back to Harlem?"

He searched her face. "Ay yo, where I know you from?"

Warmth spread through her body and she couldn't stop the smile that captured her entire face. "You've probably seen me around, maybe online. I write for *The Real*." She laughed. "Actually, you would be my first story."

"Your first huh?" Tracy nodded, the smile would still not leave her face. "Yeah I know you, you caught my dunk earlier. A lot of the shit you post is ill."

Tracy motioned over to Lindsay. "Who you with? Is it cool if we ride?"

Cam'ron nodded over to his friend. "Just me and my man. Pooch, is it cool if they ride?"

"Hell yeah." Pooch promptly put his arm around Lindsay and they all made their way to the parking lot. Tracy spotted Lindsay's friends helping a blonde into their car. She elbowed Lindsay, who burst into a raucous laugh. She was gone.

Cam stopped in front of a drop top Mercedes. "Pooch, how 'bout you and home girl hit the back seat?"

"Hell yeah."

Cam'ron headed towards the passenger door. This time he spoke to Tracy. "You drunk too?"

Tracy quickly straightened herself. "I don't get drunk."

"Cool, 'cause I am. Can you drive stick?"

"I can drive anything." Tracy slid into the driver seat, put the car into 2nd and sped off. Cam pressed a button, the top went back, and the moonless sky enveloped her. It was the most fun she ever had. When they emerged from the Triboro Bridge Tracy pulled in front of IHOP. Cam looked around.

"Aren't you hungry? Come on let's leave them and me and you get something to eat."

Pooch sounded his agreement from the back seat. "Hell yeah."

Inside their booth, Cam sat with his back against the wall and his legs spread out in the seat. Tracy removed her tape recorder from her clutch. "How is it that you've remained relevant for so long?"

The conversation flowed well and over pancakes and coffee, Tracy's cherry was popped.

Tracy met Lindsay for drinks a couple of weeks later. Tracy lifted her glass to her. "Girl last time I saw you, your legs were hanging out of a backseat."

Lindsay smacked her teeth. "Bitch, that was weeks ago. On to the next. Let me order a fat ass drink 'cause I'm doing a seven day cleanse starting tomorrow."

"You look good. You could tighten your stomach a little, but just lay off the bread. Cleansing has too many ups and downs. It's better to be consistent."

"Yeah you can say that because you're not around these model bitches all day and these stuck up designers."

"I guess you got me beat there."

"Yep, but one of those designers, who shall remain nameless, slept with one of Diddy's producers, fucked around and fell in love, and just found out the nigga is engaged. She gave me her two tickets."

Tracy perked up in her seat. "To what? To the all-white party?" Lindsay nodded. Tracy stood up and did a shimmy. "Oh yeah."

"Don't act like you haven't been before."

Tracy bounced her shoulders up and down. "Fuck that, I'm not acting. I haven't been before."

"No one ever told me that niggas in Rochester are country."

"And no one ever told me that niggas in the city don't appreciate shit. I guess sometimes you have to see things for yourself." Lindsay fronted like Tracy embarrassed her, but she kept inviting her to places.

"Ok little miss appreciative, you should let me style you for the day." Tracy hesitated. "What? Bitch, you should be thanking me. Everyone knows I got skills."

Lindsay found Tracy the perfect dress in a vintage shop in Park Slope. She made her an appointment at a Dominican shop on 118th although she still insisted that Tracy "needed to lose the India Aire bullshit and have some tracks sewn in." They had a brunch of bagels and tequila spiked orange juice the day of the party. "Okay, come on let me work my magic." Lindsay zipped her into her dress and applied double sided tape to the arm straps. "Remember, it's all about the fit." She used finishing spray on Tracy's now straightened hair and put concealer under her eyes before whisking a brush along her cheeks. "You already have wonderful skin, but a little concealer and blush goes a long way." Lindsay coached her on how to stand, but when she passed her a pair of five inch stilettos, Tracy held up a hand in protest.

"Uh no. Aren't we going to be on grass all day?"

"So?"

"So? So, I need to be comfortable and relaxed. This might be my big break."

"Bitch, you already got your big break. Cam'ron."

"Interviewing a rapper after an evening at the strip club isn't exactly original or provocative. That's not what I came to New York for."

Lindsay snorted. "Whatever, just try not to get too star struck on me." Tracy ignored her and reached for a pair of teal wedges. "Those actually work. Okay hurry up, the car should be here any minute." Lindsay bounced up and crossed the room in hurried steps. Tracy turned to follow her, but was stopped by her own reflection. She looked beautiful. She rolled her eyes and laughed. Lindsay did have skills.

Lindsay also talked nonstop all the way to the Hamptons. As the terrain transitioned from steel and glass to grass and sky, butterflies began to dance in Tracy's stomach. She half-way listened as Lindsay droned on. "This bitch talking 'bout I broke her hair off. No, bitch you broke your hair off. You had me bleach it blonde and then didn't take care of it. Who the fuck doesn't know that you have to deep condition your hair every week?"

"You do?"

"Yes, you do."

"Did you tell her that?"

But then Lindsay was on to another subject. Another example of how she was smarter than somebody else and how they were hating on her. Tracy laughed. Lindsay was funny and she did know a lot. Well, she knew a lot about make-up and fashion and celebrity gossip. Her life was fast paced and her mind moved too quickly to ever consider matters of importance. The car stopped.

Lindsay was on the moment they stepped out. She tossed her head back and headed straight towards the step and repeat. Tracy hung back. She couldn't have asked for a more beautiful day. The sky was a delicate powder blue and the sun was warm and welcoming. Everything around them was green and lush. Tracy took a long inhale. She hadn't realized how much she needed a break from the city.

A man came from behind her and threw his arm around her shoulder. Tracy looked up at him in surprise. Busta Rhymes was grinning back at her. "Good shit, huh shorty?"

Tracy laughed. "Yeah."

"This your first time?"

"Yeah."

"Okay cool, Ima show you how it's done." He grabbed Tracy's hand and directed her towards the step and repeat. Cameras flashed. "Busta over here, look this way." Tracy watched him pose. He started off with his face scrunched into a grimace, his hands clasped before him. He yelled over to Tracy. "I like to start with my hardcore shit." He grinned as she laughed and struck a more comical pose. "But fuck that, it's all about the fun. Ay yo, get a picture of me and my shorty." Tracy joined him and hollered as he lifted her off of her feet. Cameras flashed. He put her down and she wrapped her arms around his waist and smiled brightly. "Bust, what's her name?" Tracy stopped smiling and looked directly at the gruff man who asked the question. "Tracy Mitchell, representing *The Real*." She put a hand on her hip and smiled over her shoulder for one more picture.

Busta was waiting for her when she was done. "You write for *The Real?* You must be really good, that's a dope mag." He kissed her on the cheek. "Don't have too much fun, ma."

Around the grounds people sat or stood in clumps. She grabbed a drink and watched them. The athletes were the loudest, the models hardly talked at all, and it seemed like everyone else couldn't stop talking. People were smiling, but something about it felt stiff. This was the biggest hip-hop event of the year and she had absolutely no desire to work the crowd today. Today she was going to have fun. She finished her drink and closed her eyes and rocked to the music. A waiter stopped to offer her an appetizer, but she didn't recognize what he was holding out to her. "What is—"

"It's Moroccan spiced salmon and it's good." Ashton Kutcher stepped in front of her, grabbed one, and walked off. Tracy shrugged, smiled at the waiter, and plopped one into her mouth. It was good. The flavors seemed to jump off of her tongue.

She milled around after that. She spotted Lindsay a couple of times, but didn't go to her. Instead, she tasted everything that was offered to her. After seven servings, and three glasses of champagne she was full and a little tipsy. She walked a bit up a grassy hill whose incline let her see the festivities, but gave her a good distance from them. Unfolding and sitting on the oversized handkerchief she brought for just this purpose, she felt at peace. She opened her purse, pulled out a joint, and took a long inhale.

She took too big of a pull and ended up in a coughing fit. A woman spoke behind her. "Easy tiger." She turned to see Nicki Minaj, a female rapper who was making her way up the ranks, standing there. "Damn you brought a blanket? That's a good idea."

Tracy scooted over. "You can sit down."

Nicki sat down slowly, filling up every available inch of the handkerchief. They were shoulder to shoulder. She crossed her legs in front of her and nodded towards the party. "Looks like they're having fun."

"Aren't you?"

"I'm working. Manager told me I gotta make sure everyone sees me, make sure everyone hears my name. I feel like a damn politician."

Tracy exhaled and nodded. "Well Nicki, I already know your name so you can relax. Want some?" She held the joint out to her. Nicki took it and blew out a graceful gush of smoke. "I've never heard a female spit like you."

"Yeah, how's that?" She passed Tracy the joint back.

"You have moments where you spit hard like Fox or Kim, but it's something completely different. You don't really do that gangsta bitch stuff. And yeah you got that New York Carribean flow, but it's more—"

"Theatrical."

"Yeah theatrical. That's exactly it."

"Theatre inspires me. I want to bring those characters to hip-hop."

Tracy passed the joint back to her. "Characters in hip-hop?"

"Yeah, look around, all of this is fake. They want everyone to think it's real, but be quick to say it's entertainment. Enter-tain-ment. They're characters paid to amuse and distract. I get it. But me, I'm gonna flip it. The whole world gonna know I'm acting and they're all going to fucking love it." She titled her head back and exhaled. Then she snapped her head and smiled and batted her eyes at Tracy. When she spoke it was in a strange British accent. "And they all gonna know that I'm directing the show darling."

Tracy looked over at her and then back at the crowd. She watched as Just Blaze told a joke, watched the gorgeous women around him laugh—some girlishly boisterous, some demure and restrained. All of it on cue. To the right of them, three punk rock dudes looked cool and unkempt even in their white. As Tracy watched them, she noticed that the tallest one took a sip from his drink robotically, like his arm was programmed to raise the glass to his lips every six seconds. She looked back at Nicki. "'All the world's a stage', right?"

Nicki smiled and nodded. "Yep. That's why I'm gonna wear a mask."

"That's not theatrical, that's gimmicky."

Nicki rolled her head towards her. "Nah, the mask Paul Laurence Dunbar was talking about. The mask is going to protect me. I can look out from it, but no one can see in." She waved her hand towards the crowd. "I'm not going to let any of this touch me."

Tracy nodded and pulled out her recorder. "Well, I gotta let you know that I write for *The Real*. You should let me interview you."

Nicki looked her straight in the eye and held her gaze. She flicked the remnants of the joint. "Fuck it, why not?" The interview was ill. That was Nicki's first major cover story and it took her career to the next level. Tracy followed her evolution and felt proud of and sad for her.

Of course, that story did wonders for Tracy's career too. She instantly became the editor in chief's favorite. Jimmie sent her to Italy to interview Common. She was flabbergasted. "You're sending me to do it?"

"Who else would I send? Our ad sales tripled after the Minaj issue." He stared straight at her. "But more than that, your piece said something. You managed to use the music to expose the politics. You were direct, but subtle. That's why I started this magazine."

Tracy nodded. Her face warmed with pride. This was why she was here. Her dream was coming true.

And Common was the most interesting man she ever met. They strolled around the Piazza Navona, and then dined on mussels and clams. He smiled as he talked, but Tracy couldn't hear him, all of her focus was on his lips. She had to remind herself that she was at work, not on a date. Yet, when Common took her hand and led her back into the perfumed evening, butterflies danced in her stomach. They walked in silence towards the main drag and stopped alongside the road. Their eyes met. She was ready to say yes to whatever he said. He turned from her a bit and hailed a taxi. Her heart sunk. He opened the door for her. "I had a really good time, it's just---"

Tracy interrupted him. "It's just an interview." She managed to get in the cab before her tears came. That night, she could not sleep. She tucked a pillow in between her legs, but it was not enough to suppress the wanting. She got up, took a cold shower, and sat in front of her laptop. Once beams of sunlight streaked into the room, she gave up on capturing the magic she had felt. It was gone now anyway. She ended up with a direct piece that juxtaposed Common's influence on hip-hop and film to Italy's romance and poetry.

If she wasn't writing, she was tracking down stories, or had her sleeves rolled up alongside Jimmie.

"What the fuck type of lead in is this?" He read, "*Though devilishly handsome, it is Nasir Jones' quiet introspections that gets panties wet.*' Who the fuck wants to read that?"

"Our readers. And if you read the research that you pass off to me, you would know that forty percent of them are female. And I don't need any stats to tell me that that's going to double with this issue. Nas is the sex symbol of a whole generation of women. I wrote the damn thing and I still might buy a copy."

"Fucking groupie."

"Hater."

But Jimmie was cool and he was passionate as hell. He wrangled with A&R's and publicists to secure artists, shook down folks to sell ad space, personally edited each piece, and in a pinch even did graphic design. Tracy wanted to learn everything that he knew. A year quickly flew by.

She interviewed Drake over linguine and Chianti. Disembarking the train at 125th street she felt like weeping. What had she done to deserve this life? This was everything. She stopped and got a cup of coffee from the bodega before climbing the three flights of stairs to her apartment. Her apartment was tiny and the stairs were a menace after a long night, but it was hers. She kicked off her boots and flung her coat over the futon. A scratched mahogany desk took up most of dining/living room. On top of it, her laptop beckoned to her. She stripped down to a camisole and panties, rotated her neck, and sat down to what she knew was going to be a long night.

At first her fingers trickled across the keyboard, struggling to keep up with her ever changing thoughts. A couple of times she was stuck; reduced to biting her nails and muttering to herself. An idea would finally take hold and then she pecked slowly, struggling to find the words that captured the essence of what she wanted to say. She finished her first draft at 5am and slept until noon. She showered, jumped into skintight jeans and an oversized sweater, blended concealer under her eyes, wrapped a turquoise scarf around her untamed mane and headed to the office. She walked a block north and then joined the surge of people descending into the earth. Below they waited for the train. A pretty Japanese girl was cocooned into her own world, courtesy of Beats by Dre. Two older men sat on the bench. They argued over a crossword puzzle. A teenage boy had his arms wrapped around his very pregnant girlfriend. Tracy wondered what the Japanese girl was listening to. She wouldn't have been surprised if it was Drake. Hmm. She took her notepad out. Maybe she could work that into her article. The train came and she pushed her way on and slid into an open seat. The aluminum cage rattled along steel tracks and her pen ran furiously over the pad. Phrases kept shouting to her. At this rate, she could probably submit her draft tomorrow. Good. Jimmie had been riding her hard these days. It was like he had lost all consideration for the creative process.

The Real was housed in a plain faced office building in Concourse Village. A magazine as fanatical about hip-hop history and culture as they were, couldn't have been anywhere but the Bronx. The security guard in the lobby waved to Tracy. She walked down the hall and opened the third door on the left. She used to love coming here, used to love passing the fiberglass sign that spelled out *The Real* in graffiti letters. Now there were ten people who worked there and a constant cloud of noise. It was like there was a contest to see who could talk the loudest. Today, she needed to show her face and let Jimmie know that the story was coming.

She opened her laptop and checked her email. Iman, one of her line sisters had just gotten engaged. Tracy smiled and clicked away her congratulations. Cool. A wedding in DC would be a nice reunion for them. Lord knows there weren't going to be any weddings in Harlem any time soon. She hadn't had a good date in months. Well she had had a perfect date, but it couldn't be a date because it was work. Jimmie was talking on his cell phone when he walked past her desk. Tracy smiled and gave him a thumbs up. He nodded and kept moving. She waited five minutes before packing up and leaving.

She grabbed a coffee and hiked the eight blocks to the library. The hollow stillness calmed her and words gushed through her fingertips. Three hours later, she finished the draft with a smile. On Monday she and Jimmie would argue over the editing, but right now she was triumphant.

She decided to write another piece while the iron was hot. She blogged occasionally for *On the Rag*, a feminist newsletter that covered every topic from dating to sex slavery. Today she penned 500 words about how to have a good hook up. *"If you find yourself horny and bored or even lonely and resigned, it's probably time for a good hook-up; your battery needs to be recharged. Remember ladies, a hook-up is not a one-night stand. No one is talking you into it. You are in control. So dress for the type of night you want to have. You're not about to meet your husband, you're going to meet a new penis. Show some skin. When you see your reflection, your own response should be, "Damn!" Then go out and own that night. Dance as much as you want to, drink as much as you can handle. Then find the hottest guy in the bar and stare him down, I guarantee he will walk over to you. Now all you have to do is tell him how you like it. This is your night, he better fuck you right.* She rattled off the rest and headed back to Harlem, her mouth watering for a fish fry. Though she was ever conscious of maintaining her size eight figure—thick enough to keep a brother's attention, but slim enough to catch a white guy's eyes, she had an inner fat girl that had to be satiated.

Lenox Lounge not only had the best fish fry in Harlem, it would also be a great setting for her video blog—"New Girl in the City." After receiving such tremendous feedback on her social networking pages, she decided to launch a blog of herself frequenting different food spots in New York. Her last post of drunken exploits at the 24 hour seafood spot on 125th had gotten over 5,000 views. Today's post would be calmer. She took a seat at the counter, propped her Go Pro up and began talking. "Welcome to another episode of New Girl in the City. I'm Tracy and right now I'm at Lenox Lounge, home of the best fish fry in the City. Ain't that right Tony?" She turned her camera towards the grumpy waiter who had just taken her order.

"Get that shit outta my face."

Tracy laughed and turned the camera back towards her. "I didn't say the service was great, but the food will make you slap your mama." Her phone buzzed. It was Francois, a Haitian line cook she was seeing. She kept talking to the camera. "I don't know why this guy keeps calling me." She let it rang for a moment before putting it on speaker phone.

"Hello?"

"Damn, I thought I was about to watch you ignore my call. That would have been depressing."

She swiveled around in her seat as he walked up to her. He kissed her full on the mouth. "Hey pretty lady."

She broke the embrace quickly and smiled tightly at him. "I suppose absence does make the heart grow fonder."

"Especially when it's forced on you. Woman, I've been calling you."

"And I've been busy. Say hi to the camera."

He faltered for a bit, but then plastered on a grin. "Hi world. I am Francois, one of the best chefs in the city. Ask my girl here—"

Tracy scooted closer to him. "He definitely has skills. No one is cooking like my man. His food is soulful, but has precision; everything is so well balanced, cooked to perfection. If you're ever in the city, make sure you check him out at Kingston's on Broadway and 7th." Francois was cool so she didn't mind bigging him up. He made her jerk chicken quesadillas on their second date that were so good she let him eat her afterwards. Unfortunately, she lost all interest after she came. He kept calling and she wanted to like him, but there was just no spark.

Her food arrived. She ate it slowly, seductively, as she narrated into the camera. "I wish y'all could taste this. The seasoning is bold, but delicate." She licked her fork. "And the texture, crisp on the outside, but soft and warm in the inside."

Francois threw an arm around her. "Yes, it's very soft and very warm in the inside. That's the best part."

She rolled her eyes. "Alright folks, thanks for watching. This new girl in the city is out." Francois handled the check and she promised to call him.

She went home changed into a tube dress and blazer and headed to Shrine. The sound of a bluesy bass guitar greeted her as she slid inside. A sexy brother with dreads eyed her. She held his gaze and smiled at him. After five minutes, she gave in and ordered a drink. He sidled over to her soon after that. Of course his cheap ass waited to approach her until after she bought her own drink. She knew that trick.

"I'm sorry, I couldn't stop watching you. You are really beautiful."

Tracy smiled. "And I'm sorry, but I'm really not interested."

She turned from him and stayed and watched four acts. Then she hopped a train and met some girls in Time Square. They drank pitchers of margaritas in The Lounge, a chill mixed spot that had hip-hop karaoke. It was a little hokey, but funny as hell. They left and cabbed it and went to a party in Soho. She got home around four, but was still restless. She grabbed her phone and scrolled through some texts before putting it down again.

The next day she climbed the fire escape to the top of her building, lit a joint, and looked over at the city. This was her weekly ritual. Harlem was quiet on Sundays. At first she attributed that to the ingrained reverence Blacks have for the Lords day. She liked that. Then she started to liken it to the only rest day of the slaves. That she did not like.

*   *   *

Two more years went by. *The Real* was doing better than ever. Bigger artists came and so did an even bigger staff and so went the familial intimacy. There was always a hoop to jump through now. There were more publicists trying to steer the direction of her interviews, more ankle grabbing to secure artists, less pieces about social issues. Jimmie would not relent with the editing now. The witty edge in her pieces was whittled down to passive aggressive musings. This was not *The Real* that she had loved. This was not why she had come to New York.

She could see now where *The Real* ended and where she began. She made time to date. Her schedule and social circle eliminated regular guys. If she wanted to have longevity in her career, artists—no matter how much of a gentleman they were or how sexy they looked when an Italian moon danced on their features—were out. So were music execs. Athletes were cool, but often too self-absorbed for anything substantial. Financial guys were the worst and actors were just strange.

There was always something to do and Tracy was determined to not let anyone outwork her. Though she was in the center of the music she had loved so much, she found herself trapped outside from all of it. At album release parties, music blared and liquor flowed, and she didn't feel a thing. At concerts, she watched everyone with their arms raised and wondered just what they were celebrating. At radio parties, jokes were told and she laughed, but it didn't warm her. Something didn't feel right. It wasn't fun anymore. She was always tired, always stressed, and less and less proud of every new issue. She found herself crying out to God again. She didn't know how long she could keep this up and she didn't know what else to do.

The Tragic interview broke up her fog. 3,000 miles up in the air she reviewed her notes, tried to get a feel for who he really was. She knew he was a church kid, born and raised in Oakland, played three instruments, did a tour in Iraq. And she really dug his music. His first mixtape was an underground smash that even had Brooklyn heads nodding. No one could deny that he could spit. His political commentary was reminiscent of Nas, his playarific tales rang of Too Short. Tragic could just as easily rap about fucking hoes as raising Black men to have honor. He was a breath of fresh air and was quickly signed to a mega label and immediately deemed the protégé of Skillz, a legendary rapping producer. Though Skillz' production was the perfect backdrop for Tragic's flow, Tracy wondered if there was a riff there. Sonship didn't seem like Tragic's style. That could be her angle.

She closed her notes and looked out of the tiny hole that was masquerading as a window. The sky was a dreamy blue that sent her mind to daydreaming. She should take a vacation. She should go somewhere and let the ocean heal her. But she didn't have anybody to go with. She pulled the window shade down.

Her mind was back on business as soon as the plane started its descent. Tragic had been communicating with Tracy sans publicist or assistant and insisted on picking her up from the airport. She was barreling towards ground transportation, shades on, phone to her ear, prepared for him to be late, when she saw him walking towards her. He hugged her before taking her carry-on bag. "It's good to finally meet you."

Tracy smiled. He was real. Unassuming in his khaki shorts, white tee, and Adidas they made it to his car unmolested by fans. The car itself, a Saturn Astra, was not likely to give them away. Tracy put on her seat belt. "I see you're low key. Or is all of this just for my benefit?"

"Shit, it's for my benefit. I got a daughter and I don't plan on ever having to blow motherfuckers up in order to feed her again."

"Yeah I read somewhere that she's the reason why you enlisted. Good thing for her conscious that you made it back."

"She wouldn't have ever known about that."

Tracy turned to look at him. "I guess your family's not like mine. With us, every sacrifice is published, the appropriate appreciation must be paid." She put her fingers on her cheeks and lifted to fake a smile.

He laughed. "Guess you know a little something about that."

She knew a lot about that. Her future had been planned and prayed for since the moment her mother realized she was pregnant. When she was thirteen her father had worked enough double shifts at Kodak and her mother had cleaned enough houses to move them from their apartment that was a stone's throw away from the projects, to a pocketbook house in Brighton, a suburb with the best school district in the county. Every other penny had been saved for her education. She went to the University of Pennsylvania instead of Howard, but was happy to make her parents so proud. Of course, the shoe dropped on graduation day when she announced she was moving to Harlem to write instead of going to law school. This time she would not be dissuaded. She had done her duty, the rest of her life would be for her.

"Used to. My parents moved back to Guyana last year. Hallelujah, I can breathe!" She laughed. "What about you? You close to your folks?"

"We starting the interview all ready? I can't feed you first?"

He parked the car on Seventh Avenue. Walking towards Jesse's, a natural soul food restaurant that he swore could put Sylvia's out of business, Tracy could barely contain herself. She could just envision the zoot suites of the '50s, Bobby Seale walking the street in his black leather in the 60s, afro glistening in the sunshine. She wanted to soak it all in.

Inside, smell of fried chicken and framed photographs greeted them. A few patrons sat along a glistening counter. A plump woman with a huge smile and gap to match spoke. "Hey Blake, go ahead and have a seat." Tracy followed him to a booth in the back. He slid down across from her. "First time in Oakland?"

She laughed. "Is it that obvious? I'm sorry, but this is so exciting. A major movement in history, started right here. Were your parents panthers?" She motioned toward his right forearm; which was covered with a mural. She made out RIP dates and images of Tupac, Malcolm X, bible verses, army tanks, bubble letters, an infant's face, and Huey Newton.

"No. In the beginning people used to be scared by all of that. Niggas talking about communism and self-sovereignty, and there being no God, no one wanted to be associated with that. It didn't get fashionable until the leather and guns came out. Towards the end there were too many rules, too many bodies, and too much talk. Niggas got tired of listening to that shit." He rubbed his arm. "All of this right here is just a physical manifestation of everything that has gotten me here."

"You ever worry that niggas will get sick of listening to you?"

"I never wanted them to listen to me in the first place. I've been shy my whole life, always stayed to myself. This rapping shit is a complete and total accident. I started spitting when I was first shipped to Iraq. Lupe said 'Hip-hop saved my life.' That is some real shit. I woulda went crazy had I kept all of this in. It just kept coming out. All of it. But there you go trying to start the interview again."

She tilted her digital tape recorder towards him. "The interview been started. You forgot what I'm here for?"

He took the recorder from her and pressed stop. "Not yet. Let me feed you first, show you my city. How you gon interview somebody you don't know?"

She raised her hands in surrender. He was cool. And when Jesse herself placed a steaming plate of fried catfish, rice, black eyed peas and greens flavored with organic smoked turkey, she didn't have any protests. The food was just as amazing as he said.

She spent the entire day with him. On their way to his barber he beeped his horn at a stocky dude on a bike. "What up ol' big head ass nigga."

The guy on the bike laughed jovially. "Same shit my nigga."

Tragic chucked him a deuce and sped back up. "That nigga's sister used to suck everybody off." In the mall, he slapped some dudes up, nodded at a few females, and stopped for a couple of pictures. Seeing him here was no unusual occurrence. In the sneaker store, a bow legged kid with freckles in a striped uniform handed Tragic a box of sneakers before he could even open his mouth. "Good look Tony. Tell your mama I said hey." This was his first hometown performance since going major, but it was obvious that he was no stranger to his city. They went to his weed man and then back to his ranch style home in a middle class neighborhood to change.

"Make yourself at home." Her eyes darted around the moment he disappeared down the hall way. Pink converses were next to the door. In the kitchen, a fourth grade report card was on the refrigerator and Heineken and a pizza box were the only things inside. Back in the living room a picture of a snagatooth girl smiled at her from the mantel. She wondered what type of father he was. The sound of his steps behind her interrupted her thoughts. She turned to face him. He still had on his clothes from earlier, but he added a thick rope chain and the new sneakers.

"You look good. How come you don't have a picture up of you with your daughter?"

He shrugged. "I'm home now. I don't need pictures."

They headed to the arena. She was surprised that they hadn't linked up with any of his homies. Most of the artists she met hated being alone. "Where's your entourage? They meeting us up there?"

He laughed. "What entourage? Niggas stopped fucking with me when I came home. I was fucked up, bad. I was on pain meds, drunk, high all of the time. Used to just zone out. They told me I used to say some wild shit. And I'm a mean drunk, started wailing on 'em. Can't blame niggas for not dealing with that. I don't blame my baby mom either."

"What about now?"

"Now I'm good. But I don't have no friends, don't have no girl. It's just me and this music. I might roll one up, kick it, look out when niggas need help. But I don't have no one around me."

She held out her recorder. "Except for journalists."

Again he clicked the device off. "Just vibe with me man. You're not going to deny a fan are you?"

"You're a fan?"

"Oh yeah. You write some real shit. Like, some mags kiss artists ass. Your stuff is positive, but there's an edge to it. It's like you hold a camera up to motherfuckas, and you ain't photo shoppin' shit."

Heat ran to Tracy's face. He was a fan of *her* work. "Thank you."

"No doubt. And those videos you make are funny as hell. That's why I was hyped to meet you. You seem like a fun person to be around."

Tracy watched him as he spoke. A lot of artists liked to kiss up to her, wanting her to paint them in the most favorable light. Tragic seemed sincere though. Shit, she was fun. She wasn't walking around with a stick up her ass, afraid to have a good time. Maybe it was New York that had been bothering her. A change of scenery and a new friend might be just what she needed. She shrugged. "Yeah I am."

He laughed. "That's what I'm talking about. I like your energy. I need that right now. Just build with me. You can start the interview the second I get off stage. I promise."

His show was amazing. It felt more like a one man Broadway play than a rap concert. There were no hype men, just him and his deejay. He led the crowd through songs, stopped to give personal anecdotes about the making of the music, the time he got pistol whipped after he tried to rip off a dealer, the friends he had lost. Then the Skillz produced electric guitar chords of his newest single dropped. He jumped up and down, ran across the stage. He screamed into the mic "All I got is this here pen/And if I die, Lord please let me in/Soul so dark, heart full of sin." Tracy was mesmerized. A host of new questions came to her mind.

Tragic was covered in sweat when he met her backstage. He lifted Tracy off of her feet and swung her around. She didn't mind. And when he passed her a blunt she only hesitated for a moment. It wasn't that she made it a habit to smoke with her interviewees, but she felt like she had made a new friend. She needed that right now. Plus, there was no way she could refuse some Cali weed; that would almost be sinful.

*   *   *

She was floating, boundless; suspended in a nothingness. Then light began to trickle in. At first she was puzzled by it, a bit intrigued by its spreading presence. But then it was the only thing she could feel and she was awake. She opened her eyes. Where was she? She was laid out on a bed. It was still made. Her eyes quickly roamed over the room. She was in a hotel. Was she alone? Her heart quickened. Everything was quiet save for the sound of a distant vacuum cleaner. She gingerly ran her hands over her body. She was fully clothed. When she got to her face, there was something wet, something thick. Oh God. She hurled. For a few moments, her body heaved in convulsions. Then she was drenched in sweat, crying and gagging until there was nothing else to come out.

She closed her eyes and tried to remember. She remembered Tragic swinging her around after the show, her coughing after hitting the blunt, their laughter. She noticed the tape recorder on the night stand. She stared it, afraid of what it might say. Finally, she crawled over to it and pressed play. His voice sounded distant, haunted. "Everybody so shocked that I made it on the scene so fast. They don't understand that I was sent here. This was destined."

Her own voice was feathery. "Sent here?"

"My steps are ordered. Everything that I been through. My pops was a pastor used to beat the shit outta me and quote Scripture. 'Chasten thy son while there is hope, and let not thy soul spare for his crying.' Now I don't know if the good book meant that you break your kid's ribs. But apparently it did, because nobody did nothing."

He went on to tell her about his first excursion in Fallujlah. "Niggas here think they know about war. They think their little pea shooters and petty ass beef is a war. No a war is when you suit up in 110 degree heat and march down a street who's name you can't even pronounce and a IED goes off and you see your man tore in half, literally torn in half. Intestines oozing out. That's war."

The conversation lightens when he speaks of his daughter. "That little girl is a straight character. She's girly as hell, only wears dresses, but at the same time she's a little tomboy. I mean she got a mean cross over. Imagine a little girl breaking someone's ankles in a dress." Tracy could make out the sound of her own laughter, it was throaty and short. The interview darkens again when she asks about his mom. "It'll be the best day of my life when that bitch dies." But it wasn't until the end of the recording that her blood ran cold.

"Yo, what the fuck did we smoke?"

"A little of this, a little of that. Welcome to the West Coast nigga."

Her voice is panicked. "What?"

"Don't trip, go with it. Relax your mind baby. That's what we do with this music. Right beat, right flow, we can say anything. We ease it in, nice and smooth, you hardly feel it." He started to freestyle. "Niggas is tripping/'cause when my pen get to leaking/ the demons in my head take over/start barking and speaking/Hot bitch/Fat ass/So we freakin' this weekend/legs part/soul open/that's when I sneak in." He laughed. "We get over a million motherfuckas singing along to that and we got something."

"We got a war playing out in front of everybody and they all pretend not to see it. It doesn't matter how many YouTube videos people make, how many of our secrets get leaked, no one believes it, no one cares. We read the little chats and laugh. People talkin' 'bout, 'They don't mean it like that.' What the fuck else could we mean?"

"We?"

"I told you I was sent here. I was six months in. They sent us to disable some bombs. I hadn't even been trained in that shit yet. They talking 'bout it's field experience. Half a kilometer in, one detonates. I don't remember the rest. One minute I'm walking, sweating from the heat and nerves the next minute I'm in the infirmary. Skull cracked. It was touch and go for a few weeks. But someone came to see me."

"Who?"

"He told me that I would rap. That he would give me the words and that my music would pierce hearts."

"Who?"

"He said I would win souls for him. He said that the music is just the beginning. By the time the battle comes we'll have enough people on our side."

The recording stopped there and though it was over three hours long, she didn't remember any of it. When she sat down at her laptop to write the story her hands shook. She didn't want to listen to the tape again; she didn't want to think about the things Tragic had said. She didn't want to think about what wasn't on the tape.

He said a battle was coming and she believed him. Something had been off recently. She felt something different when she listened to the music. It was almost like a presence, like an aroma that only she could smell. She would look at those around her and see that they were totally unaffected. So she dismissed it until she sat down with an artist and felt its presence again. And there it was when she opened a final copy of *The Real*. Something tugged at her. It whispered secrets into her ear. The real music had been kidnapped. What stood in its place was an evil impostor. Hip-hop was no longer the music of the people. It no longer gave a voice to the abandoned and disenfranchised.

The new hip-hop, the clever impostor, had millions hypnotized through super powered headphones and lulled into a false consciousness. In this grim fantasy love was ridiculed, women were fucked, and money was plentiful. Real niggas didn't hold hands or have feelings or give a fuck about anybody else. Ex correctional officers were rapping about flipping bricks and teenagers were spitting "bang bang" and niggas were dying in the streets. Souls were being won for the devil.

She slammed her laptop shut. She couldn't write that. What proof did she have? She wasn't some half-baked conspiracy theorist or desperate preacher. Maybe she had misunderstood what Tragic said. "People talkin' bout, 'They don't mean it like that.' What the fuck else could we mean?" She held her face in her hands. There was no misunderstanding that. He had been very plain all along. All of them had. The enemy was hiding in plain sight.

Tragic was right, the lyrics spoke for themselves. He wasn't using subliminal messages hidden in beats; he was getting people to speak a spell out loud. Tracy had to figure out a way to get people to realize that. She opened her laptop again, but it was like her fingers were frozen. She couldn't type a word. What did she need to say anyway? She would just transpose the tape and let everyone see for themselves. Jimmie probably wouldn't even run it. He had turned into a complete kiss ass recently. She swept her arm across her desk and everything went crashing to the floor. She sobbed into her hands. This would ruin her. But she had become a writer to tell the people the truth. This was why she had dreamed of Harlem her whole life. This was why she was here.

Jimmie called her into his office. For the first few seconds he was silent. Tracy stared back at him. They had come so far together. They had both been searching for something. What that was wasn't revealed until now. But Jimmie looked weary and she could not begrudge him that. Everything was about to change. Finally he spoke. "Are you sure?"

She placed a copy of the recording on his desk and walked out. He ran her story in its entirety.

The back lash was swift and the internet was abuzz. The purists said *The Real* was always too critical of artists. The hipsters said her article was slanted to jump on the illuminati bandwagon. The females said Tracy was a hater who half of the industry had ran through. The preachers said people had much too literal an interpretation of the Bible. The Battle of Armageddon was an allegory. And the industry said the story was completely untrue and was a publicity stunt of a desperate mag; hip-hop was not intentionally contributing to urban violence, it simply was reporting it. People put too much pressure on rappers, they wanted celebrities to raise their kids. Hip-hop had always been a report on the ghetto, not the cause. It could not be blamed for what was happening in the streets.

Tragic said nothing. He didn't have to. He had wanted that article to be printed, the world's response was confirmation that his plan was working. The music had truly brainwashed them all. The battlefield was ripe.

Jimme told her it would all blow over. "Take a few days off, don't respond to any of this. No tweets, no statuses, nothing." Two weeks later he called to say she would have to issue a public apology. His tone was stern. "I can't believe I let you talk me into running that piece."

"What are you talking about? I didn't talk you into anything. You heard it for yourself--"

"Yeah? Well, no one believes it."

"Oh they believe it, they just don't give a fuck. That's why you started this magazine. The people need to be woken up! You so busy selling ad space and kissing ass that you're missing the whole fucking point. We are *The Real*. We expose the truth, we shake people when they don't want to hear it. How can we stand by and let these motherfuckas cast spells that are killing our people. These motherfuckas are killing our people! You think the homicide rate in Chicago is an accident? We have to wake everybody up." Her heart beat wildly as she clutched the phone.

Jimmie sounded exhausted on the other end. "Tracy, how can I do that if I don't have a magazine? Tragic's label could shut our lights off. Issue the apology or find another profession." He hung up. She never spoke to Jimmie again.

No other editors were interested in talking to her either. Her emails and calls and even her visits to publications that used to swoon over her were fruitless. No one was available. Even *On the Rag* ignored her. So much for sisterhood. The posts on her social networking were so vicious that she shut them all down. Her bank account was quickly dwindling and her phone was blaringly quiet.

It didn't matter anyway, she could no longer write. She sat in front of her laptop and pecked away but the words were empty, their meaning blank. It was the same thing with her journal, she filled the pages with mad scribbles, the paper ripped where she pressed too hard.

She had to do something. She temped, but that money was barely enough to cover rent. She went to see Stephanie, her recruiter at the temp agency.

"I need something that pays more."

Stephanie's gray eyes were warm. "Look hon, I like you. You get good reviews from the jobs I send you out on, but unless you get hired directly, there's nothing I can do."

Tears welled up in Tracy's eyes. Her life had been reduced to rubbles. She had no friends, no money, no prospects. Hadn't she done the right thing? Why was everything that she had ever dreamed of being snatched away? She ran her hands over her face. She had to get it together. But she couldn't stop the tears and soon her entire body was shaking, consumed with her hopelessness.

Stephanie's words broke through her sorrow. "Have you thought about substitute teaching? The pay is pretty good."

It took three weeks for her to apply at the New York City Department of Education, be fingerprinted, hired, and then sent on her first teaching gig assignment. Her alarm went off at 6 am, she had never woken up so early in New York before. She showered, dressed and caught the bus to 135th street.

The A. Philip Randolph Campus High School was sprawling. She pushed through hundreds of kids waiting to be scanned and admitted. A gruff security guard pointed her towards the main office where she was given a key and directed to the basement. She would be filling in for the shop teacher.

The room was cavernous. Work tables and benches filled the center, while heavy machinery was lined up along the right wall. Bird houses in various stages of completion, were sprawled across a table. What the hell were these kids gonna do with a bird house? Tracy thumbed through the packet of work she was supposed to give them. It had pictures of various tools and screws and a brief description of each. They were supposed to write a paragraph that explained which tools they used to complete their bird houses and why.

The bell rang and Tracy steadied herself. By the time the bell rang again, she had nineteen students sitting before her, sixteen of them boys.

"Good morning." No one returned her salutation. "Well as you can see Mister Moore is out today."

"And as we can see you fine as hell. Damn baby, what's your name?"

"Well, it certainly isn't damn baby. What's yours?"

"Michael."

"Okay Michael, read number one."

He looked at her hard for a second. "These are pliers. Pliers are a hand tool with hinged arms that end in jaws—"

He actually listened to her. But the student next to him was a different story. "I ain't reading."

Tracy narrowed her eyes. "Yes, I can definitely tell that you 'ain't reading.'"

A few students laughed. The boy set his jaw. "Yeah, so move on."

"Can't you read?"

"Yeah, bitch I can read."

Ooohs filled the room. "I'm a bitch because you're either too stupid or too proud to read two sentences in class? Or am I a bitch because I look better than your mama and any chick you could ever bag." She stared him down. "Is there anything else you want to say?" The class was silent now and Tracy quickly smiled at the student to the right of him. "Why don't you show him how a real student does it?" The boy obliged her and she blew a deep breath through her nose.

That kid had been so quick to snap on her. He called her a bitch as smoothly as if it were her name. All of that because she asked him to read? Tragic's words rang in her ear. "We ease it in, nice and smooth, you hardly feel it. Niggas is tripping/'cause when my pen get to leaking/the demons in my head take over/start barking and speaking/Hot bitch/Fat ass/So we freakin' this weekend/legs part/soul open/that's when I sneak in. We get over a million motherfuckas singing along to that and we got something." Children were most affected by hip-hop's poisoning. They grew up in a world shadowed in spells, their reality was dimmed by materialism and emotional detachment. The end result was an entire generation with no trust, no love. Perhaps there was still hope in trying to reach the youth. Hadn't the future always begun with them?

Everything that she had been through had led to this moment. She had dreamed of Harlem, not because she was supposed to be a writer, but because she was supposed to teach. Her dream wasn't dead after all, it was reincarnated.

She emailed Miss Pratt, her elementary music teacher who used to run the Black History assemblies. Miss Pratt had put Tracy in the choir even though she couldn't sing a lick. Somehow she discovered that Tracy could write. Tracy needed her help again now.

Miss Pratt, you said I would meet my future one day and I did. Because of you, I became a writer at ten years old. Even after my family moved to the suburbs, and all of my problems were supposed to disappear, the words would not leave me. I marched steadily towards what I knew to be my destiny. I came to Harlem and I used my pen to tell the stories of my people until I discovered a truth that they didn't want to hear, wouldn't dare to believe. I walked to the Brooklyn Bridge on Tuesday. I couldn't step on it though, I feared the desire to jump off would be far too strong. But today a new future greeted me. Today, I became a teacher.

*   *   *

Miss Pratt wrote her back and told her all about what was going on in Rochester. There had been four school superintendents in the last ten years, the district was in a severe deficit, extracurricular activities had shrank and the graduation rate had plummeted. *"Tracy, we need good teachers. There's an accelerated graduate program that would put you in your own classroom in September."*

2

*"I do it for the young kids who need to be advised.
And they wonder why his soul forever cold.
It was three words that he was never told."*

-.38 Spesh

"These 3 Words"

TRACY DROVE AROUND DOWNTOWN her first day back and gasped when she got to Main Street. What had they done to Midtown? She pulled over and walked up to the remains of what used to be the epicenter of the city. There used to be department stores, All Day Sunday--an upscale urban boutique, a grocery store, a monorail. Dancing dolls from foreign lands used to mark the hour. During Christmas, there was a Black Santa Claus whose wintry land sparkled and beckoned. It used to be magical. She couldn't believe that all of that was reduced to the rubble and the abandoned cranes and trucks that she stood in front of. A man walked past her, "Excuse me, when did they do this?"

He shrugged. "I don't know, maybe two months ago."

She came to learn that a lot more had changed since she had been here last. Low rent was the one good thing about Rochester's decline and she loved her apartment. She would have never been able to afford this much space in Harlem. Nestled on a one-way off of Monroe Avenue, she had the bohemianism that her soul desired and the grim realities of the city's crime at her doorstep. There was a natural food market around the corner and prostitutes in its parking lot at night. Her neighbor had a rainbow flag that hung proudly and dozens of visitors that never stayed for more than five minutes throughout the day. Her place had hardwood floors and big windows and a ceiling with a delightful slope. She filled it with pieces from Craigslist and garage sales and thrift shops; the result was a colorful and warm haven that was telling of her artist soul.

She subbed during the day and went to class at night. Her program was for career changers who wanted to teach in an urban setting. The thought was, trained teachers with real world experience would fare better in the classroom. It was a theory that Tracy didn't completely buy since most of the people in her cohort were idiots. There was Carleen, math wiz, turned housewife, turned would be teacher. She was anxious and patronizing. "I mean those poor dears don't have anybody to show them how to live. I just can't imagine what it's going to be like in the classroom." Then there was Earl. Black, ex jock, and dumb as bricks. "I mean some of them kids real smart. Just gotta know how to apply it. We got crack dealers doing major arithmetic. Just gotta get 'em in the books."

But the course work was fascinating. She learned about educational policy. Gone were the days when the 'slow' kids were in a different class. Brown vs. Board had been reinterpreted by No Child Left Behind. It was discriminatory to place disabled students in separate classrooms. Teachers now had to read and implement students' *individualized educational plans*—thick packets that described the student's deficits and strengths at length and the necessary strategies to accommodate them. She took psychology classes to understand the mindset of teenagers, literacy classes that taught her different ways to increase reading comprehension, assessment classes that taught them how to write lesson plans that met several learning styles. She attended seminars on bullying, child abuse, trauma. Statistics cited that 35% of the city's students had experienced trauma, their brains permanently altered because of it.

When she wasn't working or studying, she was restless. She didn't miss the speed of NYC, but she did miss the energy, the potential that lingered in the air. None of the friends that she graduated with were coming back. Rochester was too broke and too slow for them. Most of them landed in Atlanta. Her friends that didn't graduate were too dim for her. They had babies and drama and few aspirations. So she went to sorority meetings, joined a church, worked out, met a fuckable guy named Jason. Spring turned to summer.

The course work intensified and she and the rest of her cohort now had the additional task of student teaching during summer school. It wasn't that taxing for Tracy though. Her cooperative teacher was a very cool guy from Uganda who made it apparent that he wanted to fuck her. His advances were subtle enough that she could pretend not to detect them and he in turn let her do whatever she wanted. He handed her the reigns on her very first day. Later on, she regaled her cohort with stories about how she led the class through grammar exercises, the essential question, and a discussion of *Invictus*. She was certainly feeling like the master of her fate these days. There were endless papers to write and group projects and sample lessons. Bloom's taxonomy, *The First Day of School*, Piaget, and *Strategies that Work* were crammed into her head.

Summer melted away and they eagerly awaited their assignments for the upcoming school year. It was tedious, as the school district struggled to reinstate and place the thousands of seniors who hadn't graduated in August as expected, and had yet to age out of the system. Tracy received her assignment the last class of their summer session and the week before school was to start. She was going to Booker T. Washington.

Earl elbowed her. "Be careful girl, that's the worst school in the city."

Tracy shrugged. "Aren't they all bad?"

*　　*　　*

At 5:47 a.m, the parking lot of Booker T. Washington High only had three cars in it. The sky was an indigo blue, the moon long gone, the sun making its glorious arrival. The tranquility of the moment calmed her nerves a bit.

Her hands shook on the door handle. She exhaled, "I can do this." Outside of the car, she steadied her hand to swipe her badge at the sensor. A click sounded her admittance into the school.

Her low heels echoed through the hallway. In the office, the head secretary was just taking her seat. She glanced stiffly in Tracy's direction, forcing her to swallow the good morning that was forming in her throat. Tracy turned away and checked her mailbox. It was empty except for a union flier and investment agency advertisement.

She had cleaned and disinfected her classroom the day before, but it still smelled of stale summer. She cracked the window and was rewarded with a gust of twilight air. Rays of amber reached across the sky. The knot in her stomach loosened.

Hurried footsteps came next. A short, Puerto Rican woman stuck her head in the door. "You got the gig."

"I'm sorry?"

The woman smiled. "You were coming in when I left my interview. I prayed that you would get the job."

"I'm sorry, have we met?"

Her visitor stepped into the doorway. "Nope. I just knew that it was the right thing to do. I'm Jahirym. Jahirym Hernandez."

"Tracy Mitchell."

"Lots to do, right? Have a good first day. Let's talk later." She was gone as quickly as she had come.

Soon there were streams of teachers passing by her door. Jen Witfield, a special education teacher, stepped fully into the room. Her eyes roamed over everything before she spoke. "Looks like you're all set up here."

"Just about."

"Just try to survive the first day. Most of these kids are hopeless; we got all of the district's throwaways. You just remember that no matter what happens, it will be better tomorrow."

Tracy looked up sharply from the email she had been reading. "It will be better today."

The knot in her stomach retightened when the buses pulled into the loop. She and a few other teachers stood in the hallway. A perky older brunette winked at her. Tracy smiled in return. A gruff bald man crossed his arms. "Just 190 more days of this shit." Miss Hernandez waved to her from a few doors down.

Nervous laughter was heard next as students began to trickle in. Most wore new clothes and unsoiled sneakers. The girls smelled of hair spritz, they waved their hands as they spoke, acrylic nails accenting their speech. The boys walked with the wide shuffle required to keep their sagging pants up. Everyone was upright, aware of the mass appraisal. These kids had come from phased out schools and had been bused from all over the city. Everyone would be eager to make a name for themselves. Tracy understood the importance of this too. She needed to assert her dominance immediately, her reputation had to be solidified at once.

The bolder kids relished the charged atmosphere. Alpha males and females could be spotted in the saunter of their strut, their shouts of "ay yos" and "hey girls" were trumpets announcing their arrival. Profanity rang out amidst the cloud of chatter, kids who traveled solo walked a bit quicker their eyes took in everything around them, this was a new jungle to navigate.

She said good morning to those individual kids as they passed. It had been her experience that these kids were the most dangerous. Already outcasts—and trying not to be fucked with--they had short fuses and could be quick to cut someone or throw a chair at a teacher. She was mindful to address larger groups too. Her years as a city student and stint subbing had taught her that the more sociable kids were actually more vulnerable and secretly longed for their teachers' approval. A smile and an acknowledgement went a long way with them. Still, most didn't respond to her greeting and she didn't expect them to. Not yet anyway. She was just tilling the soil at the moment.

Thirty-one kids stared at her after the bell went off. She swallowed and plunged forward. "My name is Miss Mitchell. I will only answer to Miss Mitchell. You may not call me Miss or Mitch or anything else that isn't my name. I will address you by your name; you will treat me with the same respect. I might as well tell you now that I want you to learn. I will not give you busy work and I will not insult your intelligence with fill in the blank nonsense. I will push you, but I will do everything I can to help you. If you are not here to learn, then you need to see yourself to the door. You will not complain about having to do work, you will remain in your seats, and you will raise your hand to speak. Again, if that's a problem, there's the door."

She heard snickers and a couple of girls smacked their teeth. But when she raised an eyebrow, and looked directly at them, they lowered their eyes. No one moved and no one spoke. She touched the screen of the smart board. An hourglass appeared and a digital voice sang out, "Five minutes."

"We start everyday with the warm-up. The warm-up is designed to shift your thinking to the topic of the day's lesson. It is a very simple question that allows me to see what you already know or what you remember from the previous class. You do not have to copy down the question, but you need to restate the question in your answer."

Nothing and everything stood out from that first day. She said every word carefully and watched for the reactions they solicited. Some kids were bored, they had heard it all before. Others were defiant, eager for a chance to test her. But still some were interested, relieved to be in the hands of a capable teacher.

Her first weeks passed by quickly. She led the class tightly, every minute was planned. She rarely sat down. She led them through grammar exercises, telling them that standard English was the difference between minimum wage and management. She nudged sleeping students as she passed, kicked their desks if they didn't sit up fast enough. Students came to the smart board to place semi colons and dashes. They hesitated when asked to read aloud, and wrote slowly. She complimented and corrected. She arrived early and left late. She went home and spread the day's events out in her mind. She went to class and listened to her cohort as they exchanged stories about lazy, disrespectful kids. She went back to work and tried all over again.

3

"I like the way you be with all that personality,
but I got flava too, you need to get with me"

-MC Lyte

"I Wanna be Down Remix"

ON ELECTION DAY SHE was a nervous wreck. She snapped at Tyrell, a sweet kid whose ADHD kept him in perpetual motion. "Ty, we don't have time for this today." She hurriedly scribbled out a pass to the bathroom and laid it on his desk. "Go take a walk." She left work right after dismissal. At home she stripped down and plopped down in front of CNN. Obama truly had the world on his shoulders. Yet it appeared that he remained everything that a Black man should be—resolute. How could anyone not love him?

At eight, she joined a bunch of black professionals at Crush to watch the results. Crush was the buppie social hub. During the week there were poetry readings, live bands, and comedy. On the weekends, the deejay was great and the crowd liked to dance. On election night it was packed. Brothers wore button downs and too tight jeans and hard bottom shoes. Sisters wore blazers and scarves and Louis hand bags. Tracy supposed it was the uniform of educated Black folk. She stuck out in a tailored leather jacket, peasant shirt, pale blue tights, and thigh high snake skinned boots. A few women looked at her and turned away; a couple of Alphas hugged her and promptly went back to their conversations.

She ordered wine and milled around by the bar. She heard snatches of conversations. "The problem with the city schools is these teachers don't relate. Who cares about Shakespeare when your mother's a crackhead?" Tracy turned in the direction of a nasally voice. It belonged to a petite woman that she knew to be a chemical engineer from Greenwich, Connecticut. Like she knew what the fuck she was talking about. A trio of men to the right of her were debating which luxury car was a better value. A couple behind them were not so quietly cheering every time Romney won a state.

She moved to the other side of the room where there was an empty seat across from a chestnut colored man. They locked eyes. She approached him. "Is anybody sitting here?" He shook his head no. Guess he was too fine to speak. Tracy knew that type. She pulled the chair back a few inches away before sitting down.

They didn't speak to each other for another hour. Romney was on top and Tracy had switched from wine to martinis. "I hope this motherfucker doesn't win."

The man spoke for the first time. "He won't."

When Ohio went Blue and Obama was declared the winner, she couldn't help but jump up and hug him. This moment had to be sealed with human contact. And when his arms closed around her, enveloping her in his scent, she wanted to hang on. She managed to pull away after a few moments. She stared at him and he held her gaze. She stepped back and bumped into one of the Alphas who pulled her towards the bar. "Trace, we gotta do a shot." His grip on her arm was strong, his joviality forced. She freed her arm and turned back towards the man, but he was gone.

A couple of weeks passed before the first snow fell. It was a feathery snow that fell to the earth like dandelion fluff and melted instantly. After dismissal, Tracy sat at her desk and watched it. She sighed and went over a mental to do list. She had made the copies, called Ryan's mentor, sent a condolence card to Soror Molly. She still needed an oil change. She turned back to the snow and sighed again. There was no one to buy a scarf for, to cuddle up next to, to even send a happy first snow text.

She turned from her musings, packed up, and headed to the gym. Her love life had been reduced to occasional romps with Jason and the flirtations she shared with men at the gym. These men worked and worked out there and smiled at her and looked too long when she pranced by in yoga pants and sports bras. They made her fantasize about long days in bed, hand holding, and movie dates. But she turned down all real advances. They were either too corny, too old, married, or too thugged out. Plus, she couldn't afford awkward run-ins at a place she frequented so often.

She had a good workout and headed to the mats for her cool down routine. Pushing her body beyond comfort, she breathed deeply and leaned into her stretches. She noticed the man from election night when she stood up. Today, he looked even more handsome bench pressing. He didn't grunt or strain when he lifted, just focused on smoothly maneuvering the weight. Something about that focus held her attention. He sat up and noticed her.

Busted, she smiled and walked over to him, "Are you finished?"

"You about to bench?"

"No, but I need someone to walk me to my car. I parked in the garage."

"We'll walk with you." His friend answered. Tracy hadn't noticed him before. His lined face and bulky build suggested a prison background. Tracy did not like the intrusion, but couldn't think of a way to get out of it. The trio fell into an uncomfortable silence.

"This is it", she said relieved once they stopped in front of her coupe. "Thanks." She didn't hesitate further to get inside and drive off.

She spotted him again a few weeks later. He nodded in response to her smile. She tried to shake away the familiar stirring the nod caused inside of her. She was just about to start her abdominal routine, but couldn't stop herself from getting up and walking over to him.

She asked, "Did you already do abs?"

"Yeah, but I'll do 'em again." She showed him the sequence and he joined in. Though he struggled at times, he didn't seem embarrassed by it. "That's some workout", he said after they finished the last set. "You leaving now?"

"Yeah."

"Need somebody to walk you to your car again?"

This time they both smiled. It was only five o'clock and she was parked right in front of the building, but she didn't decline the invitation. The silence was comfortable as they walked through the gym's doors. She snuck peaks at him. He had defined cheekbones and almond shaped eyes. His frame was solid and basketball sleek. She remembered the way his arms felt around her.

He nodded when she pointed to her car right in front of the building. "Can I call you sometime?"

"Who are you going to ask for?"

"I was getting to that. What's your name?"

"Tracy. Yours?"

"X."

"Like the rapper?"

"No. My name is Oxford, but everyone calls me X."

"So your brothers are Cambridge and Canterbury?"

"That's clever. I'm the only Brit. My brothers names are Princeton and Harvard."

That's clever. He said that with authority. He moved with authority too. She rattled off her number and he put it in his phone. "How old are you?"

"Twenty-four." She didn't add that she was turning twenty-five in a couple of months. No need to think about that. "You?"

"Twenty-nine."

He called a few days later. At the sound of his rich baritone she found herself agreeing to go out to dinner with him. She hadn't been this excited about a date, since, since ever. Something about X struck something within her. She felt like she already knew him.

The last time she had clicked so quickly with someone had been Tragic. She thought about waking up in that hotel room and shuddered. Nothing like that would ever happen again. She would meet X at the restaurant. She would lead the conversation and she would signal the completion of the date. She was in control.

Even after this declaration though, Tracy was still nervous. She stood in front of a full length mirror and ran her hands over the tight, gray, sweater dress she had chosen for the occasion. The dress was seductively casual and clung in the right areas that she was so determined to keep in line. Regular exercise kept her waist narrow, her thighs thick, and her ass tight. Her jet black, kinky hair was pulled back in a tight bun that made her eyes look even more slanted. She finished the look by dusting powder over her coffee colored skin and rubbing gloss over her full lips.

She was purposely fifteen minutes early when she pulled up to the Italian Steakhouse. She had a pre-date ritual. She liked to take a moment to hope for the best, picture herself smiling and nodding demurely, plot the witty things she would say. Her ritual was shot when X pulled alongside her. So went being early.

She slid out of the car and walked over to his cherry red Lincoln MKS. He responded to the question in her eyes. "What? I'm never late."

He slid his arm around her waist before leading her to the restaurant and away from the warnings that sounded in her mind. Inside, he pulled out her chair and let his eyes linger on her face once he sat down. "I'm glad we're finally here," he said after they ordered.

"Finally?"

"Yeah, I've seen you a few times before election night."

"Really?"

"Yep. At the gym, you're always by yourself. I like a woman who can stand alone and I like those blue shorts you wear."

"Thank you." She sipped her water. "So let me ask you, what are we doing here?"

He leaned towards her. "You know what we're doing here." He let that statement hang before licking his lips and leaning back in his chair. "Do you want to see a magic trick?" She nodded, eager for a distraction. "Okay, see this salt shaker?" He lifted it up as if she couldn't see it from where it sat at the table. "I'm going to make this ordinary run-of-the mill salt shaker disappear." He covered the salt shaker with the napkin and slammed his hand down on the table. The napkin flattened with no salt shaker underneath it.

She laughed and clapped. "How did you do that?"

"I can't tell you all of my secrets."

They chatted about nothing in particular: sports, music, movies. She laughed often and felt completely at ease. He smiled a lot, listening more than he talked. Afterwards, X walked her to her car and opened the door for her, leaning in close enough for her to catch another whiff of his scent. "Good night."

Her voice caught and she cleared her throat. "Good night."

It wasn't until she was lying in her bed that she remembered that they hadn't discussed the first date essentials. She didn't know if he had a girlfriend, a felony, or kids.

She still didn't ask those questions when he called and asked her to go to a basketball game a few days later. Shivers went down her spine when he put his hands on her hips, and directed her through the crowd towards their seats. "So you got a man?" he asked during a time out. He looked over and waited for her response.

"No. Do you have a girl?"

'No."

"Why is that?" It was her turn to peer in his face and search for red flags.

"No particular reason."

"You're a man of few words."

"I use enough."

"Do you? I still don't know anything about you."

"What do you want to know?"

"How do you make your money?"

"The hard way."

She raised an eyebrow. "And how exactly is that?"

He shrugged. "Does that matter?"

"Uh, yeah."

"Why? I'll just say this: I make enough to live in a way that is suitable for right now. I make enough to take care of you if it came to that." He waited for her response. She turned her attention to the game instead. The other team won. X took the outcome well. He shook his head and turned his attention back to her. Tracy on the other hand sulked. The Razorsharks should have won. They were better. Why hadn't they played like it? He was quiet while she whined, then grabbed her by the shoulders. "You can't be so affected every time something that you don't want happens."

Tracy brushed away his hands. "I don't need you to school me, remember that."

At dinner, she didn't eat or talk much. Instead, she watched his lips move, followed the curve of his smile as he talked. He was smug, cocky as shit.

"You like hip-hop?"

She almost laughed. What an understatement. She used to eat, breathe, shit hip-hop. But she didn't want to go into all of that, didn't want to discuss heart break. "Yeah."

"You heard that Kendrick Lamar? Yo, I haven't heard someone switch the game up so much since Kanye came on the scene." She smiled, remembered the first time she heard *College Dropout*. She was a sophomore at UPenn and played the album non-stop. She had never heard someone rap about college and racism and family obligations and the perils of consumerism before. She had never heard someone tell her story before. Of course the Kanye that she interviewed years later was way different than the one she initially fell in love with. But the brilliance and the passion was the same. And Kendrick Lamar, his album was mind blowing. Cinematic and gritty, he was a poet, a wordsmith. He told tales that captured the very essence of all that they were. His music stimulated her mind, gripped her heart, made her weep. Why did Black people have to have it this hard? She would kill to be able to write like that. A few years ago she would have died for a chance to interview him.

"Yeah, he's an artist. I so respect that."

"And I so respect you. You're not from around here."

She titled her head towards him. "Born and raised right here."

He lowered his voice. "You don't have to prove that to me. But I bet you haven't been living here for the last few years."

"What makes you say that?"

"I can tell. All of this hasn't touched you yet." No one had ever spoken truer words about her. Her parents had done the right thing and got her out of the city before its stench had seeped into her pores, before its claws had marred her spirit. Now being back home, she felt like an alien. Who were these people who didn't dream and didn't care about their own lives?

She looked away. He was cocky, but the way he carried it was subtle, refined even. He didn't talk much, rarely said anything about himself. She looked back at him and saw wisdom and pain in his face. What secrets lay behind those eyes? She wanted to hear them all. She wanted to allow this man to unburden himself, to touch the innocence she knew was deep inside. How is it that he too had managed to remain unscathed by the city?

She was bugging. It was obvious what he was into and that was obviously wrong. She was glad when he finished his food. Glad when he dropped her off to her car.

4

"Five in the air for the teacher not scared to tell those kids that's living in the ghetto... that the world is theirs"

"The Show Goes On"

Lupe Fiasco

On Monday morning, Tracy woke up in the dark. It seemed like she could never get enough sleep. It was dark when she woke up in the morning, dark when she left work, dark when she came home. And cold was darkness' constant companion. The cold crept in her bones and slowly suckled at her energy. She was exhausted. She kept very still and tried to block out the alarm clock's sound. She could call in sick. She could sleep for another hour, arrive late, and say that she overslept. But there was no time to waste and she didn't want a sub in her room.

Hot water in the shower beat the sleep out of her. She thought of the students she was going to see, of the students she hoped not to see. She ran over her lessons in her mind. They were reading *Native Son* in Princeton, her honors class. Her other classes were knee-deep in the poetry unit. She had led them through a discussion of Claude McKay's "If We Must Die" the day before. The poeticism had been lost on Yale, a class full of teen mothers, foster kids, and parolees. Howard dug the poem though and she was excited to hear their original poetry.

She raked through her closet and settled on a thick navy dress with designer tights, and suede booties. Outside, she swore. It had snowed several inches overnight. Fucking around with this snow she was going to be late and ruin her boots. She started her car and reentered her apartment to change her shoes and check the news for school closings. There were none. Why was it always so fucking cold here? She turned the television off, went back outside, and quickly brushed her car off.

She made it to school with three minutes to spare before her first class. The old brick building was plain and sad, as if the walls themselves settled for a life devoid of note. Inside, the hallways were dim and narrow. Fluorescent lights and egg-shell colored walls were not enough to brighten the place up.

Tracy spoke to each kid she saw as she made her way up to her third floor classroom. Most of them greeted her by name even if she didn't know theirs. At first she attributed her popularity to the fact that she was one of a few Black teachers. Later, she surmised that it was because she was one of the few teachers who acknowledged their presence; who still had a smile left to offer. It wasn't until she was walking through the cafeteria one day that she got a glimpse into what her reputation really was.

Kareem, one of the fuck ups from her Yale class spoke. "Hey Miss Mitchell."

"Hey." She hadn't bothered to ask him why he wasn't in class earlier, she was actually grateful that he had been absent.

His friend spoke to him. "Damn, she a teacher?"

"Yeah, she look good right? But don't get it twisted. I bet Miss Mitchell will whoop a nigga's ass. You see her arms?"

Tracy had chuckled to herself. Today she made it to the second floor landing when she saw Mr. Burke yelling at a group of female students. At six feet, two hundred and fifty pounds, he towered over the girls he was addressing. "Why are you late? You need to go to class so you can at least learn enough to fill out the welfare application."

Tracy's blood ran cold. Instead of continuing up the stairs, she approached the group. "Good morning." The offending students said nothing; they had been shamed to silence. Mr. Burke turned and went into his classroom. Tracy turned to the girls. "Now you go to class and make him a liar." They filed off. It wasn't surprising that he spoke to students like that. During the first week, in the copier room, he had asked Tracy where she went to college. When she told him that she had gone to the University of Pennsylvania he asked, "Oh so you had an athletic scholarship?"

She had learned to keep her head down and focus. She rarely talked to white teachers. In one of her graduate classes, her professor had warned of the dangers of going into the teachers' lounge. It was all too easy to pick up a negative attitude, all too easy to join in with the complaints. Yes, the school was underfunded and the student body was comprised of the throwaways--kids whose parents had not had the resources or determination to either move away or send them to private school. Even some of those parents who lacked in these areas had sense enough to lie and claim that their kids lived with well-to-do aunts in suburban school districts. Of course, the charter school wave added another dimension to the dynamic. These start ups sprung up across town and only accepted city residents and promised to deliver a curriculum that was engaging and geared towards college readiness. All of the parents with good sense had run to sign their kids up. Who could blame them? Tracy wouldn't send her kids to a city school either. She felt like she was walking the prison yard sometimes. However, the throwaways deserved to learn too and the deliberate pains that were taken to deny them of that right made Tracy all the more certain that the key to the future was with them.

So she didn't venture far from her room and she made the best of the four walls she was given. She had bulletin boards covered in colorful felt and topped with exemplary student work. Each one of her classes was named after a prestigious college. In addition to

Howard, Princeton, and Yale, there was Berkeley and Tuskegee. Her lessons tapped into student interest. She juxtaposed poetry with hip-hop lyrics, showed cartoon clips to illustrate a theme, called student homes for 'no reason', and always played music. Her students had learned not to make requests and just enjoy the vibe of Lauren Hill, Marley, and 2pac. It was the vibe of revolution.

She had just put away her coat and purse when the bell rang. Her first class was Yale and most of them were late. Tracy smiled at the six students who were on time. "Go ahead and start the warm-up." She sat down to do her attendance and Dejanik walked in a few seconds later. Her stilettos made a mechanical sound as she made her way to the back of the class. She flipped her red and blonde weave before speaking to Tracy. "I need a pencil."

Tracy didn't look up from her computer. "So?"

"So, can I get a pencil?"

This time Tracy looked over at her. "You're late, you're unprepared, and you don't even know how to ask for something--"

Ryan strolled in at that moment and interrupted her. He talked loudly into his cell phone. "Yeah man, I told that bitch—"

"Get out."

Ryan stopped in his tracks. "Man let me call you back, my teacher is tripping." He tucked the phone in his pocket.

"Get out, you clearly didn't come here to learn."

Ryan laughed. "Miss you tripping. But aight. I'ma get a pass from Mrs. Smith and then you gon' let me in."

Tracy laughed too. It was no secret that Ryan was the principal's pet and he invoked her name every chance he got. "I don't care if the superintendent gives you a pass. You're not getting back in here today."

The bell didn't ring fast enough. The students got up. Most didn't bother to push their chairs in or take their work with them. Tracy shook her head and went around, tossing everything in the recycle bin.

Howard filed in and were greeted with Tracy's cheery smile. They took out notebooks and got to work on the warm-up.

"Now this sounds like a simple question, but I really want you to reach into that critical thinking. What effect does setting have on literature?" There was a faint murmur of conversation as late students slid in and greeted each other. Tracy turned and snapped on LaShonda. "Late students enter class quietly. Talking and tardiness don't go together."

LaShonda smiled guilelessly. "My bad Miss Mitchell."

Daquan raised his hand. "Setting can have a physical impact on the characters."

"That's an interesting point. How so?"

"Well, if the character is claustrophobic or something they're going to be real sensitive to what's surrounding them. Ah check me out." The class laughed and Tracy smiled. The boys had taken up competing with each other to raise the best points in class.

"Can a setting have a mental effect?"

Jeremiah jumped in. "Yeah, like if everything around you is f--" He caught himself. "If everything around you is negative that will impact your mentality."

"How so?"

"If you grow up seeing everyone around you in the drug game, bangin', then you're going to think that's all that you can do too."

"Does that happen around here?"

"Hell yeah." Tracy raised an eyebrow. "My bad Miss, but you already know the answer to that."

Tracy nodded. "Okay class, let's go ahead and take out our homework." There was the sound of collective groans and shuffling of papers. "Oh come on, don't act like you didn't have enough time to do it. Chanelle, I bet you had enough time to go to that teen party at Vixen. Bradley, I know you had enough time to watch the Dolphins get whooped."

Most of the students had their sonnets. Tracy set the class up in groups of four. They were instructed to have each student read their piece out loud. Afterwards, the group would give feedback, saying two positive things and one suggestion for improvement. Tracy walked around the class to monitor.

LaShonda's group was off task. "I'm just saying. 2 Chainz is the hottest out right now."

Tracy interrupted. "I know him."

"Yeah right Miss."

Tracy took her cell out of her pocket and pulled the picture up. "See." 2 Chainz had his arm around her. His eyes were low and Tracy was smiling brightly into the camera. He had been high as a kite that night, funny as hell. "Did you know that he went to college?"

"Miss what was you doing with him?" LaShonda raised her eyebrows.

Tracy narrowed her eyes. "What *was* you doing with him?"

"I mean what were you doing with him?"

"I interviewed him. I told you I'm a writer."

Lashonda smiled. "I know Miss, I'm just messin' with you."

Tracy moved on to another group. "I liked the way you rhymed your words, but why did you keep saying street? I understand repetition and all, but I don't think it works here." Vivian, one of her brightest spoke lightly. Tracy was just glad to hear her participating in class at all. She was glad that she felt safe enough in here to do so.

Tracy lingered with another group. One of her favorite students, Andre, a syrup colored boy with cornrows and Tru City tattooed on his neck, was reading his poem. "All I have in this life is me. I dare not dream of more. I follow what I do not see. Sometimes just breathing is a chore." His voice was low, heavy lashes covered his eyes.

"Nice use of meter Andre. What emotion are you trying to convey?"

He tried to stop the smile from spreading across his face, but Tracy still saw it. "I don't know Miss. The speaker, he doesn't feel nothing no more."

"What's that?"

"The speaker doesn't feel anything anymore."

"Why not?"

This time when he spoke, he looked directly at her. "Because he used to believe that everything would work out. Now he's seen so much. His hands ain't clean so he can't blame anybody. All he can do is what he's been doing."

"Okay so the poet, you, has the additional task of expressing that frustration, that numbness, that hidden hope. The speaker hasn't given up. If he had, he wouldn't see anything wrong with what he was doing." She gave him a meaningful look before moving on to the next group.

After Howard, Tracy had a free period. She thought about what Andre said. He had been placed in her class a month ago after being in juvenile detention for two years. He always spoke slowly, as if he was carefully selecting every word. He wrote in the same matter. Tracy had been taken aback when she read his essay on *Romeo and Juliet*. The prompt had asked him to define love based on the action of the characters. He said that the title characters' love for each other was enhanced by the death of their cousins. "Nobody can claim to be in love without first feeling the sting of a loved one's death. Death makes us love the living."

When Tracy had complimented him on the depth of his observations he was visibly embarrassed, but smiled for the first time. He was quiet in class, took notes, and always did his homework. He was the ideal student, but she doubted that he would graduate. She could tell from the things he wrote that he doubted that he would even be alive to see graduation.

She made it a point to encourage Andre. Tracy gave him brochures for colleges. She hooked him up with the counselor so he could go on college tours. She told him to research countries he would like to visit. She wanted to do anything to let him know that there was more to life than just Rochester.

Behind her desk, Tracy shook away thoughts of Andre. This was not a movie where the super hero teacher swoops in and saves the ignorant masses. She was just here to expose these kids to something different. They would have to want more for themselves. She could not do that for them. She checked her email and laughed at the latest email chain between her line sisters. Friends in her life had come and gone and she felt very blessed to have found a lasting sisterhood.

Next, she checked her cell phone. X hadn't called her after their last date and she wasn't surprised. She knew it was for the best, but she missed him. Her heart fluttered when she saw an unread text message from him. It read, "I can see that it is going to take a little more time to get you on my side. That's okay, I appreciate hard work. See you soon." She smiled.

The rest of the day passed by in a blur. Mondays normally did. She made copies, graded papers, mapped out a unit outline. Tidbits of gossip were exchanged with Ms. Hernandez. At a quarter to four, she left for her sorority committee meeting. They were putting on their most popular fundraising event and it had to go off perfectly. The chapter also stepped at the banquet every year so there were practices on top of the planning meetings.

At nine thirty Tracy made it home. All she wanted to do was pull the covers back and close her eyes. At her door, she saw lilies on top of her mail box. The card was signed by Jason.

Jason Colton was an amateur boxer she had met at Crush when she first came home. He was a smooth talker and sexy enough that Tracy ignored his many short comings and screwed him from time to time when her body cried out in its longing for a man. Jason hadn't fought competitively in years, but his status as a Rochester celebrity allowed him to still think very highly of himself. He got hundreds of likes and inbox messages from half naked women. He liked to tilt his phone towards Tracy as he slowly scrolled through his facebook. She bit her tongue to keep from laughing and pretended to be mad. It was a small price to pay really, he screwed her brains out and filled the testosterone void in her life.

Of course, her dealings with Jason didn't remain that simple. First, it was his fourteen year old daughter, Nikki. Tracy didn't even find out that this kid existed and went to Washington High until after she and Jason were already intimate. With over 1200 students in the building, Tracy had never met the girl before. She had always kept her professional and personal lives separate. Her affair with his messy ass ruined all of that.

One Thursday, Miss Dawkins--a black math teacher, came up to her in the hallway during passing time. "Girl did you see Nikki's father? He is fine."

Tracy could have choked. "He's here?"

"Oh yeah, he's here."

At that very moment Jason walked up to them. Miss Dawkins grinned from ear to ear at his arrival. "Nice to meet you", he crooned as he gently shook Miss Dawkins's hand. She looked like she could melt. To Tracy he said, "See you later baby", and kissed her squarely on the mouth before walking away.

Miss Dawkins squealed after him. "Girl, why you didn't tell me that you were dating him!"

Tracy was livid. Later, she firmly told Jason that she did not appreciate him coming to her job and being so affectionate. It was completely unprofessional and she valued her privacy. He said that he wanted everyone to know that she was his. Why was she always tripping, being so secretive?

After that, Nikki, Jason's daughter, looked knowingly at her. Tracy wanted to run and hide in shame. She could just imagine what her students would think, what they would say. A week later Miss Dawkins burst into her classroom during a planning period. "Please tell me that you didn't know that man is married."

Miss Dawkins's tone had a sternness that Tracy didn't understand. "What man?"

"Nikki's father."

Tracy felt like air was leaking out of her. She walked to a student's desk and sat down. "He's married?"

"See, I knew you didn't know. You wouldn't do no shit like that. See girl, I was telling Nikki how her father is so fine. And she said, 'don't get excited 'cause my daddy is married.'"

Tracy thanked her for the information and told her that she needed to go to the library. In the bathroom, she took a moment to collect herself outside of Miss Dawkins's scrutiny. She blotted her face with a wet paper towel, tried to talk down her anger. How the fuck was Jason married? There was one toothbrush in his bathroom and never any toilet paper, he was always in the club, and he fucked anything moving. Tracy hadn't cared, hadn't made any demands of him. She dealt with him because he was predictable, safe. It could have been the perfect situation, why did he have to come to her job? Why did he need for her to pretend like they were in a fucking relationship? He had to be trying to get his wife mad. He was going to have her caught up in some straight foolishness because he needed attention.

Tracy dragged through the rest of the day. She kept running Miss Dawkins's words through her mind, picturing Jason's slick ass smiling down at her. He did really want everyone to know she was his, he needed them to.

She called Jason. She asked him how his day was and plainly told him that she did not want anyone to know about their involvement and hoped that a married man would appreciate that. She was very calm. He told her that he didn't give a fuck what she hoped, that his marriage was his concern, and if she and Miss Dawkins continued to interrogate his child he was going to call the school board, schedule a meeting with the principal.

She was breathless when she ended the call. She didn't have any feelings for Jason, but she certainly wouldn't have opened her legs to him if she had known how destructive his desperation was.

She remembered all of this as she picked up her lilies and deliberated whether to throw them away or not. She breathed in their light scent, and made her decision. Jason was pathetic, but he had chosen her favorite flower. Inside, she cut the stems and put them in water. She then stripped down to her bra and panties, tied her hair up, and got into the bed. Boris Kudjoe was leaning into her, she reached up and groped his bald head. He was just about to kiss her when the phone rang. She pulled him to her, but his face faded away and all she could hear was ringing. Awake, she reached for her phone and answered it.

"What you doing?" It was X.

"Sleeping. What time is it?"

"A quarter pass 11. I wanna see you. Let's take a drive. The roads are clear."

She was suddenly wide awake. "Okay, I can meet you in half an hour."

"Come on pretty girl. Let me pick you up. I will never come to your house uninvited." She relented and rattled off her address. In fifteen minutes, X was waiting outside of her door.

He greeted her with a kiss on the cheek when she got inside of the car. "You're in the cut, right in the heart of the city, but not too many people come down these one-ways."

She nodded her agreement. "Yeah, but you'd be surprised at what goes down on this street."

"No I wouldn't. I know them homos across from you move major weight."

"Yep, like clockwork." She relaxed into the seats, looked out the window and sighed. It was a perfect night. The streets were empty and glistened under the fresh snow. Overhead, the sky was a tranquil midnight blue. The moon stood alone, keeping vigil--waiting for a long lost lover. Maybe she had found hers. That thought surprised her, and she looked over at X and quickly looked away.

"I love to drive around on nights like these. Lets me think, lets me dream." He put his hand on her leg as he spoke. She didn't remove it, though him knowing what her neighbors were up to was not lost on her. He drove to the top of a parking lot and switched off the radio.

In silence they looked over at the city. The skyline hinted at the promises of grandeur Rochester once held. Her parents said it was the place to be in the '70s. The industries were booming and the people were determined to change the world. Now the industries were shipped overseas and the residents were a shadow of their former selves. She, like everyone else who couldn't leave or was determined not to, was bracing herself for worse days to come. The violence worsened every day and could no longer be contained to the hood. A teacher had been held-up in the school's parking lot a few weeks ago.

X took his seatbelt off and turned to face her. He placed a hand on her cheek and looked at her intently. She looked down.

He waited until she lifted her eyes. "I will never let anything happen to you. I need you to trust me."

"I don't even know you."

"Yes, you do."

He put his seat belt back on and eased out of the lot. They rode in silence. This time she couldn't appreciate the stillness of the night, or the moon's luminous simplicity. She had never felt like this before. He was right, she felt like she did know him. But what she knew scared her. How could she tolerate his profession?

When they reached her apartment, he got out of the car and walked over to her side. He opened the door and held her hand as she slid out. Without warning, he brushed his lips against hers, let them linger, and then deepened the kiss. With one hand nestled in the arch of her back he eased his tongue into her mouth. It was thick and agile, rousing a passion in her that she no longer wanted to control. He tasted like cinnamon.

5

*"Hey if I were you, it would be me
that I'd go home with."*

-Andre 3000

"Green Light"

ON FRIDAY AFTERNOON, SHE waved goodbye to her last student and wished them all safe weekends, and headed to her car. The weekend was here and soon so would Monday and the worries and routines of the week.

Nothing exciting had happened. No major incidents at work. Jason had called her several times and she wasn't even tempted to pick up. X hadn't called. Maybe she should get a dog. She shook that thought away. She wanted some excitement, not mess.

Her eyes scanned the road for cops before she reached into her purse and pulled out her phone. Her intention was to delete X's number, but she couldn't do it. She settled for dialing her sorority sister.

Thalia was one of the best things about being back home. At 5'1, 100 pounds, Thalia talked more shit than anyone Tracy had ever met. There was a brash confidence to her that must have aided her in corporate America, because at the age of 31 she was named Regional Executive Accountant for Bausch & Lomb, and sent to revitalize their Rochester plant. Seeing that Bausch & Lomb was one of the city's biggest employers, Thalia had made it her business to establish herself in the community. Underneath her power suits and perfectly relaxed hair she was a sistah, through and through.

"What you doing?"

"I was thinking about getting my pussy ate, but Terrance here doesn't know what he's doing."

"Shut up. Can he hear you?"

"I don't know, he's in the other room. I don't care. We need to go out. Get some fresh meat."

"The last time I went looking for some fresh meat I ended up with Jason's rotten ass."

Thalia laughed. "Yeah you're right. What am I talking about? There's going to be plenty of men at the banquet. Let's just go out and have fun. Let's get cute, get drunk, get feisty. You know?"

Later, Tracy stepped out of Thalia's Lexus and instantly adopted a new personality. They were in the Black club district and robberies and assaults were not infrequent here. Tourists were targets. Tracy made it clear that she was a native with her stern expression and purposeful walk. Thalia was from Georgia, but her sassy walk and attitude did not exude southern hospitality.

Their walk to the club could have been used for sociology lecture on the dynamic between Black men and women. Guys hung idly around, hurling cat calls and sexual explicative to the women of their liking. "Hey sexy, chocolate." "Oh girl, I like your style, you're different" were directed towards Tracy. "Ay yo, little mama" "Hey red bone" were reserved for Thalia. Neither woman lost stride.

Once inside, Tracy relaxed a bit. The heat produced by moving bodies enveloped them. They quickly became part of the surging crowd; the entire place pulsated.

"Let's get a drink." Thalia was pressed against Tracy at the bar. She was wearing black patent leather boots with five inch stiletto heels. Tracy, always height conscious when she was with Thalia, wore flats. Tonight the two were almost shoulder to shoulder.

They yelled to be heard and laughed at nothing in particular. A part of the club experience was pretending not to notice the dozen men staring at them. One particularly brave fellow stood next to Tracy and eased his arm around her waist. Thalia commented immediately, "Nigga, you awful familiar. I guess this round is on you, huh?" He paid for the long island iced teas which they drank quickly. This was not a night for casual sipping.

The reluctant buyer lingered. He seemed to be at a loss for words and was obviously taken aback by Thalia. He didn't know what to do with his hands. They were in his pockets, on the bar, grazing Tracy's hip. He spoke too slowly and was too short. He was screaming something about the weather when Tracy said, "Thanks for the drinks. Have a good night."

When Tracy turned and walked away, Thalia was right on her heels. Tonight was only about having fun. It was about being under the influence of strong drinks and good music; tonight was about being the desire of as many men as possible and leaving them all disappointed.

As the alcohol spread through Tracy's system she felt lighter on her feet. She eyed men brazenly and took up more space with her dancing. She lost her reservations and let the music move her. She and Thalia screamed along with the lyrics. "All I want for my birthday is a big booty hoe!" At 1:35 Thalia nudged her and she remembered herself. They always left before two, before the clubs officially closed and chaos broke out in the streets. They were trying to party, not die. Tracy felt a bit unsteady when she maneuvered the steps. She laughed and straightened herself. Thalia was lither, occupied with her iPhone, presumably making arrangements for later.

"Ay yo, ma," Tracy ignored the cat call and kept moving. Men were even more aggressive after the club in their last-ditched frenzy to go home with somebody. Women who couldn't figure out a way to tactfully disarm their advances risked being called everything but their names or even assaulted. Tracy wasn't having it.

"Tracy." She snapped her head around to see X standing in front of a Range Rover. Tracy warmed at the smile that was planted on his face. She walked over to him. His arms were already outstretched for a hug. She felt that familiar feeling when they closed around her.

He whispered in her ear, "I know the type of woman you are. I'm going to earn you. You'll see." He broke the embrace. Looking up at him Tracy felt a pull on her heart.

"I'll call you." She walked back towards Thalia.

"Who are your friends?" A huge man stopped next to X and gestured towards them. He had to have been at least 6'9, 300 pounds. He was the color of ginger snaps and judging by his serious expression, he was in charge.

"Uncle Derek, this is Tracy, the woman I'm seeing."

He said *the*, not *a*. That one preposition kindled the pull on her heart again. Thalia sidled up to her and was unusually quiet. "Girl, who is *his* friend?" Tracy shrugged the question away. She didn't want to miss what the huge man was going to say next.

"I like them. Bring them with us."

X raised his eyebrows at Tracy. It was an invitation, a challenge. Tracy felt like accepting and she was pretty sure about how Thalia was feeling. Still, she followed female club etiquette and posed the question, "Do you want to go?"

Thalia was already walking over to the Range. She introduced herself and the bigger man loomed over her, swallowing her hand in his, already captivated.

There was a strange vibe in the car. X drove, a sober silence radiated from him. Derek chatted Thalia up and kept looking into the rear view window to see her. Thalia stared back at him. Tracy averted her eyes. X kept his on the road.

The SUV was soon out of the club district and gliding into an area that was known as 'ghost town', aptly named as the streets were always empty after sun-down. Ghost town was the most treacherous part of the city. There everyone, those in and outside of the game, had an equal shot at being held up, stabbed, or shot. If Thalia had an idea of where they were going it didn't show. Tracy crossed her arms tighter around herself.

The car stopped on a dead end street in front of an empty house. They all got out and X put a hand protectively around her waist and led the way. She remembered what he had told her the last time she saw him. *"I will never let anything happen to you."* She relaxed a bit and an inconspicuous door opened and they all went inside.

It was an after-hours spot. There was just one room which was covered in plush navy blue carpet. A bar covered an entire wall, leather couches covered another. Marijuana smoke hung heavily in the air, there wasn't an empty glass in sight, Slaughterhouse played in the background. It felt like a different world.

The men escorted them to the bar and retreated. Tracy followed X with her eyes as he walked away. She turned to Thalia. "So?"

"So this is different." Thalia winked, "Maybe it'll be good for you. You've started to act like an old lady."

"Is that right?" Tracy leaned in closer even though they both could hear each other fine. "And what exactly is different about this?"

"Bitch, don't play dumb. You know what I'm talking about and you know exactly what he's into. It's not my scene, but I'm nobody's judge and jury. Just be smart."

Thalia held Tracy's gaze meaningfully. This was why she made six figures. She had a knack for sizing up situations and a willingness to gather new experiences.

The men returned and champagne was brought over. Tracy wondered if they were celebrating something. Derek filled her in, "You know, I'm not around women like y'all every day. Shit, Junior never brings women around. I'm honored." He tipped an imaginary hat and was rewarded with Thalia's laugh.

The quiet that followed was thick with what was not being said. Tracy barely sipped her champagne. She was sobering up and trying to figure out how to act in this new environment. She scanned the room. A few mellow men, bobbed their heads to Max B and exchanged quiet words. X's friend from the gym mouthed along with the lyrics and jabbed a finger towards an imaginary opponent. Two men had their arms around ghetto trophies--girls with fake hair and lashes, skimpy clothes and succulent asses to fill them out.

"You know I get sick of hearing this shit. Whatever happened to love?" Derek smiled at Thalia as he spoke. She didn't return the gesture. He persisted, motioned for the bartender. "Antoine, have them put on something slow." Al Green's classic, "Let's Stay Together" began to play.

"Come dance with me." Tracy glided off of her stool at the sound of X's command. She reached up to wrap her arms around his neck and nuzzled her head against his chest. His spicy, earthy scent was intoxicating. His body was hard and solid against hers. His hands rested in the small of her back.

She didn't notice anything else. People were probably watching them, they should have been. Something major was transpiring, something rare. And though no words were spoken, their meaning was palpable. Their simple two-step was the conversation. Her fingers tapped against his neck, asking, questioning. His kneading hands on her waist, acknowledged and released her doubts and fears. When the music stopped, she knew what she wanted.

They sat at the bar for over an hour; none of them wanted the night to end. Thalia regaled the entire group with stories about Augusta. She even had X roaring with laughter. Tracy talked about sports—their beloved and doomed Bills. Derek talked about the election and local politics. X talked about music.

She leaned into him. "Okay, so who's your favorite member of The Lox?"

Thalia snickered. "She can talk about this shit all day."

"Styles P. Gotta go with the Ghost. Who's your favorite member of Wu?"

"Sorry old man, Wu Tang is a bit before my time."

He nodded. "My oldest brother played them nonstop. Favorite R&B artist?"

"John Legend. Yours?"

"Al Green." She nodded. That explained the intensity of their dance.

The two men she noticed earlier, ditched their trophies and approached the group. X acknowledged them. "What up 'Riek, Sean."

They both slapped him up. "Can't call it. Just got a little something we need to holla at you about." X got up and led the two a few feet away.

Derek cleared his throat. "Well, I guess we should get you ladies home."

"Yes. You gentlemen have definitely shown us a good time." Thalia smiled tipsily.

X returned to the group and held out a hand to help Tracy up. They shared another silence as she met his eyes and accepted his outstretched hand. He didn't break the embrace and continued to hold her hand on the way out. 'Riek and Sean's girls stared unabashedly at her. X was the second biggest catch in their pond and here she, a stranger, had managed to reel him in.

*   *   *

On Sunday morning, her alarm rang out, interrupting a dream about X and signaling that it was time to visit the House of the Lord. She went to church two times when she lived in New York. The first was too small and too loud. The second was too big and too pompous. She didn't have time for church anyway. It was different in Rochester. Her spirit felt heavy, it needed a release. She had brought the subject up to Thalia over lunch a few months ago.

"What was it like your first year here?" She dunked her chicken wing into the bleu cheese.

"Cold."

She laughed. "Yeah, I know that. But how did you feel?"

"Girl, stop trying to Dr. Phil me and take your ass to church."

"Do you know a good one?"

"Go to Love Temple."

Tracy had been skeptical. What kind of name was that for a church? Love Temple? It sounded like a cult. However, she felt a peace she had yet to find anywhere else the moment she entered the sanctuary. She didn't go every Sunday, but lately she had been going more often than not.

Today she made it there just as Pastor began his sermon. "This isn't a cult. God gives us free will because He wants us to choose Him. I'm not saying don't have fun, don't live life. You shouldn't be a hermit. You should be in the world but not *of* it. But your idea of fun should change. Jesus came so that we may have life and have it more abundantly."

People in the church were nodding and agreeing with Pastor. They shouted the Scripture in unison. Pastor had taken a breath and collected his thoughts. He looked as if he was straining to hear every word from God and deliver it in a way that his flock would receive. Tracy prayed that his words would fall on fertile ears.

"So what does having life more abundantly mean? First thing that comes to everyone's mind is blessings. Oh, I'm waiting for a blessing. I know I'm getting a blessing. A blessing is right around the corner. You woulda thought blessing owe you money the way you stalking it. You woulda thought blessing was a refund check the way you checking your mailbox." The congregation chuckled.

"Life more abundantly means that you have more of life. You notice more of life. The Holy Spirit fills you with joy so that you actually appreciate that life. We spend almost all year waiting for summer. The kids want to be out of school, we all want to go to barbecues, and the beach, to Darien Lake. Then what happens when summer hits? You go around saying for a week, 'Isn't it nice outside? It's so nice. I can't wait to go outside.' Next thing you know, you're by the water cooler and you say 'Isn't it so nice outside?' and the negative fool who you don't even like says, 'oh it's a little too hot for my taste.' And now for the rest of the summer you talking about, 'it's too hot.'" More laughs from the onlookers.

"What has happened is you have let the world get into your thoughts, your personality, your desires, your character. You have spent seven months cold, cooped up, miserable. Here you have your beloved summer and you're complaining! Oh my Lord! That is being of the world. You can't let the world dictate what you want, how you talk, how you act. You don't need to seek validation from the world because you're getting it from our Holy Father."

"When you have life and have life more abundantly you receive blessings and you actually cherish them. You don't just stick out your hand and start asking for the next thing. You're praising and worshipping God not because of what He did for you, but because of who He is. You take the time to remember that it is through God's majesty that we have summer and that even in the winter God is working some things out for you."

"So when you're a Christian it's not fun to listen to music that speaks of death and destruction. It's not fun to go out somewhere where your total worth is measured by how you shake your butt. You don't watch movies where life is taken away casually. Not because you're not allowed to. There's no commandment against it. It's not a sin. It's only a sin if you let your mind wander down the path those things promote. But I don't see how you couldn't. Nobody but crack heads are in the crack house."

Tracy clapped along with the congregation. She turned the pastor's words around in her mind. He was right, there was no denying that. But the abundant life that he spoke of seemed, well…boring. She liked to go out, she liked R-rated movies, and despite her best attempts not to—she still loved hip-hop. She loved the Lord, but she didn't want to be married to church--avoiding every imaginable evil, condemning every sin, missing out on so much of life. And she didn't want to be the church's mistress either. In high heels, tight skirts, saying "I'm blessed and highly favored" while baking cakes and laying on her back for the few bachelors.

She was just trying to live her life the best way she could. Jesus had to understand that.

Back at home, in sweats and a wife beater, her hand stopped midway between the plate of marinated salmon and the foreman grill. She was sick of eating alone. She wanted to cook for X. Feed him, watch his lips wrap around the fork. She wanted those lips on hers.

She called him. "Where are you eating Sunday dinner?"

"I'm not. What's up?"

"You should come get a plate."

"Just a plate?"

"Yeah, just a plate."

She was wet when she hung up the phone. She ran her hands down her body and contemplated whether she should change clothes. Her old UPenn sweats had seen better days, but they were uber comfortable. She decided to keep them on. She wanted him to see her, the real her.

She was buttering the rolls when her doorbell chimed. She wanted to run to the door, but the butterflies in her stomach slowed her pace. Butterflies? It felt so silly and so good.

In the peep hole, X's face was hidden behind two dozen assorted roses. She squealed and flung the door open.

"That's so sweet."

He kissed her and ran a hand over her face. "You're sweet."

She blushed and stepped aside, granting him access to her home. "Come in." He stood in the middle of the space, taking everything in. He walked over to her overstuffed couch and picked up one of the emerald green, suede throw pillows appreciatively. He ran his hand over a hand crafted coffee table and stopped to browse the titles of novels on her mahogany book shelf. He noted the African sculptures and black and white photographs.

"Your place is like you."

"What do you mean?"

"It's warm."

"Warm?"

He stepped closer towards her. "Yes, warm."

The butterflies in her stomach were dancing. She looked away from him. "Why don't you take a seat?"

She unwrapped the roses and held them over the sink gingerly. She ran luke warm water and used kitchen scissors to cut the stems in one swoop. They billowed out in the vase, their lushness instantly transforming the room. She leaned in close to them, letting their velvety petals graze her face. Yeah, she wanted to feed this man. She set down the plates and a pitcher of homemade lemonade. She raised her fork to her lips when he interrupted her.

"Do you mind if I say grace?"

She shook her head. "Not at all, please do."

"Lord, thank you for this food, for this moment. Amen."

She laughed. "Straight to the point."

"Never a reason not to be." He took a big bite of food and nodded appreciatively. "It's good."

She smiled. "Thank you."

"I never got around to asking you what you do."

A few months ago she would have been too proud to say she was a writer. These days the only thing she was writing were lesson plans. "I'm a teacher."

"Word? What subject?"

"English."

"I could see you doing that. You like it?"

She paused before answering. "I do. It's just not what I thought it was going to be." She hadn't said that out loud before, had tried to stop herself from even thinking it.

"How so?" He dipped a piece of asparagus into the lemon butter sauce before pushing the whole piece into his mouth. She watched his lips.

"Well, I was living in the city, as a writer. Everything was perfect and then everything wasn't. I had no idea what I was going to do. Had to make money so I started substituting. I loved it. So I emailed one of my former teachers. Great lady, she did thirty years in this district." She tsked. "Shit, I'll be lucky to do three. But anyway, I emailed her and she told me about this graduate program that would put me right in the classroom. So I came home."

"You look around and see that Black people have it worse than ever. We have the lowest life expectancy and the highest rates of unemployment and incarceration. No march, no speech is going to save us from that. We've been there and we've done that. And now the system is so entrenched that we wouldn't even know what to protest in the first place. These kids listen to pure rubbish all day and when you talk to them, you realize they really don't give a fuck, really. They have nothing to live for. So education is the only way to make a difference. But it has to be specific, it has to be thoughtful, it has to be deliberate. Because once a people have nothing to lose they fight back, they rise up. If we could just tap into that, if these kids could just apply..." She trailed off and took a sip of her lemonade. "It really could change their lives."

He just looked at her for a moment. His eyes were warm as if he were seeing her for the first time. Heat rushed to her face and she lowered her eyes. Finally, he spoke. "You really believe that?"

"I don't know. I can't stand some of 'em. Like they come to class, don't do shit, don't even try to. Most of the other ones are sweet, dumb as hell. You ask 'em 'Why?' and the first thing they say is "I don't know". They don't even think about the question. Then there's some that's smart, but act dumb. Like when did it become shameful to be intelligent? I guess you can chalk that up to the Trinidad James of the world." She sighed. It felt good to be able to say these things. She would feel like a race traitor if she said this in front of her cohort. She already had to suppress the urge to get offended every time they said something negative about the kids. Ultimately, truth was truth. Still, one sideward glance from Tracy and her colleagues would adjust their tone or stop talking all together. The fear of the angry, Black woman came in handy sometimes. She smiled "But still even in the midst of complete hopelessness there are some that have that spark, that are really trying to make it out. Those are the ones that I really love."

He nodded. "And those are the only ones who have a chance. Problem with the schools is they're trying to save everybody. God doesn't even work like that. You make a choice to walk with Him or you make a choice to walk away."

"What choice have you made?"

"Baby girl, you shouldn't have me in your house if you have to ask that question. What type of niggas you deal with?"

Heat ran to her face. "Hard to tell who's who these days."

"No, it isn't. It's actually easier now. You judge a man by what he does. What he stands up for. If it's nothing, then he's nothing. Every good tree bears fruit. The schools need to chop the rest of 'em down."

"Yes, but with the right push—"

"Fuck that. They're holding everybody back. It's not their fault, the system created 'em. But whatever, for our purposes"—he waved his hand between him and her--"For our purposes, they gotta go. There never was a successful slave revolt in the States. You know why?"

"There was always an informant." She was quiet. Just like slave owners strategically employed tactics to reduce their fine African specimen to cowering chattel that either in glee or pure fear of the Godliness of their masters revealed plots that could have changed the course of history, the education system had lobotomized a once vibrant people into welfare recipients and call center employees and prisoners. X wiped his mouth. "You can cook. I've never had stuff like that at somebody's house."

She waved a hand. "That was nothing."

"Oh really? Okay, I see you. And it's healthy too right? That's how you keep that banging body?"

"Ah that's corny." She laughed.

He smiled. "We can't all be as cool as you."

They settled in on the couch and watched *Overboard*. It was a classic romantic comedy and one of Tracy's favorites. Tracy was surprised by the intimacy of the moment. She couldn't believe they were sharing sofa time. It was comfortable. It was exciting. It was how she had imagined a relationship to be.

He played in her hair, wrapped and unwrapped the kinky strands around his fingers. She scooted towards his touch. His hands in her hair were so relaxing that she dozed off. A knock at the door woke her up.

"Expecting someone?"

"No." She rose and went to the door. What if someone had followed him here? She glanced back over at him. He was calmly looking at her, but seated on the edge of the sofa. She looked through the peephole and almost swore. It was Jason. Again, she glanced back at X. "Excuse me for a moment."

"Nah, let him in."

She felt guilty and then immediately admonished herself. She wasn't doing anything wrong, she had nothing to hide. She opened the door wide. Jason was standing there, all dressed up and ready to lie. He wore a suede blazer that was too light for the weather, a maroon button-up, dark jeans, and a pair of tan and maroon loafers. What a clown.

He was about to attempt to kiss her when he spotted X. Always cocky, he stepped in as if he owned the place. Trying to work his Don Juan magic, he pecked her on the cheek.

"I didn't know you had company. You don't waste any time do you?"

Heat rose to Tracy's face. It was all she could do not to slap his smug ass. "What the fuck do you want Jason?"

He was visibly taken aback but he recovered. "You."

His simple affirmation enraged Tracy. "You can't be serious." She wanted to cuss him out, but remembered that X was sitting behind her listening to every word. "Listen, we're done. You hear me? We're finished. I would appreciate it if you left right now and never came back."

Jason didn't seem to hear her and didn't seem to care that X was staring him down. In fact he seemed to appreciate the audience. He relished this opportunity to mark his territory. "Baby, I know I messed up. Just let me explain. I want to make everything right." He looked around the room and spotted the roses. "So you liked them? The lilies weren't doing the trick so I decided to try something different."

Confused she turned around and looked at X. He was now on his feet with his hands crossed behind his back. Jason had left those roses?

"She asked you to leave. Leave." His voice sounded like thunder. She never had a man defend her before. She moved to diffuse the situation. "Thanks for the flowers Jason, I'll call you later."

She stepped towards him and towards the door. But Jason wasn't going for it. "You better tell him who I am."

Tracy almost laughed. She had never known anyone who was so deluded. He was a fucking loser. Did he want her to say that? She struggled to find the right words.

X beat her to it. "Him doesn't give a fuck who you are."

Jason brushed past her and addressed X for the first time. "Nigga, I don't want to hurt you. My hands are on paper. I would kill you."

"Yeah? Well, I got something that ain't on paper."

Jason faltered. He seemed to see X for the first time. "This is the company you keep, Trace?" Tracy didn't answer him. She almost felt sorry for him. "Ok, well I'll be looking forward to your call." He backed away and didn't turn around until he was a foot away from the door.

Tracy's hands trembled when she locked it behind him. That could have ended a dozen different ways. She was thankful it didn't conclude in injury, death, or arrest. She tried to settle herself before she faced X.

"So you didn't get me those flowers?"

He smiled, "Not this time. Hey, look I have something I need to do. Thanks for dinner." He moved towards her and lifted her head towards him. Still smiling, he took his thumb and wiped off the place where Jason had kissed her cheek. With a quick peck on her lips and a swift swat on her ass he was gone.

Tracy stood in the same spot for a moment. Did that just happen?

The rest of the day was uneventful. She talked to Thalia and summarized the Pastor's message. Thalia loved the Word, but was not a fan of church. She preferred to sleep in on Sunday's with her current squeeze. Still, every Sunday night she asked Tracy about the message and noted the Scriptures.

After their unorthodox Bible study, Tracy filled Thalia in on the rodeo that occurred earlier. "Girl, you shoulda let him shoot Jason's bitch ass."

"Ok. Will do next time."

In her bed, X consumed her thoughts. She wanted to feel his lips again. She wanted his arms around her. She wanted him inside of her. But she couldn't act on those wants. There was no telling what he thought of her after today. She needed him to want her. She had to wait.

6

"Mind tellin me no, body tellin me exit.
Breasts said yes, give me more wet kisses
Uhh, twist my body like the Exorcist"

-Foxy Brown

"Get Me Home"

MONDAY REARED ITS UGLY head quickly. In her first period class, they were reading August Wilson's *Fences*. Denzell, a laid back street kid, was playing Bono. "Naw....naw...you mean if the nigger knew how to *drive* he'd be alright. Been fighting with them people about driving and ain't even got a license.'" The class erupted in laughter.

Tracy smiled herself. "Denzell read that line again."

"'Naw....naw...you mean if the nigger knew how to *drive* he'd be alright. Been fighting with them people about driving and ain't even got a license.'" There was less laughter this time.

"Again."

"'Naw....naw... you mean if the nigger knew how to *drive* he'd be alright. Been fighting with them people about driving and ain't even got a license.'"

"What point is Wilson making here? How can we relate this to what we know about the time period?"

Deja raised her hand. "The Black people that moved up North during the Great Migration didn't get the same jobs as white people."

"Exactly! So how did Troy get a job as a driver? What does it say about his character? Denzell."

"He not afraid to speak up for himself?"

"Are you asking me or telling me? Strong writing makes a clear statement."

"He got the job because he went and talked to the union. He's a leader."

"Exactly. You drew your own conclusion based on the text. If you can do that on the test, we are going to murder that thing."

"Hell yeah." Tracy narrowed her eyes at him. "My fault Miss. But I'ma kill that test though." He turned his attention back to the play. "'Mr. Rand know you ain't got no driver's license?'"

The rest of her day flew by. Before fifth period she was standing in the hall herding in students when she heard LaShonda cursing.

"What the fuck do you mean, you don't care? I got his seed bitch." She was yelling at Nicole, a curvy freshman who had just come off of a long term suspension.

"Like I said, I don't give a fuck. You can get over it or you can give me the round."

Tracy surveyed the situation. Onlookers were quickly gathering around the girls. The security guards were on the other end of the hall. She yelled to them, but they couldn't hear her over the rumbling of the crowd. She could go inside her classroom and call the fight into the office. They would then dispatch over the radio to the security guards. But by the time they made it through the crowd, LaShonda would have gotten her ass whooped.

Tracy forced her way through. She half pushed, half tackled LaShonda into Miss Hernandez' room. She closed the door behind her and told Hernandez to call the sentries. Angry tears ran down LaShonda's face as she continued cursing at Nicole through the door. Her act was convincing enough, but Tracy knew that Lashonda was scared. And hurt.

When the guards finally made it down the hall, Tracy's heart rate had returned to normal. Both girls were taken to the administrator's office. She couldn't believe she had done that. One of the teachers in her cohort told her that she saw a teacher rolled out on a stretcher after trying to break up a fight. She couldn't believe that she had put herself in such a precarious situation.

One guard, Freeman, a well-built man well into his forties couldn't believe it either. "Girl, you crazy. You shoulda just let those girls fight. Ain't no sense in trying to talk life to the dead."

Tracy didn't respond. He was the dead. He was a middle-aged toy cop who chased every skirt in the building—student and staff. He used to bring Tracy little gifts every day until she told him in no uncertain terms that she wasn't interested. She turned on her heels. She had a class to teach.

After dismissal, she emailed the administrator about the fight and asked him to set up a mediation. She doubted that he would, but it was best to ask. She found herself grading papers mindlessly. She wanted to think about something other than work. She wanted to talk to someone who understood. She dialed X before she could talk herself out of it.

He sounded hurried when he answered, "Hello?"

She suddenly didn't know what to say to him. She didn't want to come off as thirsty. She had just seen him yesterday. "Hello, this is Tracy." She cursed herself after she said the words. Of course he knew who it was.

"Why, hello Tracy."

"Hello Oxford. I didn't want anything. Guess I just wanted to hear your voice."

"Good 'cause I want to see you. Where you at?"

She should have been on her way to step practice, but the banquet could wait. Her man wanted to see her and she wanted to see him. Her man? She needed to calm her ass down. "I'm at work, but I'm finishing up."

"Yeah? Don't you and Thalia have to plan for that event?"

He had been listening at the after-hours. What didn't he know? "I don't *have* to do anything."

"Okay tough guy. Meet me on Magnolia and Seward."

Magnolia and Seward was located on the southwest quadrant of the city. The ride in her Accord became noticeably rough when she entered the area. There weren't many tax payers over here and thus the area was then last to receive basic services—garbage disposal, plowing, street repair. She hit a gigantic pot hole and swore. "Why don't they fix this shit?"

Tracy pulled into the lot that X described and waited. She considered locking her door, and then was disgusted with herself. Still, she was relieved when X pulled alongside her.

"Hey baby." He slid into her car and pecked her on the lips before putting on his seatbelt.

His kiss and casual use of 'baby' quickened her heart. She pulled out of the lot. "Where are we going?"

"To work."

"To work?"

He directed her down a side street. Her face was hot and she gripped the wheel tightly. After taking a quick left down an alley and a right on a one-way, they ended up on Jefferson Avenue. She knew where she was now.

"Pull over here." She eased behind a dumpster, giving them full view of the corner store across the street. Three guys were standing near the door. X adjusted his seat and leaned back.

"You see the one in the green vest?" The one he was referring to drank from a brown paper bag, but he his gaze was steady. "That's Sonny. 'Bout seventeen years-old, looking after his two little brothers. Mom died of cancer a while back. His auntie and them smoke through the foster care money."

An older man with a severe limp and old leather coat approached the store door. He stopped and spoke to Sonny. Sonny didn't respond.

"That's Ray. Ray's an old timer, been out here for as long as anyone can remember. Petty hustler, pretty decent thief. Used to be able to empty a house out in thirty minutes. I saw that nigga on the block once selling a refrigerator. He had a stroke few years ago, so now he just boost. He went up North a couple of times all fucked up like that." He looked directly at her. "I know niggas was doing him dirty."

Tracy looked away. It was a gray day, so cold that the sounds of the street seemed to be hushed. Cars crawled by, slush splashing against their wheels. The mounds of snow that the plows left pressed against the curbs were rock hard and littered with garbage. A woman and two small children walked past the store. Their gait was hunched, they folded their bodies against the cold and kept their eyes on the ground to avoid ice. Two teenage girls passed by on the other side of the street. They avoided the icy sidewalk and instead walked on the edge of the road. One wore a yellow coat bunched up at her hips.

X shook his head. "That's Melvin's daughter. Hot in the ass. Ten degrees out here and she got her coat pulled up like that. He rolled down his window. "Tonya!" The two girls stopped. Tonya spoke to her companion briefly and sauntered over to the passenger side of the car. Her smile froze as she got closer to the car and realized that it was X who had summoned her. "Something wrong with your coat?"

"No X." She pulled the coat down. It now stopped mid thigh. "What you doing out here?"

"Little girl, you don't question me. Where you coming from?"

"School."

"School? Where your book bag at?"

"I left it at school. Too cold to be carrying that around."

"Not too cold for you to be strutting around out here though. I guess you don't need books. Cute dummy. That's what you trying to be?"

"No X."

"Take your ass home. Now." She walked away without another word. To Tracy he said, "Pull in front of the store." She pulled out in a wide swoop just as someone in opposing traffic was trying to make a left. The driver rammed on the horn. X shot her an annoyed glance.

Sonny approached the car. "What up X."

X reached out the window to slap the young man up. "Same shit. 'Riek been by here?"

"Not since this morning."

X nodded. "Looking slow."

Sonny shrugged. It's the fourteenth. But you know niggas gon' get them checks tomorrow and it'll be flooded."

"No doubt. Aight man, stay up." He rolled his window back up. "Make a left at the light." He talked as they drove, stopping only to tell her when to turn. "You know everything is a business. People are people. It's a shame that you have to micromanage niggas. But unless an employee sees value in what they're doing and has an investment in their organization, they will half-ass. They'll cut corners and that will inevitably fuck up my money."

"So what do you do when that happens?"

He looked at her. "You shouldn't have to ask that." He had her stop in front of what appeared to be an abandoned house. "I'll be right back." He slid around the back of the house and disappeared.

This had to be the trap. Rochester winters were brutal and there weren't many Sonnys who would bear the cold and stand out on the block. Illegal electricity was hooked up in traps and customers were serviced through the windows. This system had a lot of flaws. Traps were susceptible to police raids and burglaries.

How would she know if something happened to him? Should she keep the car running?

What the hell was she doing out here? She should be at step practice. She would be laughing to herself at the annoyance on Thalia's face. She herself would be irritated with Diane, a wanna be diva with little rhythm, and too much attitude to spare. She had been lost in her thoughts, sitting there for ten minutes, when X tapped on the window. Startled, she jumped in her seat. He slid into the car shaking his head.

"You have to be more alert. You know where you are, don't you?"

"Yes, I know where I am. But didn't you say that you wouldn't let anything happen to me?"

"I can't protect you from everything. You have to use your head--"

"This isn't what I had in mind when you said you wanted to see me." She pulled off and was driving faster than she needed to on the slick roads. If she disposed of him immediately she could still make it to practice.

"Slow down."

She cast him an icy glare and shifted into fourth gear.

"What are you doing? Slow down."

She pulled over. "You don't tell me what to do. I don't work for you so don't talk to me like that. What are you doing? Did I ask you for a tutorial on drug dealing?"

"How you gonna teach them little niggas if you don't understand where they come from? You looking right at it, but you don't know what you're seeing. This, this right here is the land of the forgotten." He nodded towards a dilapidated house. "You see these houses. What do you think goes on inside? Who do you think sits in your desks?"

Her chest tightened and she lowered her eyes. X lifted her head. "How you gon' be with me if you don't understand what I do? Stop fighting me baby. I can show you things, I'm sure there's a lot you can show me. There's no time to spoon feed and sugarcoat everything."

"What makes you think I want to be with you?"

He was quiet for a moment. "I know the way I feel and I know the way you feel about me."

Subdued, she eased the car back onto the road and drove at a slower speed. She turned the radio up in an attempt to gain composure. Did he know the way she felt about him? She wanted to slap him, to kiss him, to rip his clothes off. She wanted him. She wanted to confide in him, to trust in him, she wanted to be free to love him.

She sighed. That was it. That was the simple truth that she had been running from for a while. She wanted to be in love. This wasn't the kind of man that she was supposed to do that with.

"So how did it go?"

His smile was cryptic. "I straightened things out."

When they pulled back into the lot, there was an awkward silence. "I'm going to come by later."

She wondered how late later was. She wanted this to be the night. "Okay."

He leaned over and kissed her. His light kiss was sweet and engaging. She felt herself being swept up. She leaned into him, into the feeling.

*   *   *

She went to step practice, better late than never. When she entered Soror Kim's house she could feel the tension. Thalia, as usual, was at the helm.

"Okay, I know everybody has varying step experience, but we all know what a ripple is right? I don't want to be presumptuous so let me define it. A ripple should be a series of individual definitive beats. So Diane, why the fuck do I hear you, when I should only hear Chantel?"

Tracy almost choked. Thalia was always a straight shooter, but today she was a marksman.

Diane, the color of vanilla wafers, turned red. She blinked a few times before answering. "Yes, we do all have varying step experience. Some of us are more versed in things that actually matter. Thalia, you are crass, and a piss poor representation of *my* beloved sorority. I'm out of here." She picked up her Juicy couture duffel bag and sashayed out. The door had barely closed when everyone started speaking at once.

"Okay, ladies let's take a five minute break. We're going to have to change formations because Diane is not coming back." Thalia turned and hissed to Tracy, "Girl, where the hell have you been? You can't leave me here with these half-stepping skaters."

Tracy laughed. She felt giddy.

"Oh no, I know where you've been. You off getting dicked down and I'm here with these dumb broads."

"You are a crass and piss poor representation of my beloved sorority."

"Can you believe that bitch? I just couldn't take it today. I don't have time to be tiptoeing around incompetent people's feelings today. The banquet is in two weeks. We have more layoffs at work. The painters keep fucking up my condo. I couldn't deal with her bullshit today."

Tracy studied Thalia for a moment. "Layoffs? You're going to be alright though, right?"

Thalia chuckled. It sounded force and hollow. "I don't know. Buy me a drink after this?"

"Yeah, of course."

The rest of practice was grueling. Nerves were on edge and everybody was ready to snap.

"You said it was an eight count."

"Why do we have to train? That's not even lady like."

"We need to drill the opening step. *Some* people are not precise at all."

That last comment was a shot at Tracy. She wasn't the best stepper, but she was definitely the most enthusiastic. She really threw herself into every step. What did precision have on showmanship?

When they wrapped, Tracy was drained. It was a true exercise in patience to work so closely with so many women and for free. She had learned in situations like these, where opinions were abundant and tact was scarce, that it was best to just be quiet. That wasn't always an easy feat.

"You wanna get a drink like this?" Tracy gestured towards their clothes.

"No, I wanna get several drinks like this."

Tracy followed Thalia to Shooters, a quaint bar in the 19th ward. This side of town housed working class Black folks and was where Tracy was raised before her family moved to the 'burbs. Most of the people in Shooters were friendly, but gave you room to breathe. It was the perfect place for a vent session, well spaced with everyone immersed in their own conversations. They sat at a table in the corner.

The owner came over. He had an earnest good nature that instantly softened their moods. "You ladies slumming it today?"

Thalia, always the charmer flashed him a grin. "Joe, I'd have you know that this is by far the classiest establishment this side of the Mason Dixon line." To Joe's delight, she poured her southern accent on extra thick.

They ordered rum and cokes. Tracy waited for Thalia to speak. "I feel like I've been set up. They said they sent me here to revive this site and when I do, it's still not enough. What more do they want? I've cut costs by 23 percent. Do you know what I had to do to cut costs by 23 percent in one quarter? I'm tracking everything, every expense report, every performance evaluation, every fucking staple. Yet, my site is still flagged for low productivity. I can't let any more people go and increase production. I think they were going to shut us down regardless of our performance."

"But you would still have a job right?"

Thalia shrugged. "Doesn't look like it."

Tracy knew better than to try to coddle Thalia. "What would you do?"

She shrugged. "I have some money saved up. I would be okay for a while. I'll find a job. It's just that the market is shrinking up here. This town is dead. I would probably have to move. Again."

Tracy nodded. "Well, you've been complaining about our humble city since I met you."

"Yeah well this cold ass shit box has grown on me. So have you." She paused, and mulled over her next words, "The people here are real, I appreciate that. And you're the best friend I have ever had."

Tracy was touched. She had never had many friends and Thalia had always been there for her. She was smart, funny, nonjudgmental, candid… "Thanks Thalia, so are you."

They sipped their drinks and planned. If she were laid off, Thalia would stick around for three months and apply to jobs across the country.

They were on their third drink when X called. Thalia raised her eyes brows.

His voice sent shivers up Tracy's spine, "Hey baby, are you home?"

Tracy looked over at Thalia. "Not yet."

"Okay, cool. I'm going to wrap things up and then I'll be over there. See you in an hour."

She struggled to find her voice, "Okay." She slipped her phone back into her purse.

"Let me find out your ass is in love."

"Girl, please."

Thalia shot her a look. "This is me you're talking to. Remember, be smart." She stood up.

"Where are you going? We haven't finished our drinks."

Thalia picked up her nearly full glass and downed it. She followed suit with Tracy's. "Have fun." She grabbed her coat, said goodbye to Joe, and was gone.

Tracy shook her head. Thalia would be just fine. The alcohol had warmed her blood and X's call had warmed her body. She paid for the drinks and made her way to her car.

At home, she showered and contemplated what to do with her hair. She settled on pulling it back from her face with the jade combs Thalia had bought her in Japan. Feeling exotic, not to mention tipsy, she oiled herself in Jasmine oil and slipped on a knee length red silk kimono, another gift from Thalia. The elegant fabric hugged her frame and didn't leave much to the imagination.

Next, she lit candles around her apartment and turned off all of the lights. She felt cliché, but wanted this night to be special. She sat on her bed, Indian style, and waited. The bell rang as she was wondering if she had completely lost her mind.

She took a breath to steady herself before opening the door. He just stared at her. This thing between them was so powerful that there was no need for words. There weren't any that would match the intensity of the moment. She stared back at him. He licked his lips.

She stepped aside so that he could enter. He scanned the room before turning back to her. She walked around him slowly, allowing him to see her at every angle. She helped him out of his jacket and felt like she was watching herself. She was ready to put on a show.

Now, as she sensed his lust, she became primal. This man would know her. He would savor and remember her. She would make sure that the mere mention of her name would arouse him. He would take her to places she had never been and she would do everything in her power to return the favor.

She pushed him against the wall. On her tiptoes, she rested her lips almost against his. Her breasts were rubbing against him and she could feel his manhood growing. Every so gently, she kissed him. She took her time. She nibbled at his lips and let her tongue explore. He reached for her, but Tracy was running this show. She shifted her body and danced her tongue around his earlobe. With building fury she sucked and licked his ear. He was growing harder against her. She unzipped his sweatshirt and he put his hands up so that she could remove the white tee underneath it.

She attacked his nipples next. She devoured each one, letting the heat of her mouth arouse him. She bit gently and was rewarded with his low moans. She worked her way down his torso. His body was hard and chiseled.

On her knees, Tracy unbuckled his belt and pulled down his jeans. He wore blue pinstripe boxers that she didn't remove. Instead, she hovered, letting the anticipation build. This was not a time to be coy or to ration out her skills. She wanted him to know just what she was capable of. She reached into the slit of his underwear and eased out his manhood. It was a thing of beauty. Its length and girth called to her. She looked up at him, he was holding his breath. His desire catapulted her to the next level. Wetness pooled between her legs.

She rubbed him against her face, swirled her tongue against the length of him, taking care to add deliberate force to the center vein. She bathed him in her saliva. The heat and suction of her mouth was creating an inferno. Finally, she took him fully into her mouth. Her full lips nestled tightly against his skin. It felt like home. Her tongue slivered about, caressing him; writing timeless love letters.

Against the wall, X's stance was weakening. He burrowed his hands in her hair and pushed himself further against the back of her throat. He felt so good as he filled every inch of her mouth. He was throbbing against her lips. She gagged, but didn't stop. There would be no stopping. He had cast a spell upon her and now was her time to work her magic.

He was thrusting himself against her faster now. His moans were deep and guttural. Tracy moaned in response. Their muffled voices were singing a duet. She looked up at him again and he stared down at her in amazement. The room was thick with their passion. She stood up. She was enjoying having him at her mercy and so she pushed him into her bedroom. He stumbled on the jeans that were still wrapped around his ankles. He took them and his boxers off.

Once X was seated on the bed, Tracy slowly slipped the kimono down, letting her fingers linger on her naked skin. She made sure he was watching before she removed a condom from her nightstand and got back on her knees. She took him into her mouth before smoothly sliding the condom on. Their eyes never left each other's when she straddled him.

Tracy was wet and hot, and X inside of her was like rain against a wildfire. He filled and soothed every inch of her. She had never felt this way before. She thrust her hips and moved her ass across him, pushing him further inside of her with every movement. Their bodies found a natural rhythm. Their kisses were sloppy, he jammed his tongue into her mouth. His hands never left her hips. He was urging her to move faster, she was begging him to get deeper. He pumped faster, he was too deep now, she felt a pressure building up that she could not control. She tried to pull away from him, but he was everywhere. It felt so good and hurt so bad.

She couldn't control the frenzy that was building in the deepest part of her. She moaned and clawed at his back as she struggled to hold on. Her eyes were shut tight and the blackness she saw was interrupted with flashing colors of red and yellow. Then everything inside of her erupted and she broke into a thousand pieces.

Everything had gone quiet. She was still, panting against him. Her head was nuzzled against his neck. His words brought her back, "Go ahead and say it."

"Say what?"

"Say you love me."

He pulled her face to his and peered into her eyes. She didn't say a word. She didn't have to. He already knew.

In his arms she felt more alive than she had ever before. She didn't have the energy anymore to fight it, to question it. He was a high that she intended to ride until it crashed. Everything just felt so right.

*   *   *

Just before dawn he kissed her and told her that he had to go. Barely conscious, she grumbled a response before she fell back to sleep. When her alarm went off she woke up with a start. Already she was reaching out for him. She smiled and shuddered at the thought of last night.

At work she could barely contain her elation. She hummed to herself as she walked around and monitored the students. The kids noticed her chipper mood and responded in suite. When the Howard class came in, Tracy was sure her day was going to get even better. That was until she saw Andre. Andre came to school every day because it was a condition of his probation, but it would have been better for everyone, if he had taken this day off. His face was swollen and puffy. Two of the fingers on his left hand were broken and in a splint. Tracy fought the urge to embrace him.

An uneasy quiet fell over the class. Andre was the definite elephant in the room. None of the students were bold enough to ask him what happened or to tease him. They didn't even dare laugh, lest he think it was directed at him. Tracy went about the lesson as normal. Andre didn't look at her for the entire class.

At dismissal, she gestured for him to stay. "Who did this to you?" Her voice shook.

"Come on Miss", he kept his eyes glued to the floor.

She stared at him a second more, but knew there was nothing she could do or say. Still she persisted, "Will they kill you next time?"

He raised his eyes. What she saw there, chilled her to her core. He didn't care if he died.

7

"You see right through me. How do you do that shit?"

-Nicki Minaj

"Right Through Me"

A WEEK BEFORE THE banquet and Tracy couldn't wait for it to be over with. The daily practices and constant obsessing over checklists was fraying her nerves. On a Friday night she found herself sitting on Thalia's living room floor instead of on X. A fact that she was not too pleased about. Still, she had duties to fulfill and so they were going over the last minute touches. Thalia was pacing back and forth with a notepad.

"Diane insisted on being in charge of the centerpieces. I told her to go to Michael's and call it a day. But oh no, that just wouldn't do it. And where are the damn centerpieces? Knowing her, she ordered some gaudy ass Louis Vuitton bootleg shit."

Tracy shook her head. She knew better than to interrupt one of Thalia's tirades.

"How long did you spend trying to find a baby doll shirt that would fit Iman?"

"Three weeks."

"Well, I told her that a 2x was the largest you could find and that she needed to go have it taken out. Her fat ass talking 'bout that's her size. Bitch got more rolls than Old Country Buffet. Who told these big bitches they could step? I'm telling you, we need to have auditions next year. Did you talk to the people at the hotel?"

"Yes, I talked to the people at the hotel. They will have the room set by 4. They know we're coming at 5. Girl, the banquet is already sold out. Everything is going to be fine."

"I'm the president of the chapter. I know the shit is sold out. The banquet cannot just be fine. We have to outdo ourselves every year." She continued to rattle off more tasks that needed to be done.

By the end of the evening Tracy had had just about enough of Thalia. "Okay boss bitch, I'm outta here." Thalia in turn gave her the finger. Tracy laughed and gave her a kiss on the cheek. This girl was like a big sister to her, tiffs and all.

She wished X would come over. She wanted desperately to plunge into this love affair. She wanted lazy days in bed. She wanted to dream together. She wanted to cook him breakfast in the morning, fuck him all afternoon, and lay with him all night. She wanted to feel his heart against hers. She wanted to be his helpmate and she wanted him to be her rock. She wanted carefree times with his arms wrapped around her, where they could recklessly plan and execute a future together. Of course, neither one of them had time for that.

She had only seen him once since their bout in the sheets. She had prepared a quick dinner, but X had left soon thereafter. "Business," he had said unapologetically. He called every day, but it wasn't the same. Had he lost interest in her after hitting it? That seemed too simple for him, but it wasn't impossible.

*   *   *

When the banquet finally came, X was the last thing on her mind. She surveyed the lavender and silver decorated hotel lobby. White coated waiters walked around and filled everybody's champagne glasses. At $150 a plate, only the city's most prominent African-Americans could attend. The men talked about the square footage of their homes while the women endlessly complimented each other.

They were the Talented Tenth, ranging in color from damn near white to blue black. They were doctors, lawyers, judges, politicians, athletes, corporate executives. They claimed to go to these things because they helped underprivileged students, but in reality they went because it afforded them an opportunity to celebrate themselves. They laughed and lifted glasses to all that they had overcome, to all that they had accomplished. They had avoided crabs in a barrel, studied hard, networked well, smiled at their white counterparts who underestimated them, and managed to downplay their weaknesses. They would always be on the folds of the American Dream, but in that tucked away space, they had created something that was just their own.

Tracy stood on the edge of the lobby and watched them. She envied them a bit. Did she have that much grace? Would she ever look that elegant? She watched the curve of the ladies necks, their impeccable posture. She wondered if they learned that in Jack and Jill. Her line sisters told her about the etiquette training they endured as children. She didn't know what the double-dutching and opened fire hydrants of her childhood had trained her for.

Her friends from that time wouldn't fit here. She could imagine how loud Tinesha would be right now. She would smack her teeth at the ladies' looks of reproach and object to Tracy's gentle chiding. It wasn't like Tracy fit in with Tinesha's crowd either. They had linked up when she first came home and went to a French Montana concert. She plotted the quickest route to the emergency exit, and shook her head at the opening acts. Girls with pounds of weave and short skirts danced, more like stripped. Tracy marveled as they clapped their asses and dropped into splits. They were doing all of this for a $50 prize that the MCs mentioned and dangled before them like a carrot. Two girls had danced to three songs and ultimately a tie was called. Neither one of them saw a dollar.

Tracy hadn't forgotten where she came from and didn't feel like she was better than anybody else. It was just that all the acrylic nails, tattoos, and stifled potential repulsed her. Those things always had. She had always been different, had always wanted more. Looking at the banquet's guests she wasn't sure what more she was seeking. She wasn't like these people either, didn't know if she wanted to be.

But tonight she did look like them. She wore a red, curve hugging, backless, calf-length BeBe dress. Her hair was pulled into a bun, her make-up artfully applied. She had turned more than a few heads tonight, she saw one woman squeeze her husband's arm as she passed.

She was almost back at her table, when she saw X. It was as if everyone else had disappeared, he was all that she saw, all that she felt. She floated over to him, taking in how good he looked in his tuxedo and red bow tie. Unsure of how to greet him, she stopped a foot shy of him; just close enough to smell and feel his heat.

"Come on give it to me."

"Give you what?"

"The double kiss. Isn't that what y'all bougie niggas do?"

She kissed him on both cheeks and laughed. "That's what they do." She tapped his bowtie. "This is a nice surprise."

"Yeah, I thought it would be better that way."

"So you like what you see so far?" Her grin was mischievous.

"I sure do."

The evening was perfect now. A soror gestured to her wildly. Well, maybe the night wasn't perfect yet. Tracy nodded towards her and put a hand on X's shoulder. "Well you know I'm working so I'll see you later." She sauntered away and looked over her shoulder to make sure he was watching her go. He was.

She had time to stop by the table during dinner to greet all of her guests. They were an assortment of people she knew from the school district, grad school, and the young black professional crew. They complimented her on her dress and the event. She only heard X.

He was completely at ease, even in this crowd. As usual, he wasn't talking much, but he looked like he was in charge as he listened attentively to her guests. He draped an arm around Tracy's chair. She leaned in closer to him. "Enjoying yourself?"

"I am now. You've been working the whole room, haven't had time for me."

She couldn't tell if he was joking or not. For once, he had to wait for her. "Business baby. You came by yourself?"

He shook his head and pointed across the room to Derek. He was dressed in a tuxedo too, but it looked almost comical on his gigantic frame. He and Councilman Brooks were engaged in deep conversation.

"Now that's business baby."

"How do they know--?"

"Real estate."

Thalia motioned for her and Tracy dutifully pulled herself away from the table. It was time to start the step show.

Their theme was the paparazzi; they were celebutantes running away from overzealous cameramen. They were dressed in black slacks, black baby doll shirts, and black pumps. To finish the look off, they wore oversized sunglasses and pink scarves.

The lights went down and the ladies sashayed out into their formations chanting, "When you see me don't be mad 'cause my nose's in the air/you know you like the way I twist my hips and swing my hair/cause I'm a lady first and second to none/so just sit back and watch cause we've only just begun."

They stomped and stood frozen in their formations. The crowd cheered them on. "Okay, I see you Thalia", "You better work it ladies" "That's right, swing that hair!" The distinct pitch of their sorority's call rang throughout the banquet hall.

They stepped with force, precision, and their trademark sassiness. They glided into the different formations and struck poses that would have made a supermodel envious.

When it was Tracy's turn to start a step, she sashayed across the floor. "Sorors, do you know what they say about us?" Her sorors responded to her, "No, what's that?" "They say that we're too pretty to step. She stopped and shook her hair. "But let's show 'em how these pretty girls get down." She put extra drama and flair into her moves and the audience ate it up. When they strolled off of the stage to Keri Hilson's "Pretty Girl Rock" they were rewarded with a standing ovation.

In the restroom, Tracy was beaming. She grabbed Thalia by the shoulders, "See girl, I told you we were going to kill it."

Thalia was just as enthusiastic, "And did you see who's here?"

"Who?"

"Derek."

"Yeah, I know."

"Did you see him rubbing shoulders with damn near every politician that's here? How does he know all of them?"

Tracy shrugged. "Real estate."

Thalia raised an eyebrow, but didn't comment further. Their sorors were hugging each other and laughing. All of the stress was worth it.

After she cooled down, Tracy changed back into her dress. She was anxious to get back to X, but he wasn't at the table. She searched for him and was stopped constantly by people who wanted to congratulate her. She smiled respectfully, hardly hearing a word.

After a few minutes, Tracy resigned herself to having a good time without him. It wasn't as if they had come together. He wasn't really her date. This was her night. She relaxed, had a glass of champagne.

She was laughing with Henry, a professional, albeit not starting, running back, when X spotted her. He nodded at Henry and pulled her away. "You were great." He was looking at her with an intensity that she had missed.

"Was I?"

He ran his hand down her bare back, "Yes, you were. Yes, you are." A heated silent moment flashed between them.

Derek interrupted them, "Ah, the belle of the ball."

She smiled up at him, "I'm afraid that honor goes to Thalia."

"Where is she?"

As if on cue, Thalia walked over. She wore a skintight black dress with a plunging neckline. Only Thalia could look so sexy and sophisticated at the same time. "Here I am."

Tracy shot X a pointed look and they returned to their table. Dessert had arrived, a decadent piece of moist, chocolate cake, drizzled with raspberry sauce, accompanied by a scoop of vanilla ice cream. Tracy dove into hers, swirling the spoon around the sauce and letting it linger on her tongue. She stopped once she noticed that X wasn't eating. Instead, he was watching Thalia and Derek. They were still chatting away, but standing noticeably closer. Each time Thalia laughed, she touched him.

"What is it?"

"How well do you know her?"

"Very well. I keep good company." Her smile went unreturned. The deejay played "Reasons" by Earth, Wind, and Fire. Tracy could not resist the urge to dance. "Come on youngster, let me learn you something real quick."

They did an easy, close two-step. She was riding on a cloud, induced by his hard body against hers and its sweet pungency. She came crashing back down to earth when Diane called her name.

"Tracy, well look at you."

Tracy stepped away from X and looked at her quizzically. The two weren't exactly on speaking terms. "Yes, and look at you Diane."

"Well, aren't you going to introduce me?" She was looking at X with a brazen interest. It was unmistakably sexual.

"Looks like you're doing a fine job of introducing yourself."

X stepped in to diffuse the cattiness "Hi, I'm Oxford." He shook Diane's outstretched hand, but moved closer to Tracy.

"Hi Oxford. I'm Diane. Are you a close friend of Tracy's?"

Tracy's face was hot. "Oh yes," X said and rested his hand on her ass. "We're the closest of friends."

Diane turned a shade of scarlet and abruptly excused herself. X pulled Tracy back close to him. "Definitely not my type." Tracy laughed. Women like Diane thought they were everybody's type.

She hadn't had this much fun since she'd moved back. It was good to be carefree and elegant and admired. It was good to hobnob with the city's finest and still be herself. It was good to be with her sisters and show what a woman should be. It was even better to be on X's arm.

"Any business tonight?"

He nodded in Thalia and Derek's direction, "Doesn't look like it. Come to my place with me."

She had been waiting for this invitation. She was eager to see where he rested his head, eager to peel away another layer of him. She smiled her agreement.

In his car, she stole looks at him. His focus was on the snow covered road in front of them, but he occasionally smiled in her direction. She wondered what it would take for him to lose his control. What it would take for him to fall in love with her.

She turned her attention from him and looked outside of the window. Gusts of wind sent snow swirling about in tuffs. It was a starless night and the crescent moon looked lonely in the inky sky. She hoped her nights of loneliness were behind her.

She had wasted her time on little boys who hid behind their money or their status. Men like Jason who spoke words with no meaning and did things with no purpose. They were weak and they knew it, all too aware of all that they could never become. They were dangerous.

She looked back over at X. She had never known anybody like him. She had been waiting for him, for a man that could fill her up. One who's laughter could chase away her fears, who's love could inspire and empower her. She had wished for somebody to share her life with. Dreamt of being one flesh and one heart. Prayed to be a we.

X navigated hills that took them up and further away from the city. In twenty minutes they had entered Pittsford, a quaint suburb that was synonymous with old money. They pulled in front of what looked like an old farmhouse.

He parked. "No one has ever been here."

The inside was a renovated loft space. The walls were made of exposed brick and covered in framed Gordon Park photographs. The hard wood floors glistened, Tracy kicked off her pumps. She followed the sloping hall of the foyer into his living room. Nearly an entire wall was covered by a flat screen. A leather sectional dominated the other wall while a gigantic, saltwater aquarium covered the third. Tracy walked over and looked into the aquatic world. She peeled herself away from the tank and passed through the dining room. It hosted a mahogany antique table that could easily seat twelve. In the kitchen, she marveled at the black granite counter-tops and state of the art appliances. She climbed the open staircase that lead to his bedroom. There was a fire burning in the fireplace across from the king-sized sleigh bed. A black, velvet blanket covered the bed, invitingly.

Tracy turned around and faced X. Every time she thought she was getting closer to him, she realized that there was so much more to know. "I have never seen anything like this."

He grinned, "Is that a good thing?"

She swirled around with outstretched hands, "Um, yeah, I think so."

"Come here."

He kissed her and ran his hands down her frame. They made love in front of the fireplace. Later, wrapped in the velvet blanket, she asked, "What exactly did you do in order to be given the keys to the kingdom?"

"Nothing was given baby."

"Okay, what did you do in order to get all of this? Do you even know how incredible this is?"

"Tracy, what do you think I did? All of this ain't shit compared to what it cost me."

She snuggled closer to him, "Tell me."

He pulled her on top of him and pushed his fingers through her thick hair until they reached her scalp. Methodically he massaged, as if he wanted to let his hands do the talking. After a long moment had passed, he began, "I was bred for this. I'm from Forrest Hills. Queens. My mother was from a nice family. Her pops was a professor, might still be. My dad was from Queensbridge. He was deep into the game. Him and Uncle Derek, his baby brother." He paused. "Well, classic story of a good girl falling for the bad guy. My mom left everything that she knew to be with Pops. They had Prince, Harvey, and me."

"Everything was everything until Pops got killed. By this time, Prince and Harvey were heavy into the streets. Harvey got killed two years after my pops and Prince went upstate. Uncle Derek was trying to hold shit together, but competition is no joke down there. So we did what any corporation does when operating gets too expensive, we relocated."

He was quiet and continued to knead his hands against her scalp. She hardly felt them now, wrapped up in his words. She couldn't imagine loosing everyone like that. "What happened to your mother?"

"They said it was an overdose."

"They said?"

"She could barely go on when my pops died. Loosing Harvey and Prince was too much for her." *Suicide.* He didn't have to say it.

He got up and fed the fire. The flames licked and consumed the firewood, but weren't enough to warm the chill that had fallen on the room.

"So why do you do this?"

He sat back down next to her and placed his hand on her cheek. "Someone has to."

*   *   *

Tracy woke with a start. She was in the bed now, but X wasn't there. She rose quickly, wrapped herself in the sheet, and tentatively headed down his stairs.

She found him in front of the open range stove, in silk pajama pants. He hummed to himself as he flipped a pancake. He seemed different to her now. Bare.

"Morning baby."

He turned to face her and laughed. "See now that's a bad dress. Come here."

It was mornings like these that she had been missing. They ate their breakfast and then screwed again. Later, they took a bubble bath in his whirlpool tub. He soaped her entire body lovingly. He too seemed amazed by the moment. "Would this be enough for you?"

She surveyed the room and quickly nodded.

"Just wait. We're making major moves. We getting legal money now. Gotta always want more, remember that."

She didn't ask him what he meant. She was hopelessly happy, she didn't want to hear anymore.

They dried off and she dressed in his t-shirt and sweats.

"I can't have my girl walking around looking like this."

His girl? "I'm going straight home."

"Uh uh. You work hard, you should have nice things. He opened a drawer and pulled out a stack of hundred dollar bills. He thumbed through it and handed her a thick wad. "Go out and buy yourself something nice."

She had never held that much cash. "X, I don't need--"

He cut her off. "Don't you ever want things that you don't need? You deserve it. Make sure you buy some warm weather things, some nice purses, bathing suits."

"Bathing suits?"

"Yeah, what are you doing when school is out in February?"

She was turning twenty-five during February recess. Twenty-five already and her life hadn't ended up anything like how she thought it would. She shrugged. "Nothing."

"Good, we're going to Miami. Make sure you get what I told you. Only top of the line shit. We'll be there for four days, let me know if you need more money."

Business called so he dropped her off to her car. She drove back to her apartment dazed. So much had changed so quickly.

She called Thalia and could barely get a word in. "Girl, whew! That was the best banquet ever. How the hell are we going to top that next year? It was just what I needed." She said the last sentence in the breathy whisper that Tracy was used to hearing.

"So who's the lucky guy?"

"Oh no. It's nothing like that. I just feel inspired. What's up with you?"

" Same old. X has instructed me to go shopping for four days in Miami."

"So you finally found your prince huh? And he's whisking you off to the steamy beaches of South Florida."

"Uh, yeah." She laughed. Was it even permissible to feel this good?

"You got a stack, right? Come over so we can start planning this shopping spree."

"Oh no, I'm not even dressed."

"I bet not. Okay let's do lunch at French Quarter at one."

At home, she was already missing X and his luxurious apartment. She told herself to slow down. With his line of work she couldn't afford to get too attached to him or the lifestyle he offered. He had lost his whole family to this business. Who's to say that she wouldn't lose him?

She lay back down, got up, cleaned a bit, and watched television until it was time to go meet Thalia. French Quarter was an unassuming, Black owned, creole restaurant. The décor was simple and elegant and the food was amazing. Thalia was studying the menu when Tracy entered. She was glowing.

"Okay, so if you're doing Miami, there are a few must have items. You need a printed dress, Hermes scarf, Louis purse, no not Louis, that's so not you. A Chanel bag, bathing suits, ooh girl, you would look so good in an all white, Gucci bathing suit. You need a couple of new dresses, satin, with bold colors."

All of this before they had even ordered. Tracy didn't know which of them was more excited. Over her shrimp étoufée Thalia continued, "So of course you're going to want to go to New York to get all of this stuff."

Tracy hadn't planned on going back there so soon. "Thalia, I know how to dress. I'm not going to trek around the world for some clothes."

"It's not around the world, it's a six hour drive. Girl, you have to suffer for fashion. Well, since you twisted my arm I will come with you."

Tracy raised an eyebrow. "Okay, and when should we take this proposed trip?"

Thalia lifted her arm and looked at an invisible watch, "Shit, today."

"Today?"

"Yeah, let's go and make a weekend of it. You have Monday off for MLK day right?"

"Yes, *I* have the day off. You corporate types gotta work on the Black messiah's birthday."

Thalia looked away for a moment before flipping her hair. "I got laid off two weeks ago."

"What? Why didn't you say anything? Oh my God T, are you okay?"

Thalia held up a hand. "I'm fine. It's not like I was blindsided. You know I've made my plans, the wheels are in motion. They gave me a severance package, so this is like an extended vacation."

"Why didn't you tell me?"

"I didn't tell anybody. Guess I was embarrassed. The mighty Thalia, laid off." She flipped her hair again. "So you down?"

The air had been let out of Tracy's sails. She had been going on about all of the excitement in her life and she hadn't even known what was going on with Thalia. She was always so tough, so put together; but Tracy noticed a pierce in her armor. Times were hard and jobs were scarce. If Thalia, who was clearly an asset, had been let go from her job, it was not going to be so easy to find another one. Tracy didn't know if Thalia was a bit deluded or just too proud to admit that she was scared. But if she wanted to act like everything was fine, Tracy would indulge her.

She sat up straight in her seat and flashed her biggest smile. "So are you driving?"

She hurried home to pack and left Thalia to make the arrangements. She had everything she had ever prayed for. A fulfilling career, friends, love. She didn't want to thank God for X; they were fornicating and he earned a living off of sin. But X brought her so much joy that she had to thank God. After all, He knew the desires of her heart anyway.

He sounded rushed when he answered the phone, "This isn't a good time. What's up?"

"Just wanted to tell you that I'm headed to New York with Thalia for a shopping spree." She couldn't contain her giggle.

Click.

She looked at her phone for a second. The call hadn't dropped. That wasn't like him. She wondered if something had happened. Was it a bad time to talk? Why? She shook her head. How did she end up here? In love? She didn't know if she was in love, but she was definitely in something. Infatuated? Insane?

8

NEW YORK HAD ALWAYS beckoned to Tracy. There was a special energy, a tantalizing mix of allure and danger. Tracy had seen beyond the glamour and excitement and knew that at its heart, New York City is a machine--recklessly churning out outcomes,--unable to calculate emotion, unable to supply compassion. X's family had been chewed up in the city's assembly line. She herself had almost fallen victim.

Thalia was unfazed by their entrance into New York. She followed the traffic and they emerged from Lincoln Tunnel into the middle of Manhattan. Her gps was calling out directions in a chipper British voice.

"Where are we staying anyway?"

Thalia's grin was wicked, "You'll see."

"Well, can't you at least get an American to give us directions to 'you'll see.' That accent is driving me nuts."

Thalia laughed. "Naw, I get tired of listening to y'all American bitches."

Tracy's nose was almost pressed against the car window, she cracked it a little to get a whiff of the city. She breathed in deeply. There was no other place in the world like this.

They turned on Central Park West. "Approaching destination" the gps chirped.

In front of them stood an elegant, but imposing building. It was the Trump Plaza Hotel.

"We're staying here?" Tracy's words came out in a rushed screech.

"Yep."

The valet took the car and a bell hop magically appeared to take their luggage. The lobby was tastefully decorated in modern bright colored furniture. The floor and front desk were made of Italian marble and the dark colored walls screamed money.

She fell in step behind Thalia at the front desk. "We're checking into one of your two bedroom, Park view suites. I believe our accommodations have already been paid for."

"Yes, Ms. Clark. I just need a credit card for incidentals."

On the elevator, Tracy couldn't help but wonder if Thalia could afford such plush accommodations. But she didn't want to spoil the mood by asking. Thalia winked at her and led the way into the corridor. She smiled big before opening the door to their room. It was more breathtaking than the lobby. The floor to ceiling windows offered a spectacular view of a snow covered Central Park. She wished X was here.

Thalia walked around nonchantantly. She set her stuff down and said a simple, "This will do." When she walked into Tracy's room and found her sprawled across the bed she was not having it, "Uh uh girl. We did not come here to sleep."

Tracy laughed and dutifully got up. They changed and decided to eat in the hotel's five star restaurant. It did not disappoint. There was a quiet elegance about the place that suited her just fine. The waiters had a grace that was befitting of royalty; utensils clinked lightly against plates as the diners took small bites of their decadent meals. Tracy and Thalia set erect in their seats and grinned at each other.

They donned the accents of the obnoxiously rich, "Why I just cannot believe this place. I heard it was amazing and for once the rumors are true."

"Well, it will suffice. I prefer the Four Seasons or the Waldorf."

They shared a hushed laugh.

Tracy selected the fork farthest to the left and enjoyed her arugula and wild mushroom salad. She wanted to lick the plate that her scallops arrived on. The lamb was perfectly tender and seasoned. The fig tart she ordered for dessert left something to be desired. Still, it was a magical evening that she and Thalia definitely deserved.

The pregame party was on as soon as they hit the suite. Tracy plugged in her iPhone and they bumped hips and had a consultation about outfit selection. Pleased with their selections, they did each other's make-up and then changed into club wear.

A dormant part of Tracy was being awakened. When she went out at home she worried that someone would recognize her as a teacher. Here in the city she chose a skin tight dress and leather spiked booties. Her hair was piled high on her head and her eye make-up was extreme. Gold costume jewelry and a gold clutch completed the look. Thalia looked equally as sexy and the two hailed a cab to Chaos.

She had been to Chaos once before for an industry party. That night champagne had flowed freely and the same was true for tonight. Except tonight she and Thalia had their own table, they didn't have to pull strings to land on anybody's guest list, and they weren't expected to act as glorified props for some newbie's sensitive ego. But the rest was the same. Big intimidating men were at the door; appraising the women, selecting who was worthy of entry. Inside there were too many women, too many men who thought too highly of themselves, and too loud music.

They had a ball. They drank too much and danced the night away. Tracy yelled over to Thalia, "Going to the ladies room, be right back." Thalia nodded in response and continued to two-step.

Tracy was giggling to herself when she came out of the stall. A woman's reflection in the mirror startled her. Tracy glanced over at her quickly, she had a half-shaven head and six inch heels and wore a red leather skirt and a see through blouse. Tracy lathered her hands and rinsed them. She took a towel from the rest room attendant. Lindsay watched her the whole time in anticipation. When Tracy turned to go, she finally gave in and spoke. "My God. Tracy is that you?"

Tracy remembered her first all-white party, how Lindsay had dressed her and how she had gotten her big break. She would always be grateful for that. But Lindsay changed once she was dubbed *the* hip-hop stylist. She stopped inviting her places and feigned surprise when she saw Tracy at industry events. Tracy recognized the bullshit, but smiled back long enough in order to find out which one of her clients was going to be at Bloomingdales or Saks or at a Korean massage parlor. Incidental bump-ins usually made for interesting interviews. None of that mattered anymore.

"Who else would it be?"

"Wow. You seem so…different."

Tracy smiled. "Thank you."

On the way back to the hotel, Tracy laughed to herself. She was so different. She was happy.

Tracy and Thalia retired to their separate rooms. She sat on the chaise, then her bed, then the sofa--enjoying every inch of the suite. Restless still, she called X who picked up on the second ring. "So how is the big city treating my girl?"

She got a chill up her spine every time he called her that. "Not as good as you."

"Must be doing something, you're up pretty late."

"I had a beautiful night."

"I will be sure to give you plenty more of those. I can't wait to see you baby."

Butterflies swam in her stomach. "I can't want to see you too."

In the morning, she and Thalia ate a quick breakfast of toast and eggs and got started. On foot, they headed east to Fifth Avenue. Inside of Prada, they were greeted warmly. Mini sofas were strategically placed around the showroom. Each piece of clothing was given its own display. The sales clerk was helpful, but kept a nonintrusive distance. They were offered champagne that they quickly accepted and sipped as they walked around the store. Tracy purchased a pair of sunglasses, a teal mini dress, and a black, high waisted pencil skirt. She casually counted out the cash into the clerk's waiting hand.

In Neiman Marcus, she remembered a tryst with Dennis Parker, a shooting guard for the Knicks. Just the sound of his voice on the phone used to make her wet. He had brought her to Neimans, jacked her skirt up and fucked her hard in the fitting room and then bought her a Fendi bag. She found out two weeks later that she was one of his three New York girls. Today, she had a man, not just a quick lay, whose money bought her a Doonie and Burke purse and Gucci bathing suit.

Thalia bought 7 jeans, Giuseppe heels, Chanel earrings, a Louis Vuitton wallet, whatever caught her eye. Tracy wanted to caution her to take it easy, severance packages were not made for splurging. But she kept her mouth closed. Thalia was a big girl. They called it quits after six hours. The crispness in the air and the surging crowd around them added to their buoyancy.

They window shopped a bit before meeting Jasmine, one of Thalia's line sisters at an Indian restaurant in Soho. The reunion was jovial. They shared chicken tiki masala, lamb palak, nan, and bismati rice. The flavors danced on Tracy's tongue.

"You should have seen her on line. Such a shiner." Jasmine waved her hand in Thalia's direction. "She could do no wrong. Some things don't change."

Thalia interjected, "And some things do. Have you seen Michee recently? That bitch is humungous! That kid tore her up. Her shape used to be sick."

Jasmine nodded. "Yeah, it was. That's why I told Jason we need to wait a couple of years. We've worked so hard to get to this point. Why change everything now?"

Tracy wanted to change the subject. It seemed like women over the age of twenty-five only wanted to talk about men and babies. "Did y'all see the new Spike Lee movie? That man is bad."

"No, but I did catch *The Color Purple* on Broadway. I loved it." Jasmine said.

"What about *Fela*? I would have loved to see that." Tracy did miss New York's theatre scene.

"No." Jasmine turned to Thalia. "Well, another one bites the dust, Melanie and Justin just got engaged. Which one of y'all is next?" Thalia quickly laughed the question away. A smile came to Tracy's face. She was just getting to know him, now she was thinking about marriage?

Lingering hugs were exchanged before the women went their separate ways and returned to their own worlds. After a short nap in the suite, they took the train to Brooklyn and met up with Big T and Michael, members of their brother fraternity. Big T was a huge man with an even bigger heart. He played defensive tackle for the Jets before being released after two seasons. Michael worked on Wall Street and had an edge that most women found irresistible.

He was extremely fair skinned, with red hair, freckles, and green eyes. The guys were waiting for them when they entered the street level from the train. Like usual, Big T spoke first, "What brings you little ladies to the big city?"

Thalia countered with a wink, "Now T, you know there ain't nothing little about me."

The foursome attended an open mic at a cozy hip-hop spot. Tracy was quickly swept away by the music. This was the hip-hop that she loved. The hip-hop that used to keep her up nights, the hip-hop that used to fuel her pen. She felt the soulful drums of an Africa they would never experience and the angst and hope of the people they had been transformed to. Those gathered there were a testament to all that they had become. The conscious crowd rocked dreads and naturals, casually chic in their loose fitting clothes radiating an inner peace that only their kind understands. The hip-hop heads wore Yankee fitteds and bobbed their heads, managing to still look unimpressed with everything. The buppies wore slacks and ties and squeezed in a little soul between Blackberry breaks.

The wave of energy swept them to a house party. Again, the music enveloped them, forcing them to stand close and speak loudly.

"So yeah, I thought she was someone I could be interested in. T had dated her sister and told me how cool and put together she was. I saw a picture and I was like bet, set that up. She shows up to the Minor Bar. Her dress was cute, I mean kinda, but the shoes. The shoes were just wack." Michael took a conclusive sip of Heineken.

Thalia nodded her understanding, Big T shook his head. "So what happened?" Tracy asked.

"I bought her ass a drink and left. A woman who pays no attention to her shoes is skipping important details in her life. I mean can she balance a check book? Does she have investments? Can she multitask? And I'm not saying the shoes had to be super fly, but don't be a bum bitch. Shoes say a lot. I don't like chicks walking around in Louboutins, fronting like they got it either."

Tracy processed his words. In adult life there was no time to waste and conclusions had to be drawn. She chuckled to herself as she thought that X and Michael would hit it off.

They danced all night. Hearty two-steps that they remixed with old school moves. Thalia playfully sashayed around the men. Plastic cups were filled throughout the evening and a hint of herb smoke permeated the air.

The weekend flew by like a too sweet dream chased away by daylight. The car ride home was quiet. She was scared to dream too big, too hopeful not to.

9

"The system broken, the school's closed, the prison open.
We ain't got nothing to lose.
Motherfucka, we rollin'."

Kanye West

"Power"

TUESDAYS AT WORK MEANT the mandatory staff meeting--mindless gatherings where new instructions were given to address the same problem—test scores. The teachers grumbled and complained and the administrators pretended like they were being listened to.

This Tuesday, Tracy followed the herd into the auditorium. Everyone sat in their cliques, already anxious to leave. Tracy sat with the minority first year teachers, Miss Hernandez, Mrs. Wilkins, and Miss Campbell. They were all like her, eager to improve urban education, unsure of how.

The Vice Principal, a man with kind eyes and rapidly graying hair, was issuing instructions on how they should handle the upcoming visit from the State Education Department. "So we will have an administrator placed on every floor. You need to contain any unwanted incidents in your classroom. Everything needs to look orderly and in control. We cannot let the state take over our school."

"Thank you Mr. Kennedy," the head of their testing department, Mr. Warring, took the mic. "If we want to keep the state out of our school, we need higher scores. You have to incorporate the academic selection strategies that you learned last month."

Mrs. Wilkins whispered to her, "He means ass, just like him."

Tracy rotated her head in order to try to stop the anger rising in her. Why not let the state take over? These fools damn sure didn't know what they were doing. Why didn't they take a few years to fix the systematic issues in the school instead of fritting away their resources on pretending that everything was okay? They damn near cheated in order to raise test scores, grade inflation was rampant in order to increase the amount of students who graduated, behavior standards were lax in order to reduce the suspension rate. In turn, the students were receiving an education that was probably worse than what they would have gotten in the Jim Crow South.

Her hand was up before she could stop herself. Mrs. Wilkins elbowed her, it wasn't wise for probationary teachers to bring attention to themselves. Mr. Warring nodded in her direction. She plowed forward. "Four lessons is a lot to dedicate to test prep. Wouldn't it be more advantageous if we used that time on actual content?"

"Content is not enough. Students need to learn how to select their answers—"

"It takes four lessons to learn how to fill in a bubble?"

Mr. Warring's face reddened. "Last year's scores seem to suggest so. It would be more advantageous to base our actions on that, rather than on the suggestions of a first year teacher. We need to dispel test anxiety, encourage the students to actually try on the exam. If you are where you're supposed to be on the curriculum pacing charts, that leaves you with plenty of time for the test prep."

Pacing chart? She had tossed that in the garbage the second after she removed it from her mailbox. She taught to her students. She hadn't heard the word 'learn' in one of these meetings yet. All they ever talked about were tests. Then there were tests to see how the students would do on the test. Then more talk and more tests. These kids deserved more than that. They needed more.

Tracy's crew followed her to her classroom after the meeting. She was the only one of them fortunate enough to have her own classroom and it was oftentimes their sanctuary, a break from the chaos in the halls and the ineffectiveness they all felt.

"I just don't get this place. How did these idiots become administrators?" Miss Campbell took a big bite of her sandwich. Tracy could see globs of white as she talked. "Tracy, did I tell you about my date with Elliot? It was bor-ing. I mean the guy has no personality and you didn't tell me that he had acne."

Annoyed, Tracy had to literally bite her tongue in order to stop herself from telling Miss Campbell that she wasn't exactly easy on the eyes herself. Tracy had set her up with Elliot in order to break up her two year drought. She hadn't guaranteed a love connection. Mrs. Wilkins stepped in for her, "Well, Shelia, you're not that exciting."

Tracy didn't even bother to try to suppress her laugh. Mrs. Wilkins had the childlike quality of innocently stating the truth. She was pretty, but plain and Tracy's favorite colleague.

Miss Hernandez spoke, "See, that's the problem with dating. We don't date in my family, we court. A man has to come highly recommended before I would even go out with him. I know his better qualities before the first date. That's what you have to focus on."

Again Mrs. Wilkins spoke up, "And you also have a curfew."

The other women left after they had gorged themselves with the needed amount of gossip and complaining. Tracy stayed behind to run through her lesson again, she was being observed in a couple of days.

The process was simple enough. Tomorrow she would meet Miss Hancock, the head of the English department who would ask a couple of questions and make a suggestion, some minute tweak that Tracy would fawn over. On Thursday, Miss Hancock would come watch her teach. She was supposed to evaluate Tracy on content knowledge, teaching strategies, and interactions with students. But what she would be most floored by was Tracy's classroom management. She would marvel at how cooperative the students were, how they interacted with each other. Who knew that these students could behave? And it wouldn't matter that they wrote papers with citations and participated in collegial circles, and actually discussed literature—none of that would draw much attention. Miss Wilkins, Miss Hernandez, and Miss Campbell had received the same type of evaluation. Minority teachers were never recognized for their mastery of the content or their ability to teach, just as minority administrators were always assigned student management instead of curriculum or operations. They were overseers in the modern day plantation.

Tracy just wanted to receive a "proficient" rating. That score wasn't hard to come by. She overheard two teachers in the copier room saying that they gave their students candy bars from complying during the observations. Fortunately, Tracy didn't have to sink to that level. She had told her kids, "Somebody is coming in here tomorrow. She's here to watch me, not you. Make sure I don't beat y'all." The kids laughed and she swatted a kid and the class went on.

If she were in charge, the observations would be random, a bit more frequent. That way there wouldn't be any room to hide behind trick lessons. Of course the union wouldn't stand for this; they were in the business of protecting teachers, not in the business of ensuring that students actually learned. Consequently, a teacher could be mediocre and get tenure. Once you got tenure, you had to either fight or fuck a kid to get fired.

It didn't matter what she thought, what she said. Mr. Warring had made that clear in front of the entire staff. Heat rose to her face again. They were all a bunch of cowards, even the tenured teachers. They spoke boldly amongst each other, but became yes men in front of those who could actually change policy. She was going to get tenure and she was going to light this place on fire.

She closed her laptop, tidied up her classroom, and headed home. The winter air slapped her the moment she stepped out of the building. At four o'clock, the parking lot was already dark and her mood worsened. She needed to go to the gym. Besides, her man was taking her to Miami and she had to look good.

She felt better the instant she entered the gym. Even in the dead of winter there was a cheerful warmth there. She chatted with a few regulars before heading up to the cardio floor. Her headphones blasted her workout mix, propelled her forward as she punished herself on the elliptical and rowing machine. She peered over the balcony at the basketball courts. A smile spread across her face when she saw X. His characteristic resolve was gone as he worked his way back down the court after blocking a shot. She noticed two men conspicuously watching the court, but not the game. It was 'Riek and Sean, she remembered them from the after-hours spot.

A wave of longing hit her. Had it only been six weeks since they exchanged numbers here? She headed towards the courts, but faltered once she entered the male dominated area. She wanted to see X, but didn't want to interrupt the game. She was about to turn around when he noticed her.

He called a timeout and briskly walked over to her. He stood a foot away from her. "What are you doing here?"

Her cheeks burned with embarrassment. "What do you mean? I'm working out. What, you're not happy to see me?"

"I'll call you later."

She was enraged. He dismissed her as if she was some bitch on the street begging for his time. She went to the weight room and let her aggression out. She did lunges, squats, and abs until her body begged for mercy. She welcomed the attention she got from men staring at her ass in her spandex tights. Maybe she could find a new one that would want to spend time with her.

At home she replayed every exchange she had with X. He had always seemed so honest and forthcoming. She had never doubted his intentions before. But maybe he was some asshole who collected women. Maybe he thought his only relationship duty was to spend money and flatter her with a few sweet words. She had been with that type before. Maybe she hadn't made him wait long enough.

She tried to wash away the disappointment in the shower. Why did she keep jumping head first into things? In her bedroom, she looked at all of the things she had purchased in New York. She shook her head at her foolishness.

She was curled up in her armchair with a novel, when the doorbell rang. She knew who it was, but she checked the peep hole anyway. She wanted to let him in. She wished that she had never met him. Well, he was here. She could at least hear what he had to say. She opened the door midway. Instinctively, her hand went to her hip, she was ready to battle. "May I help you?"

"Come on Tracy, let me in."

"Tracy? Oh now you know who I am? Let me ask you, what are *you* doing here?" She was mad as hell. She didn't care how much money he spent on her or what he said. She was not one of his possessions or employees.

"You know what I'm doing here."

She felt like she had been slapped. So that's what it had all been about. "Goodbye Oxford". She closed the door and blinked away tears. It was better that this happened now rather than later. He already didn't have time for her. Already went missing for days and reappeared whenever he pleased. He actually travelled with guards. That's how deep into the game he was. He was callous, how could he not be? How could he know how to treat her? What had she been thinking?

* * *

Her observation went as planned. "You have such a delightful rapport with your students," Miss Hancock said before rushing out.

Three delivery men showed up to her classroom during her free period. They brought with them twelve different assortments of exotic flowers. Tracy went to each bouquet and breathed in the beautiful scents. There was no card, but she knew who they were from. She had complained to X before about how drab her classroom felt in the winter. Now he had given her a tropical paradise and even remembered to have the flowers put in kid proof plastic vases. She smiled before she thought better of it.

Sure he was thoughtful and attentive when no one else was around. Tracy tipped the delivery men and arranged the flowers around the room. He wasn't slick. Jason had used the same trick. Like floral arrangements were supposed to negate the fact that they were assholes.

In her next class, Unique commented on the flowers, "Miss, let me find out you got it like that. You dealing with a boss huh?"

"Naw, she dealing with a punk. What kinda dude gotta buy a chick flowers to get some play?" Ryan Kelly asked.

"A gentleman." Tracy said.

She couldn't stand this fucking kid. She'd called his house only to be told by his extra loud mother that she didn't know what to do with him either. She had sent him to the administrator, tried to have a heart to heart with him, prayed for him, gotten him a black male mentor, even had him moved to a different section of her class in hopes that a more positive atmosphere would kindle something in him. The principal's indulgence offset all of her efforts. Tracy had gone as far as she could go, as far as she would go. She had to conserve her energy for the kids who had a chance. She had no time for ungrateful bastards that showed up to school with two hundred dollar sneakers, but without a pen, didn't even bring a scrap of paper. Tracy had learned to back them down quickly, ignore most of what they said until they stopped coming to class. But Ryan was stubborn, persistent. It was like he took enjoyment in annoying her.

Tracy went to collect the homework from the bin when she heard Ryan talking to Unique "She must give some mean head to get all them flowers."

Tracy bristled. She could pretend like she didn't hear the comment. She could send him out, but that would be an embarrassing write up, 'Student referred to my prowess at oral sex'. No, she was ending this now. She was sick of self-entitled males and their bullshit. She turned around to face him. "Mr. Kelly, I don't share the same recreational habits as you."

The smarter students giggled immediately at what she said. Their laughs were subdued because they didn't want to attract Ryan's wrath. Tajanek wasn't as discreet, "Damn dude, she played you."

Ryan registered what Tracy said. "Yo, bitch what did you say to me?"

The situation had turned from tense to dangerous. Ryan was always defiant with Tracy, but had never been blatantly disrespectful. Tracy gauged the situation. She was nine feet from Ryan with two rows of student desks stood between them. She could push him a bit more. Even with the state on their ass, she didn't think an administrator would tolerate the threatening of a teacher.

"You heard me."

"Yo, fuck you black bitch." That stung. It reminded her of the playground taunts her dark skin attracted. She stopped herself from cursing back at him though. She was the professional. This incident would go just the way she wanted.

Ryan was now on his feet. His growing fury was not lost on her. She just had to nudge him now. "Now we both know you don't have a chance at that. Now sit down and shut up. Some people come to this class to learn."

Ryan was closing the space between them. Tracy hadn't expected that. Attacks on teachers in the city were not uncommon, but she had never worried about that before. Her students knew what time it was. She could whoop all of the girls, but Ryan was 6'2 and at least two hundred pounds.

"I will fight a bitch. Word up." His words were a declaration. Tracy caught the eye of Khadijah, a serious Muslim student. She knew if worse came to worse, Khadijah would get the security officers. Her door was open so it wouldn't be hard to hear the scuffle.

Tracy grabbed a paper weight off of her desk. It easily weighed five pounds. Adrenaline raced through her veins. "Mr. Kelly, if you put your hands on me, you won't live to tell about it." She was no longer posturing. She was ready to smash his fucking skull open.

Ryan stopped dead in his tracks. He stared at her. She stared back, her lips pressed forward, her nostrils flaring. A sound emitted from his throat, it was a cross between a growl and a yell, it rumbled across the room. Tracy prayed. He started turning over desks. "Fuck you, you fucking bitch! Fucking black bitch! Fuck you! Fuck you!"

Freeman and two other security guards rushed into the classroom. They slammed Ryan to the ground, "Calm down, calm the fuck down." Ryan struggled against them, finally stopped after Freeman pressed his knee into his back.

"I'm cool, I'm cool." They let him up. He was almost through the doorway when he turned back towards Tracy. "Don't worry bitch, I'ma catch you in the parking lot." Tracy did not break her stance or put down the weight until the locked door was closed.

Her hands were trembling, but she quickly took a seat before the students could notice. A good teacher always appeared to be in control. Tajanek interrupted the silence, "Miss Mitchell, were you really going to hit him with that thing?" Tracy shrugged.

She tried to conduct the class as usual, but the students were too riled up. Finally she gave in and let them use the rest of the time to catch up on missing assignments or independently read.

When her lunch buddies came in, they were buzzing. "Girl, the whole staff is talking about you," Tracy detected envy in Ms. Campbell's voice.

"Yeah, so what's this I hear about you threatening students and throwing up gang signs?" Mrs. Wilkins asked matter-of-factly.

"What?"

"I'm joking."

"*Mira*, weren't you so scared?" Ms. Hernandez gave her a quick hug.

Her concern touched Tracy. She was always so sweet, even on the first day of school. "Of course I was, but I was ready. These kids don't run this school, we do."

"And who is this mystery man who buys you a whole room of flowers?" Again, Miss Campbell's words dripped with envy.

"Wouldn't exactly be a mystery if I told you, now would it? You want one?" Tracy got up and selected a flower for each woman. She curtsied before she passed them out. Next, they divied up the salad that was in the refrigerator. They were deep into their food and gossip when staff members started poking their heads in the room. Most were thumbs up and other quick gestures of encouragement.

Freeman showed up after ten minutes. "See, I tried to tell you that these kids are crazy, you trying to treat them all like they're special. Most of 'em are fucking retarded."

Normally, his comment would have irritated her, but today she appreciated him. She didn't know what would have happened if he hadn't shown up. "Thank you, Freeman. I truly appreciate you getting here so fast."

He took another step into the classroom. "Of course baby girl, you know I gotta look out for you." His eyes darted around the room and he noticed the flowers. He looked a bit deflated. "Well, I guess I will leave you ladies alone."

Miss Johnson showed up to gawk at the flowers and try to pump Tracy for information about the sender. She cast a judgmental, "Umm hmm" before leaving.

When the principal, Mrs. Smith, showed up, Tracy's lunch dates quickly packed up. Miss Hernandez shot her a look of support before closing the door behind her. It was never a good thing for a principal to show up unannounced. This one in particular had a reputation for unquenchable ambition and bitchiness. She gave all four of them a similar speech when they were hired. "I would like to say that I'm happy to have you aboard, but I don't know you. You're not here because of your credentials or because I requested you; you're here because the district says we need more minority representation on my staff. You're here to fill a quota." Tracy's stomach had turned, her heart felt like it would burst through her chest. She snapped her portfolio closed and walked out. They hadn't spoken since.

Today, Mrs. Smith looked around at the flowers. "My, my aren't you popular?" Tracy didn't answer. She didn't like this woman and she didn't like her lunch break being interrupted.

The silence didn't last long. "I hear you had an exciting morning."

"You could say that."

"Why don't you walk me through it?"

Tracy retold the incident with Ryan. She rushed through the part about him commenting on her giving head, opting instead to say "he made a sexually explicit remark." Mrs. Smith watched her with unshielded skepticism. Tracy finished, "I have written testaments from six students."

"Of course. I don't doubt for a moment that Ryan acted in that manner. His home life is a wreck. And that temper of his, of course that aids him on the basketball court."

The reason for Mrs. Smith's impromptu visit suddenly became apparent. The basketball team was the only source of good press for the school. Tracy had been to a couple of games—they were very impressive. There was a popcorn machine and cotton candy, and a emcee and graphics that shot across the gym. Yet, there was little room in the school budget for field trips or art teachers or counselors. When Ryan failed her course last marking period, two different administrators came to her to ask why.

"Threatening a teacher is a long term suspension and we have sectionals coming up."

She was shocked that she wasn't shocked by what she was hearing. Ryan was going to a D-1 school, maybe even pro. That prestige was worth something. That prestige was enough to bend rules, blur memories. It was the reason why so many Black athletes went broke and got in trouble and never did anything worth a damn. The system intentionally created little boys who couldn't function in society and would never use their money and popularity for the betterment of their community. Instead, they became another example of Black ignorance and justification of white fear.

Mrs. Smith squirmed under Tracy's silence. "So what are you asking, I mean telling me to do?"

"I'm not telling you to do anything. I can understand that you were rattled by Ryan's actions. But you're a tough one, I hear you handled yourself quite fine. I'm just asking for you to consider the school's position on this matter."

She was a tough one. Was that the only consolation she was going to get? This whole conversation would have been different if Tracy were white. Mrs. Smith would be comforting her, assuring her that this wouldn't happen again, even offering her some time off. Tracy assessed the situation. She could alert the union and push for Ryan's suspension, but Mrs. Smith had more pull with the school board and they would write it off as the exaggerations of a first year teacher. Additionally, she would end up on Smith's shit list. It was hard to fire noncompliant teachers, even non-tenured ones, but it was easy to make their lives hell. She could be given the maximum amount of classes to prep for, the worst students, administrative duty. Her classroom could be taken away from her and she could be shunned to a cart--forced to commute to three different classrooms.

"Yeah, I understand the school's position. I hope you understand mine. Next time I will handle the situation my way. If you'll excuse me, I need to use the restroom before next period." She didn't wait for a response.

At two o'clock on the nose, X called her. In the middle of the commotion she had forgotten about their spat. Maybe she should tell him about Ryan. She quickly dismissed that thought. She could handle Ryan. She didn't even want to know what X would do if he knew. "Hello."

"What did you think of your package?"

"They were lovely. The kids really enjoyed them too."

"So when can I enjoy you?"

"Shouldn't you be asking if?"

"Come on, why you acting like this?"

Acting? Who was acting? Anger tightened her chest. She had been completely honest with him, open, too open. "I'm not acting, unlike you. I don't act a certain way in front of you and your friends, and then pretend like I don't know you in public. I don't show up to your house, unannounced, in the middle of the night, and make you feel like a whore."

"I didn't--"

"Whatever, X. This has been fun. But it has run its course. I hope the Miami tickets are refundable because I'm not going." She hung up before she could lose her nerve.

* * *

She was in a foul mood the next day, she hadn't slept well and the kids were particularly annoying. She looked up from the papers she was grading, Miss Hernandez was standing in the doorway. She didn't feel like being bothered with her today. "What's up?"

"You haven't heard?"

"Heard what?"

"Somebody busted Ryan's kneecap with a crowbar."

*   *   *

At home, there was another package waiting for her. She ripped through the box, found a Louis Vuitton set of luggage. The tag read, "You're going."

She ran her hands over the brown and gold leather. Imagined herself exiting the Miami airport, her Vuitton bags in tow. She shook her head. It was dangerous to entrust things—even things as beautiful as this—with the power to brighten or worsen your mood. She knew how quickly everything could be snatched away.

Her doorbell rang. She watched X through the peep hole. He looked uncharacteristically anxious. After a few seconds, she slowly opened the door. She waited for him to speak.

"Well, what do you think?"

"What do I think about what?" She crossed her arms.

"Will you come with me?" He stepped closer to her.

Looking up at him, all Tracy wanted to do was fling herself against his body. She took a deep breath to steady herself. "Why did you act like that when you saw me at the gym?"

"When was the last time you saw me at the gym before the other day?"

"Weeks."

"That's because I go to seven different gyms. Gotta switch it up." He placed a hand on her cheek. "I can't have the wrong people associating you with me. I told you, I'm not going to let anything happen to you. You think this is a game I'm playing? You think I don't want everybody to know who you are to me?"

She was softening under his words, "Who am I to you?"

"You're mine." He closed the final inches between them and lifted her head for a kiss. As if in a dream, her arms went around his neck. She was completely lost in his embrace. Their tongues danced with each other. He pushed her into the kitchen and hoisted her up onto the table. He repeated his words, "You mine" and kissed her deeply.

He moved down to her neck. Tracy moaned as his kisses deepened and he began to suck on her neck, letting his tongue run over her flesh. He unbuttoned the blouse she wore and ran his fingers over the lace fabric of her bra. He kissed and sucked at her nipples through the thin fabric as his hands unhooked her bra. Once her breasts were exposed, he squeezed one in his hands and ran his tongue around her nipple. Tracy closed her eyes and held her breath. When he gently bit down he was met with more of her moans. He took her entire breast into his mouth and sucked it ever so gently, she pulled him closer against her. Her panties were already soaked. He switched breasts, giving the other one the same individual attention before he pressed them together and really let his tongue go to work.

He moved down to unbutton her pinstriped slacks. Tracy lifted herself up so he could take them and her panties off. X repositioned himself on his knees. He started by kissing the delicate skin of her inner thighs. Tracy's wrapped her legs around his upper back and arched her pelvis towards him. He burrowed his head between her legs.

Carefully, he circled the tip of her clitoris. Tracy cupped the nape of his neck and pushed his head closer against her. He licked and sucked at her clit with more force now. She circled her hips against the pressure of his tongue. Her moans deepened and she moved faster against him. His hands squeezed the meaty portion of her hips as his tongue quickened to keep pace with her.

When he put the right pressure on the right spot, she felt herself being pulled upward. Her body shook as she climaxed. He eased away from her, wiped his face, and stood up. She was perched on the table, still soaring.

"You on birth control?"

"Yes."

He flipped her around on the table before she had time to react. Put his hands under her stomach--forcing her to arch her back, and entered her in one smooth movement. He thrust himself into the deepest part of her. One hand held her head down and the other gripped her hip. She was pinned and he pulled her against him with each stroke.

He fucked her with a controlled frenzy. "Don't you ever close the door on me again. Do you hear me?"

He filled every inch of her. She moaned, "Yes."

"I can't hear you." He tugged at her hip harder.

"Yes!"

"And don't ever fucking hang up on me again."

"Okay." She was reaching the brink, his strokes were faster now. She came again with such force that she was startled by her own screams.

In bed, she nuzzled her head against his chest, felt the rise and fall of his breath. "I don't understand you."

"What is there to understand?" He pulled her closer to him, rested his hand on her ass.

"Why do you do this? This isn't the only thing that you can do."

"No, but no one can do it like me."

"But—", her voice caught in her throat. "It's not right."

"What is right? You look around here, when was the last time you saw 'right'? I used to worry about 'right'. But you know what I realized?" Tracy shook her head no. "There's always gonna be users and there's always gonna be dealers. It's just a matter of who. And if it's us, then we can at least use our influence to keep these niggas in line. We're the last gentlemen in this shit. We make sure everyone follows the code, because without it, no one would make it out of these streets."

Tears came to her eyes. "Why does that fall on you?"

"Because I'm strong enough to carry it." He reached over to the nightstand for his phone. He swiped a few times before his baritone filled her ears. "Judges Four." His voice rose and fell, engrossing her in the story of Deborah—a mighty prophetess, judge, and warrior. Tracy sat up in the bed, she had never heard of Deborah before, had never read Judges. The Old Testament hadn't interested her much; she thought it could all be summarized with Adam and Eve, Cain and Abel, Abraham, Noah, Moses, and David. What mattered now was Jesus, all the ways of the old had passed away. But what X was reading was stirring her heart. "'Then Jael, Heber's wife, took a tent peg and took a hammer in her hand, and went softly to him and drove the peg into his temple, and it went down into the ground; for he was fast asleep and weary. So he died.'" He put his phone down and pulled her back to his chest. "So what does that tell you?"

"That's Old Testament."

"Yes, but what does the Old Testament do?" Tracy didn't answer him. She actually didn't know. "It tells of Who and what is to come. The New Testament removes the yoke of the law from us and replaces it with love. But love is the biggest stronghold of them all. I hate these niggas, but I love 'em too. You know?"

She thought of Ryan Kelly. Once upon a time, he could have been a good kid. She wondered how old he was when that hope was stomped out. Six? Three? She couldn't stand him, she didn't want to ever see his face again, but she hadn't wanted his future taken away. She shuddered. God's humbling was no joke. She had felt it herself. Her whole world had collapsed in New York. Now she finally understood why. "Yeah."

10

*"And I admit, when the time is right, the wine is right
I treat you right, you talk slick, I beat you right."*

-Notorious B.I.G.

"Me and My Bitch"

TRACY BOARDED THE PLANE behind X. She was trying to contain her giddiness and get into character. She used to do that before interviews, steal herself and remind herself that she was in control. She certainly looked good. She had her hair washed and set in big rollers, the effect was big waves that hung at the nape of her neck. She wore traveling clothes, a white camisole with an open red cardigan, skin tight jeans, and leopard pumps. She would ditch the sweater once they landed in Miami.

She eased down into her first class seat and looked over at X. God he was sexy. He rubbed his thumb over her cheek.

"So what are you looking forward to doing once we get there?"

"Getting a new connect. Right now we got a middle man in New York. Cheaper to go direct, but in this underground world of ours, it's hard to make new partners. Could be a UC, a set up, anything. But this time I gotta risk it. Gotta see what's up with this dude. That's where you come in. You're charming, you're beautiful. I'm sure he will open up to you and I'm interested to hear your opinion of him. Just make sure you listen more than you talk. Never mention the business, let me do that."

Tracy nodded. He needed her and he wasn't too proud to let her know it. "Got it. I used to interview the stars, remember? I know how to see what's what."

"Yeah I know. You think I don't notice when you use your little journalist tricks on me. You get a nigga to spill his guts. But this is still a vacation. I want you to go shopping, go to the beach, have fun. I'll be occupied most of the time, but I'll make time for you." He licked his lips.

She leaned over and kissed him deeply, sucking on his bottom lip. "You better."

"Oh and babe, none of this lovey dovey shit in front of the connect."

Air travel was another example of the American caste system. Even air could be qualified. Tracy listened as the counter agents announced the first class boarding, then the platinum reward boarding, then the gold members, the silver elite. It was funny what people were willing to spend in order to board in front of someone else--even if they still had to wait and shared the same space. And though she and X had first class tickets, she waited to board with everybody else. X chuckled when she said it made her feel awkward to be seated and waited on while those in coach filed past her. She did enjoy the amenities though. The seats were plush and she had room to stretch out her long legs. The eight people in the section were serviced by two flight attendants, the same amount that served the 200 passengers in coach.

Besides the accommodations, the plane ride was uneventful. X busied himself with a Sudoku puzzle while Tracy attempted to read the latest installment in the Tennyson Hardwick series. She normally loved reading the exploits of a Black actor turned detective, but today she could barely make out the words on the page. She looked over at X and he tapped her nose with his finger. "Relax baby, we'll be there soon." She nodded and turned her attention to the tiny window. All she saw was white as they flew through the clouds. It calmed her raw nerves.

When they deboarded, Tracy fluffed her hair and put an extra strut in her steps. She pulled out her Prada shades from her Vuitton carry on, donning a new persona.

The agent at the rental counter told them that someone would pull the car around. The air outside seemed to pulsate with warmth and promise. She couldn't remember ever being happier. When another rental agent pulled up in a convertible BMW, her smile widened. X even cracked a grin at her enthusiasm. He opened the door for her before sliding into the driver's seat. After putting the address of the hotel into the gps, he pulled off.

Racing down the highway, Tracy took in as much of Miami as she could. The colorful buildings were monuments to the city's Spanish influences, the luxury cars were a testament to the city's affluence. They exited the expressway and ended up on Collins Avenue, a busy commercial strip of hotels, restaurants, and retail stores.

Their hotel was an unassuming two story building in the middle of the strip. Once they entered the gate they passed a courtyard of palm trees, a swimming pool, and jacuzzi. Their suite had hardwood floors, minimalist furniture, and a modern bathroom. It was Miami chic to the fullest.

Three o'clock in the afternoon felt like the middle of paradise. They made love quickly before showering and changing. X donned a white, linen suit with white and silver Nike Dunks. Tracy put on a figure hugging marine colored print dress that stopped at her ankles. Big silver jewelry and turquoise Jimmy Choo sandals completed the look.

X spun her around appreciatively, "Sexy," he said and was rewarded with an open mouthed kiss. He stopped her when she rubbed her hand against his erection. "Later baby."

They walked a block over to Ocean Drive. The smell of the salt in the air made her want to disrobe and give herself to the ocean.

But, X made it clear that this was a working vacation, playtime had to be earned.

He put his hand around her waist as they walked. "We're going to a hotel party. Remember what I told you."

They entered the open lobby of the W, South Beach, which was absolutely gorgeous. In the gold paneled elevator, X pressed "PH". She remembered being here before for Fat Joe's album release party. She had felt plain amid all of the Latin beauties and was trying to work up the nerve to introduce herself to the man of the hour. He approached her actually, and said that she had the most beautiful skin he'd ever seen. She landed a cover story.

When the elevator stopped, Tracy was another woman. She still walked half a step behind X, but her saunter let it be known that she stood on her own. She walked away from X towards the edge and the spectacular view of the Atlantic Ocean. Facing out into the sun, looking down at the vigorous indigo waves, the breeze began to stir a part of her that had been dormant.

She turned away from the balcony's edge and surveyed the crowd. The women ranged from pale white to deep caramel. Their hair didn't move in the breeze though their vibrant colored fabrics flapped around their well-toned bodies. Most of them stood in clumps, looking equally bored.

The men weren't as cover ready. They must have been very rich because the hairy chests and over the hillers there certainly weren't what kept these women. They did look like money with their Egyptian linen, diamond bezels, and Italian shoes. X stood out from the group with his striking, youthful features. They all sat in the middle of the room—kings appraising their subjects.

A bar spanned one-side of the room and bacchata music played in the background. Tracy fell into an involuntary four-step. Her roommate sophomore year was Dominican and had made it a pet project of hers to teach Tracy how to dance. Though Tracy never mastered the moves, she was proficient. A white coated waiter turned to her and asked, "*¿De donde eres?*"

"*Soy Americana, pero mi familia es de Guyana.*"

"*Ah si, tu eres muy bonita.*"

"Gracias."

This quick exchange garnered the attention of some of the women. One copper colored woman with red hair approached Tracy. Her mouth was held in a smile, but there was no missing the ice in her eyes. "Are you an invited guest?"

Tracy made a show of peering down at the woman. "I am my own invitation." At that she walked to the bar and ordered a mojito. Once she had thanked and tipped the bartender, she turned around to see that she was being summoned by one of the men. She glanced at X and he nodded.

She walked over to the man that had beckoned for her. He wore a white, button down shirt and Bermuda shorts. He was clean shaven, with black hair that he wore slicked back. His olive colored skin was obviously tanned, but besides X, he was the best looking man there. Tracy urged herself not to fidget under his stare.

"Marhaba"

"Marhabtein." He was an Arab.

"You seem to be the center of attention." His English was accented with a sflight till that made him sound almost melodic.

Tracy glanced over at X, who was two chairs down from the mystery man. "Sometimes that can't be helped."

The man smiled. He watched Tracy with an amused entitlement. "Where are you from?"

"East Coast. And you?"

"I'm an Afghan."

"Really, Jalalabad region?"

Again the man smiled. "My village is 30 kilometers away from Kabul."

"Is it still intact?"

The men shared a hollow laugh that Tracy didn't understand. The man clued her in. "Oh yes, it's too profitable not to be."

She got it. Until that point she hadn't been entirely sure as to what drug X sold. She had assumed cocaine and this trip to Miami solidified that to her. But this guy was not Latin. He was an Afghani. Tracy knew that since the Taliban fell, opium production had skyrocketed in Afghanistan. Consequently, heroin was growing in popularity in Western nations; an unforeseen byproduct of the war on terror.

Again the man spoke, "So you're well traveled?"

"Actually no, I just try to be astute on global affairs."

"So you're well educated?"

Tracy laughed and flipped her hair. She wanted to change the subject. "I'm getting there."

The man cast Tracy a knowing look. "Which university did you attend?"

Why was he interviewing her? She could lie, but he would surely ask her follow up questions. What could be the harm in telling the truth? "University of Pennsylvania."

The man nodded. "Ah, we have ourselves an Ivy Leaguer gentlemen." To Tracy, he extended his hand and said, "I'm Amir."

Tracy placed her hand in his and he kissed it. "And we have ourselves a prince. I'm Tracy. I'm afraid there is no regal translation of my name."

He was impressed. "There doesn't need to be. Your elegance could rival that of a queen. Please join us." The man that had been sitting between Amir and X faded into the background and an empty chair appeared. It seemed that Amir could snap his fingers and get whatever he wanted.

"So Tracy, you have a fondness for waiters?"

So that's what had gotten his attention. The American social caste was rigid even among criminals. "I respect the working man. We're all trying to make a living."

Amir gestured towards the waiter. "It's an honest living, no?"

"Yes."

"What's honest? Settling for crumbs while the government and corporations lie and kill for trillions?"

Tracy chuckled. "And next you'll be asking me to define terrorist."

Amir raised an eyebrow and then laughed. "Well of course you've heard and considered all of this before. You wouldn't be here if you hadn't." Amir turned to X, "Oxford if your decisions in business are as wise as your choice in women, you're going to make me an even richer man." His cronies laughed, but X only nodded. Amir stood and held Tracy's hand again. "It was nice meeting you Tracy. I will see you later, no?" She nodded and watched Amir and his entourage exit the patio.

She waited for X to get up and followed suit. Again, he put his hand on her waist as they walked. She caught the eyes of the nosy redhead and gave her a curt head nod. She had indeed been her own invitation. Now it was just a matter of figuring out exactly what she had rsvped to.

Once they had exited the hotel and were a block up, her nerves dissipated. No longer able to contain her giddiness, she spun around with her arms outstretched. X too seemed relieved and laughed openly. She put her arm around his waist and asked, "So how did I do?"

X imitated Amir's accent "Your elegance could rival that of a queen." She nudged him playfully in the ribs. "Nah, you held it down. Uncle Derek doesn't know how to deal with these foreigners, that's why he sent me. I don't know how to deal with these niggas either that's why I asked you to come. Got me an Ivy Leaguer." He lowered his voice. "My parents would have loved you."

He normally was so sure of himself, sometimes downright cocky. But still, he had needed her and trusted Tracy enough to let her know that. She felt closer to him every day.

They went back to their hotel and changed into bathing suits. Her Gucci one piece had cut outs that revealed an hour glass figure. She was thankful that her hectic schedule and regular work outs had helped her lose weight. She wanted to look good for X. She knew that he liked showing her off. She liked it too. She liked that her presence made him proud, she in turn was proud to be on his arm, proud to make a statement. Did that make her a trophy? Weren't trophies symbols of honor, physical manifestions of a man's will to conquer? She smiled up at him. He had indeed won her heart. He took her hand to his lips and kissed it.

They rented a beach umbrella and laid down a blanket. As they kissed and rubbed sunblock on each other, everyone else faded into the background. He pulled her onto his chest and massaged her ass.

It all felt so good. Being with him always felt like being in another world, one reserved only for two. The sun caressed her entire being, its pull was gentle, soothing. She dozed off. When she awoke her eyes immediately went to the ocean. It's majestic waves called to her. She stood at once and ran to the water's edge, wading in quickly before the chill of the water could dissuade her. She heaved herself into the waves, leapt into the startling goodness of it all. She swam horizontally to the shore, avoiding sand bars, letting the water carry her away.

Floating in the ocean, under a sweet sun, and a loving God, she felt weightless. She felt born again. She was young. She was free. X joined her in the surf. She wrapped her legs around his torso and kissed him with abandon. He pulled at the crotch of her suit and moved the fabric aside. He entered her with a gush. She closed her eyes again and let his stroke, the sun, and the rocking waves take her away.

*   *   *

At the hotel they showered again. Tracy studied her reflection in the full length mirror. She was glad that she had made such a good impression on Amir, and she wanted to maintain it. The teal Prada dress she wore stopped mid thigh, but it hugged her curves modestly. Her wet hair was slicked into a bun in the middle of her head. She wore silver drop earrings and a thin silver watch. Her make-up added a bit of flair, a smoky eye and cognac colored lips.

The valet gave Tracy an approving look before opening her door. X raised his voice a bit. "You gon make me hurt somebody down here, motherfuckas act like they don't see you with me." X held up a fifty dollar bill, but the valet was now hesitant to approach. "What the fuck you scared of now? Shoulda been scared before. Come get this fucking money man."

Tracy stared straight ahead. What was X jealous about? Did he know something that she didn't? Was it normal for Amir to have invited her to dinner too?

X handed the keys to the valet in front of Azul. Tracy kept her eyes on the ground this time. She followed him into the restaurant where they were greeted by a drop dead gorgeous Cuban hostess. Tracy suddenly felt insecure. Miami was the home to the most beautiful and glamorous women in the world. Had she really thought she could hold a candle to them?

She tried to shake away those thoughts. She looked good too damnit. She redirected her attention to the décor. White clothed tables stood atop of gleaming hardwood floors. True to its name, beautiful blue accent pieces made the restaurant simultaneously elegant and relaxed. Floor length windows offered a breathtaking view of the ocean. The sight of the water calmed her.

They were taken over to Amir's table which was in the center of the restaurant. He sat with a beautiful woman who appeared to be of Middle Eastern descent. He stood when X and Tracy approached the table. "Oxford," he firmly pumped X's hand. "Ah and the beautiful Tracy," he kissed Tracy's hand before sitting back down. "I would like you all to meet Lydia."

Lydia smiled politely and shook hands with the couple. She was truly stunning--with skin the color of roasted pecans, high cheekbones that highlighted captivating eyes, and a smile that was welcoming and genuine. She had the poise honed in finishing schools. Tracy envied her instantly.

The men lowered their voices and busied themselves with the complexities of their industry. Tracy was relieved. Looking at Lydia she saw that she didn't have to worry about having to entertain Amir.

"First time?" She asked Tracy after the waiter had taken their drink orders.

"In Miami? No."

"I mean is this your first time?" She titled her head in X's direction. "In a situation like this?"

Tracy eyed her. "Does it seem like it?"

"Seems like you're enjoying it."

"I am."

Lydia glanced over at X knowingly. "Cherish it."

"You sound like you're speaking from experience."

"Amir was right about you. Your naivety is refreshing in this business of ours." She took a dainty sip of water. "Yes, I speak from experience."

Tracy leaned in. She wanted Lydia to confide in her. She could be a source of useful information. "You're right, I am new to this world." She smiled and arched her hand towards the ambiance of the restaurant. "So any words of wisdom you could offer me would be greatly appreciated."

"I have lots of words to offer, but you probably won't hear any of them. You're in love. How could you not be? Real men are a precious commodity these days. You have one and he loves you. This is quite obvious and this is quite a feat. And yet you don't even know how much danger you're in."

Heat rushed to Tracy's face. She looked over at X, but he and Amir were in earnest conversation. She glanced around the restaurant. Nothing looked amiss. Lydia took a sip of her wine. "You are dealing with two very destructive forces. The first being love. Which will inevitably make you do the most reckless of things. No one is immune from this." She held Tracy's eyes. "The second force is that man. Men are naturally destructive. They conquer, blaze new trails. And a man like that is even more brazen."

"Look at those two. Here with us, in this place, discussing business in such a casual way. And all around them a thousand dangers lurk. But they are in control and they know it. Of course you love him for it and so you will disregard everything I am saying. But I feel I should still tell you. You will hate him one day. That ambition will become insatiable, nothing will ever be enough. His attentiveness will be reserved solely for work. His intuition will be used to bed other women. That confidence will curdle into a demonic ego."

Tracy noticed X looking at her and she smiled quickly. The appetizers arrived and gave her a moment to retreat from Lydia's words. She put her napkin on her lap and took a quick breath. This woman did not know them. She cut into the miso-marinated hamachi slowly, and took her time bringing her fork to her lips. This time she caught Amir watching her mouth. She removed the meat off of the fork with a flicker of tongue and held his gaze as she chewed. She closed her eyes.

"I can see that you are really enjoying your food." Amir said.

She nodded. "I am really enjoying this moment." She smiled over at Lydia and put her hand on X's.

Amir chuckled. "Oxford, you're a lucky man. It's hard to find a beautiful woman who actually eats." Lydia's face reddened.

X nodded. "She's everything I need." They dined on shrimp dumplings, edamame rice, grilled lamb chop, and smoked eggplant. The mood at the table was light now. Amir steered them through gracious conversation about current events, politics, and local points of interest. It seemed like a deal had been reached.

They were ordering dessert when Tracy nearly choked on her water. Derek and Thalia were strolling over to their table. They both looked rejuvenated and Miami chic. As usual, Thalia spoke first. "We didn't miss dessert did we?"

Amir stood, "No, no you're just in time. It's good to see you Derek." Thalia and Derek shook hands before sitting down. Derek was instantly swept up in a hushed conversation with X and Amir. Thalia's presence interrupted the newly forged intimacy between Tracy and Lydia. There was an awkward silence. Thalia was oblivious. She pulled out a velvety jewelry box. "An early birthday present."

It grabbed Amir's attention, "It's your birthday?"

Tracy's face burned. "Tomorrow." X raised an eyebrow at her.

"Well open it, it's not for decoration." Thalia said.

Tracy gently opened the box and revealed a strand of ivory pearls. Thalia was grinning. "Pretty girls wear twenty pearls."

Tracy laughed. "Thank you Thalia, they're beautiful."

Derek nodded. "She has great taste."

Tracy did not acknowledge his comment. What the hell was going on between them?

Lydia interrupted her thoughts. "What we need right now is a toast."

They all raised their glasses. Amir spoke, "To new friends and partnerships. And especially to Tracy, I hope your birthday is filled with boundless joy."

The party milled in front of the restaurant after dessert. Tracy itched to be away from these people, but she waited for X to initiate their exit.

Lydia had less patience, "Gentlemen, it's a beautiful night in Miami, surely we can find something to do besides pat each other on the back and talk business."

Amir looked at her blankly, but Lydia did not fidget under his gaze. He seemed to remember himself and plastered a grin on his face. "What do you have in mind my *habibti*?"

Lydia too adorned a plastic smile, "Dear, we should all go to the mansion. Isn't that your favorite club?"

*   *   *

The Mansion was packed. Beautiful, scantily clad women walked around nonchalantly. X gave her waist a reassuring squeeze as they were escorted into the VIP section.

With Derek there, X seemed more relaxed. He had done well with hiding the strain of the pressure Derek had passed off to him. Now he was more casual, and like Tracy, seemed eager to let loose. In her ear he whispered, "You're the sexiest woman in here."

Bottles were brought over. The group toasted and slammed back shots. The tequila was ice cold and went down smoothly. Seconds later, Tracy could feel it warming her body. She sighed softly and leaned back into the sofa.

She looked around her. Derek was grinning, his big frame was pressed against Thalia. What the hell was she doing? Tracy reached out for a glass of champagne and noticed Amir. He was turned away from Lydia and angled to catch the full view of the busty cocktail waitress. Lydia was staring at him. The sadness in her face made Tracy look away.

She took a long swallow of her champagne and closed her eyes. The music felt like it was moving through her. She tapped her foot in tune to it, her head rocked to the beat of the moment. It wasn't long before that she wanted to dance. The VIP section was reminiscent of the balcony party. Everyone was either too pretty or too rich to dance.

Tracy stood and smiled over at X. He nodded and she grabbed Lydia's arm and led her out to the common dance floor. Lydia was surprisingly a good dancer. The music rocked them to and from each other. Their bodies found an easy sync and they laughed and went with it.

When her shoes began to feel too heavy on her feet, she led Lydia back to their seats. Thalia and Derek were gone and replaced with three gorgeous women. The blondest and most tanned of them was leaning on Amir. She tossed her hair back and looked over at Lydia.

Lydia sat down on Amir's lap, swinging her legs towards the girl, who was forced to scramble out of the way. She kissed him full on the mouth before he pushed her off. She knocked over a few glasses and the air suddenly became thick. Lydia sprung to her feet and Amir clasped her hand. "My *habitita*, I think you're not feeling too steady on your feet. Oxford, Tracy, we will speak soon." He pulled Lydia close to him and steered her away. X stood up and held his hand out to Tracy. She took it and he pulled her in close. They swayed for a moment before he led her outside.

She asked to drive. With the top down, and the warm night air caressing her face, she felt like she was flying again. It was an exhilaration that she never wanted to come off of. She sped back to their hotel where they ended up in the hot tub. She sat in between X's legs and he cupped her breasts under the jets. She closed her eyes and gyrated against him. When she opened them she noticed that they had been joined by another couple. She started to move away but X pulled her back into place. He moved one hand in between her legs, against her clit. "Who's is this?" he whispered.

"Yours."

"Show me."

She started to pull away again and he squeezed her hips and hoisted her on top of him. He moved her bottom out of the way and he jammed himself inside of her. His hands on her hips slammed her back into him, she rocked her hips to the motion. The liquor, the hot water, his violent strokes inside of her--hurt so good. She wanted to cry out, but feared it would intensify the punishment she was taking. She squeezed her eyes closed and shut out everything, but the feeling that was bursting inside of her. She climbed higher and higher until the only thing that mattered was the frenzy that was growing, until that exploded and she felt like she could melt.

The other couple was gone when she opened her eyes again. X delivered a final shudder and clung to her. They both needed a minute before they could stand. When they did reach their room, they fell into the bed.

In the morning, she woke up alone. On the pillow was a stack of hundreds and a note "Buy yourself something nice." She crumbled the note and threw it across the room.

She wrapped herself in a terry cloth bathrobe and tried to finger through her hair. It was a jumbled mess from last night's reckless bout in the whirlpool. Her stomach lurched and she hurried to the toilet. Her bowels emptied in a watery rush. It took a few bouts of that before she gingerly could wipe and flush the toilet. There was a knock on the door just as she was washing her hands.

She moaned and walked over to the door. "Who is it?"

"Your new best friend," the words were marked by Lydia's signature crisp enunciation.

Tracy tried to smooth her hair down before opening the door. Lydia didn't share Tracy's hangover. She damn near skipped into the room.

"So I was thinking a girls' day would be perfect for the birthday girl."

Remembering that it was still her birthday worsened her mood. She wanted to crawl back under the covers and sleep the day away.

"Don't tell me you're bummed about getting older. We're far too young for that. Once you do something with that hair of yours, no offense, you'll be stunning."

Tracy couldn't help but to laugh. She dragged herself into the shower and dressed hurriedly. Out on the strip, they walked arm and arm like old friends. Tracy was surprised and a bit worried about the familiarity she already felt for this stranger. *Remember why you're here.*

"There's a great Cuban hairdresser a few miles from here." Tracy raised her eyebrows.

"What? I'm a well-rounded gal."

"So you wanna get a cab?"

"No, my driver will take us." A uniformed chauffeur was waiting in front of a silver Rolls Royce. The heat of envy rose to Tracy's face. Lydia had warned Tracy about the dangers of this business, but failed to mention its luxuries. Tracy smiled at Lydia, but she wondered what else she had left out. Amir must own a poppy field. Whatever deal he was giving Derek and X was sure to be way more profitable for him.

At the hairdresser, Tracy listened intently to Lydia and gently prodded her. "So will I be coming to a wedding in Miami soon?"

"If Amir was going to marry me he would have already. He seems to be the picture of modernity, but believe me his roots are not. He will end up with some beautiful, educated virgin in a *hajib*."

Tracy nodded emphatically. "Men want you to submit to their will, but they hold it against you once you do. They lust after whores, but settle down with prudes. Do you think he will still want you?"

"Who is to say? I have many talents, but future telling isn't one of them." Her tone was dismissive and Tracy turned her attention to a magazine. She would stoke that fire later.

Gloria, a middle-aged Cuban woman, motioned her over. She dismissed her assistant and gently shampooed Tracy herself. She conditioned her hair and sat her down under the dryer. Tracy didn't wait an extra minute. As soon as the timer went off she washed the conditioner out and skillfully blowed dried her hair almost straight. She used smoking hot curlers to give Tracy a head of loose spirals that dusted her shoulders. Her confidence was soaring when she bopped out of the shop.

They poked around in boutiques along Ocean Drive, but Tracy wasn't too eager to part with the money X had given her. She blew the first stack for this trip. She was looking forward to using this one to pay off a nice chunk of her student loans. There would be more shopping sprees in the future.

Lydia didn't seem to be in the mood for shopping either. She bounced around like a teenager. "What we need is some alcohol, sun, and some privacy. Don't you want to see the real Miami?" She didn't wait for Tracy to respond.

X hadn't called or texted her. Lydia hadn't mentioned Amir. It was like last night had never happened. Maybe money gave people the luxury of erasing embarrassing memories. But Tracy couldn't forget the sting of Thalia's unannounced arrival and X's disappearance this morning. A drink would take the edge off.

The car smoothly climbed the hills of South Florida. They stopped in front of what looked like a gated fortress. The estate was sprawling. After about twenty minutes of an abridged tour, they ended up in the cabana area that circled the swimming pool. There was also a steam room, Jacuzzi, massage area, and bar manned by a white coated servant. Tracy was expecting the sound of Robin Leech's voice at any moment.

"Manny, two mojitos and keep them coming." Lydia's tone was curt.

Tracy bit her tongue and settled down into the beach chair. Manny placed a tall glass in front of her. "Muchas gracias Emmanuel." The mint and lime danced on her tongue and she drank half of it before she could think better of it. The sun felt softer now, she stretched out. "Too bad I don't have a bathing suit."

"No need. Trust me, Manny knows how to keep his eyes and mouth shut." Lydia was already stripping out of her dress. She revealed a lithe body that seemed to be dying to be admired. She was waxed completely clean, revealing a small birth mark. "What are you waiting for?"

Tracy felt tingly. Still, she stood up and stripped down to her black g-string. Lydia's eyes roamed her body. "See that's better."

Manny brought over lobster rolls and freshened their drinks. The combination of freshly made sushi, rum, and unshaded sun soon tired Tracy and she dozed off. When she woke up Lydia was bending over her. Tracy held her breath. "Maybe I'm not the marrying type."

Tracy couldn't think of a response and so she offered none. Lydia must have taken her silence as consent because she lightly placed her lips on top of her's. The gesture sent a bolt of electricity through Tracy. She laid very still and waited for the wave to past.

Lydia sat back up and stared at her. Tracy held her gaze. If this was a test, she passed, she hadn't rejected nor encouraged Lydia's advance. Lydia lowered herself toward Tracy again. "Can you make way your way back to the front?" Tracy nodded. Lydia moved closer and hovered over Tracy's mouth. She kissed her again and then worked her over to her ear. Lydia quickly darted her tongue around her earlobe before whispering, "There's way more to you than what reaches the eyes."

Tracy silently dressed and headed towards the front. It took all of her will power not to look back at Lydia. She had fantasized about women, but never allowed herself to act on it before. This was definitely not the time to start. Lydia could not be trusted. Her mind raced the entire way back to the hotel. She told the driver to stop a block up and she walked to the water's edge. She sat there for hours. So much was happening so fast. At times it seemed like the world was hers and at other times she felt completely out of control. She tried to replay everything in her mind, tried to see it from different angles, tried to plan her next move. But her thoughts continued to give way to feelings. She felt alive. She felt guilty. She felt fearless. She felt alone.

She was twenty-five years old. No longer a young adult, no longer able to laugh off wrong decisions, swat them away and jump into the next adventure. Everything she did from here on out mattered. And though logically she understood this, understood that she needed to exercise caution, emotionally she knew that she could not go back. Her fate was now tied with his. She made that decision the moment she stepped on the plane. She had known what was required of her, had accepted the dangers. She no longer could lie to herself and pretend that she could walk away. The truth was she did not want to. X was like a brand, her heart was seared now, it would never be the same.

He was in the room when she got back. "Where the hell were you?"

"I was--"

"Lydia's car dropped you off two hours ago so don't even try that one."

"Try what? We're in Miami, and you left me all alone. So I occupied myself. What, did you think I was just going to sit around here waiting on you?"

He closed the space between them. With him staring down on her she reconsidered her words. But she was right. She would not back down. There would be no retractions. "Who are you talking to?"

"You're the only one standing here, right? It's my birthday and you've been gone all day. Didn't say bye. Left me a note like I'm the maid."

"This is a business trip."

"Yeah, well what is Thalia doing here?"

"You stupid? Thalia is here working. The same reason why you're here."

"Oh really? Are me and Thalia doing the same exact job? No wonder she climbed the fucking company ladder so quick."

"You don't need to wonder. I tell you what you need to know." He jabbed his finger into her forehead. "And watch your mouth."

She slapped his hand away. "Who the *fuck* do you think you're talking to? I'm not on your payroll."

With one smooth motion he wrapped his hand around her throat, pushed her across the room, and slammed her against the wall. She bit down on her tongue to keep from crying out. "This is not a conversation that we're going to repeat. We could go far. We will go far if you just play your position. I can handle the rest."

He released her and she staggered to grab ahold to an end table. "Get dressed, it's time for dinner." In the restaurant, he chatted with her casually. She pushed her food around her plate and answered him with curt, one word responses. He kept talking as if he didn't notice. When she looked over at him, she felt a strong emotion churn in the pit of her stomach—regret.

*   *   *

Her eyes opened the moment light entered the hotel room. X had his arm draped over her hip and the pressure of it felt heavy, stifling. She rolled her body free from under him and headed to the bathroom. Her mind was reeling. He hadn't hit her, but he had come damn close. Was Lydia's prediction coming true? Already?

She needed time to think. She wanted to call Thalia, but now that was a conflict of interest. God, what had she gotten them both into? *God.* She couldn't remember the last time she prayed.

She quickly brushed her teeth, washed her face, and slipped into a sundress. On her way out of the door, she stopped and looked over at X. Even in his sleep he was quiet, rarely stirring or snoring. He slept like a man with no worries or regret. He looked at peace. *I can handle the rest.* She doubled back into the room and left a note. "Taking a walk."

She walked along the beach, quietly talking out loud to God. "Lord, I thank you for your lasting mercy and grace. I know I don't deserve it, Lord believe me I know. But I am so grateful. I truly am. You are the King of kings, the Host of hosts, the Most High God. You are the God of Moses, Jacob, and Abraham. You gave the world your only begotten Son. God I love you and appreciate you so much."

"Lord you know my heart. You know I want this man, but I never meant to put him before you. Please tell me what to do. Show me the way Lord. I can't do it without You."

She felt better, almost at peace. She didn't know what she should do, but she believed that she would be able to do it when the time came. Her mind cleared enough that she was able to take in the beauty around her. When she returned home, it would be to a cold hard city. There would be barren trees, slush filled streets, and an ever present darkness. She needed to make the best of this

~ 143 ~

moment. Right now she was walking barefoot on the sand, under a sun that seemed to be shining for her alone with the ocean only a few steps away.

She returned to the hotel and held her breath outside of the door. She wondered which X would be waiting on the other side. The good twin greeted her with a huge smile. "Come here baby."

She crossed over to the bed and sat down tentatively. He wrapped his arms around her and delivered playful kisses across her back. Wasn't he at least going to apologize? Was he even sorry? Well, she did curse at him. She couldn't expect a man in his position to let that ride and he didn't exactly hit her. He had actually shown a lot of restraint when she hadn't. His lips felt so good against her skin. She wanted to feel more of him; she wanted to feel all of him. She gave in to that feeling before she could think better of it. With his head between her legs she thought of Lydia's kiss and the warmth of her breath against her ear. She climaxed.

She fell asleep and was awakened by X's gentle nudges. "Come on baby, we gotta get dressed. The yacht leaves in an hour." Yacht?

They showered together. Kissing and laughing the whole time, the water seemed to be washing away the tensions of the other night. Wrapped in a towel, she rummaged through her luggage. Again she thought about calling Thalia. But it seemed so childish to call the accountant of a major drug cartel for outfit consultation.

She decided on a turquoise catsuit and silver sandals. She wrapped a multicolored Hermes scarf around her head of curls. Silver hoops and the signature silver Tiffany's bracelet completed the look.

The marina was a sight. Yachts of various sizes gleaned in the sunlight. The boats were the pride and joy of their owners, beacons in the water, standing monuments. There was Helen of Troy, Triumph, Suzanna, Glory...

Amir's yacht was a 125 foot beauty, aptly named Pearl. Just looking at it, Tracy felt insignificant. She wondered if Lydia and Thalia were going to be present. Would Amir greet her as the beautiful Tracy? What the hell did that mean anyway, was he being condescending? Did he know that his girl had an affinity for women? Were they like swingers?

X was looking at her. She feigned a smile and inched closer to him. Amir greeted them on the lower level. "Oxford, Tracy, I'm so glad you could make it."

X nodded while Tracy smiled graciously, "Who could refuse this?"

The yacht was lavish. Again, Tracy felt envious. Why should Amir and Lydia profit so much off of the poison they peddled? Amir was leading them through the state of the art kitchen to the main dining room, to the theatre…the whole thing was nauseating. They finally settled on the deck.

Tracy hadn't realized that the boat had pulled off until she looked down at the whirling water. Her mind raced along with the boat. Why was it that everybody else was able to make so much money off of Black people? Why was it that they bought Indian hair from Korean stores and clothes from white designers and sneakers from Nike and heroin that purchased Amir's yacht? Drugs would always be sold, she agreed with X on that point. So shouldn't someone Black get paid?

She leaned against the bow, the thrill of the rushing water stirring her. She closed her eyes, the sun warmed her face and the wind offered a soothing contrast. Amir elbowed her. "Not thinking of jumping, are you?"

"I already have."

He laughed, "I'm not looking forward to you leaving."

X moved closer to her and put his hand on her hip. "Business awaits."

Tracy caught his eye and flashed him a reassuring smile. She didn't want to see his jealous side again. They sipped red wine. Undoubtedly expensive, Tracy could barely swallow it. Both men seemed to be waiting for her to get the party started. "I see a few people missed the boat."

Amir shook his head. "We have finished our business I have no need to see Derek and Thalia. Lydia is feeling under the weather. I brought you out because I wanted to ask you all something."

"What's that?" X leaned in a bit.

"I was hoping that Tracy would want to stay on and work for me." He was talking about her, but directing the question to X. She bit her tongue. The unabashed chauvinism was hitting a nerve.

"Work for you?" X damn near snorted. "Why would she do that?"

"Oh, I am sure that you provide more than enough for her. It's just, she is endowed with a disarming grace. I have several businesses, she would be a wonderful addition."

"Tracy is a wonderful addition everywhere, that's why she's with me."

She cleared her throat. "And Tracy is right here." She rubbed X's arm before turning to Amir. "It's a very flattering offer. But my place is with X."

She couldn't get off of that boat soon enough. She walked before him into their hotel room. He grabbed her from behind and pushed her over to the desk. "Who do you belong to?"

"You baby."

He was grabbing at her breasts, ripping at her clothes, pulling her hair. "Take all of that shit off."

She hurriedly undressed. His kiss felt like he was trying to swallow her whole. He ran his hands over her whole body before cupping her ass roughly. "You like that don't you?" She nodded before he kissed her again. Then he was unbuckling his belt. He pushed her down. "Suck my dick." When she obliged him he held her head down forcing her to take all of him against her throat. He controlled the motion, beating himself against her fast.

She loved making him loose control. Her body throbbed with wanting. She got it now, whenever he felt threatened or jealous, he fucked her like this. "Ooh you about to make me come, you like that don't you? You're mine you know it. You do whatever I say. Yeah you swallow all of that dick. You gon swallow that cum too." He delivered one last shudder that sent his salty fluids into her mouth. She did as told and swallowed.

He lifted her back to her feet and swung her around. "I'm not done with you yet." He was rock hard when he entered her from the back.

11

"When I look into the mirror, and see my own image
I feel like there's something else far in the distance
Something I wanna see, but something that's resistant
And every day the hauntin' is growing more persistent"

-Dice Raw

"Now or Never"

THEY RETURNED EARLY SUNDAY morning and were greeted with frosty air and tufts of snow. Tracy had never been happier to be home. She understood now that winter was necessary; it slowed everything down so one was forced to think, forced to confront themselves. She needed that now. Everything about Miami had been too fast.

X too, was happy to be back. He was damn near giddy at the thought of getting the new product out on the street. How would his life have been different if he hadn't been born to a drug dealing father? He was so smart, so ambitious, he could have been anything.

Her thoughts drifted to Andre. What could he be? What would he be? Was this life all of their fate?

She stamped her feet as they waited for the shuttle to take them to their car. Was this what she really wanted? Everything could go horribly wrong at any moment. She hadn't forgotten that. And although X was so self-assured, he wasn't fool proof. He could go to prison or get killed at any time. That was the cold reality of his life and now hers.

X held her hand and waited for her to step off of the shuttle. She danced in place as he brushed the car off and watched him with a sigh. This man had completely taken over her thoughts. She used to read and dream about faraway places, plot all of the ways she would help make the world better. She started to look at dreams differently after *The Real* abandoned her and now her time with X had obscured her vantage point. To dream was one thing, to do was another. She was in the trenches now. She had never known right and wrong to be a gray area before. But every day when she went to work and peered in her students' faces, she saw a longing so raw that it hurt to look at. No one was able to fix it or even seemed like they wanted to. And though she talked to God about it all the time, nothing was changing. In those parts, with so much pain, it was even hard to mention His name. The god they heard of was a children's tale, a Santa Claus that didn't come around their neighborhood often.

Then there was X, moving about without words. He offered a way out to those whose spirits had long ago been broken by the system. He gave glimpses of paradise to those who could never rise above their station even if they tried with all of their might. He offered opportunities to those whose eyes were open, who struggled to be freed from the invisible prison that was blocking their every turn. He had given her both. It almost felt spiritual when she was with him. He took her mind and heart and body to the highest of peaks. She could lay in his arms and close her eyes and feel so far away, feel so at peace. He made everything beautiful. It was a high she never wanted him to come off of. Her lust and desire built with each hit of him. It no longer began and ended with X. Now she wanted to win. Why should Lydia live in a mansion and ride around in a chauffeured Rolls Royce while Amir sailed around the world in a yacht?

She shivered and pulled her coat tighter around herself. Why should she care about any of that? What good did it profit a man to inherit the world and lose his soul? X waved to her and she trotted out to the car. He dropped her off at home and gave her a quick peck. "This is just the beginning," he said. That was one thing she was certain of.

She was confused. Since she'd been back in Rochester, church had been her solace. It was her place to refuel and realign her thinking. But the last time she went, she felt like a fraud. There was nothing worst in the world than a hypocrite. She had clapped along and sang to songs about God's goodness and a week later, she dined with a murderer, and came close to having sex with a woman. How could God be in any of that? She could twist X's actions around in her head until they were arranged in a semblance of justice, but what she had done didn't allow such distortions. How could she go to church with that shame?

Well, she had only done exactly what needed to be done and nothing more. Right now, they needed Amir as a connect. With his low prices they could flood the market; none of their competitors stood a chance. The opposition's workers would flee quickly, like rats out of a sinking ship, no war would be needed. The bounty would overflow. X was not greedy. He would quietly cycle the money back into the city, buying vacant plots of land, shining a light into darkness. Black contractors would be used, all workers would be hired. Young men with baggy clothes and blighted ambitions would watch them from the street corner. One would build up enough courage one day to walk over to the job site. "Yo, is it true that y'all hiring anybody, even if you got a felony?" He would be told yes.

She had only acted in order to secure that. She had just smiled and listened politely. Lydia had come on to her. And though the thought of her breath against her face brought a shiver down her spine even now, she hadn't acted on it. She had resisted temptation. She got dressed for church. God knew it all anyway and He was the only judge who's verdict counted.

The church's parking lot was ridden with pot holes and ice that made the steep incline treacherous in her stick. A few weeks ago, she had rolled back and almost hit a car behind her. She started parking across the street from the church, in a factory lot, after that. The place was closed on Sundays and never complained about parishioners parking there. She later learned from X that it was a gun manufacturing plant. He said it was good to know where armories were. Today, she crossed the street as quickly as the slush would allow, with each step her foot was sucked down into the gray thickness, it was like walking in mud.

She made it to the church's lot where a jolly middle aged man called out to her. "Good morning!" Tracy smiled. Even on the coldest days, the ambassadors were stationed around to greet people as they entered. You felt loved even before you walked into the sanctuary. This ambassador was particularly sweet. Though she didn't know his name, they exchanged a hearty greeting every time they saw each other. She was greeted two more times before she made it inside. In the lobby, Viola's response to Tracy was a guttural noise in her throat. Only a Black woman could make "mmm hmm" sound so threatening. Tracy kissed the older woman on the cheek. "Hi, Miss Viola."

"I haven't seen you in a long time."

"Well, you see her now." Cheryl swooped in and pulled Tracy away. "Don't pay that heiffa no mind." Tracy laughed. Cheryl was cool. Though in her forties, she had a shape that could put some twenty-somethings to shame. She was curt to most, but fussed incessantly over those who she liked. Today, she gave Tracy a mouthful. "But she does have a point. I mean I know you young and fly and all of that, trust me I know, I used to get it in in my day, but I always made it to church. If you too tired or that thing is too good for you to get up and praise the Lord, then you need to let it go. Didn't you tell me you were going to write something for the Black History program?"

Tracy had completely forgotten. "Yes, I did. Don't worry, it'll be done."

"Mmm hmm." Cheryl's tone had a grandmother's warmth to it. "Handle your business girl." Tracy entered the sanctuary and followed the usher to a pew. She quickly got wrapped up in the praise and worship. The harmonious belting of the choir, striking of the piano keys, thumping of the drum, and chords of the electric guitar lifted her. She found herself crying without knowing why.

The message too seemed meant just for her. Pastor preached about the dangers of sin, of the wedge it created between believers and Christ. "Turn to John 8:34." The resulting turning of pages could be heard through the sanctuary. Tracy pulled the Scripture up on her phone. "I'm reading from the English standard version. "Truly, truly, I say to you, everyone who commits sin is a slave to sin." What does that mean? It means that sin will come between you and Christ. Sin will become your master. Don't you know that sin creates more sin? You start off doing one thing and that guilt eats at you. Instead of you recognizing that that's the Holy Spirit trying to correct you before you go completely off track, you feel shamed. You stop talking to God. You stop believing that He wants to bless you. Before long, that sin has grown. Now you're unable to control your flesh. You're doing things you never thought you wanted to do. Why? Because a slave cannot have two masters. Jesus himself is saying here that if you allow it, sin will rule you."

"Think about it. You hear of men just walking away from their families. You wonder, 'how can this man just leave his wife and children and simply walk away?' How can a man of God do that? I'll tell you how, he is no longer a man of God, but a man of sin. Women say, that girl isn't even that cute. What did she do to him?" The crowd laughed. "She ain't do anything, the sin did. That man fell short of the glory of God every time he laid with her."

"Repeated, unrepented sin will chip away at you. It will whittle down that reserve that God had placed in your heart. It happens slowly until one day you look in the mirror and don't even recognize yourself. Sin ain't nothing to play around with. You can't have one foot in sin and the other out. Sin will make God harden His heart toward you."

"That's what the enemy wants. He wants to take you away from God's protective hedge. Sin does that, it removes God's safety net and leaves you in the hands of the enemy. You hear me? Satan is the enemy of your soul. He came to seek, steal, and destroy. You can't play no friendly games with the devil, he's playing to win. Some of y'all entertaining him. Talking 'bout 'I'ma just do this devil, but then leave me alone'. No, it doesn't work like that. Y'all need to do what I do when I see the devil—cross the street."

"I have a beautiful wife, y'all see her." This time the audience broke out into applause as the first lady of the church blushed from the choir stand. She was a beautiful, elegant middle-aged woman. Her looks were enhanced by the genuine concern she demonstrated for the church. She often led women ministries and spent time counseling single women. She assured them that if they placed God first in their lives and preserved their bodies as His temple, their husbands would come. Looking around at the 80/20 ratio of women to men in the church, it was a message that Tracy didn't buy. Still, she loved the first lady for trying to instill hope.

"But it's not how fine she is, or how much she loves God, or how good her potato salad is that keeps me from straying. I mean I travel a lot and I see first-hand the marvels that God can make. And all of the brothers say amen." Again, the congregation laughed. "But I'm not tempting God. God has done too much for me. He has saved me from my foolishness too many times. His anointing on my life is too strong. The blessings He has given me are too bountiful for me to risk on sin."

"When you sin, you are putting that fleshly thing above God. You are risking everything that God has given you. Is that sin really worth it? Are you prepared to lose God's favor in your life? I know I'm not. We need to repent." The band quietly made their way back to the stage and the choir stood in unison. They quietly began to sang, "We fall down/but we get up."

Pastor walked out towards the congregation. "All of us have sinned, all of us. Jesus died for our sins. Glory Hallejuah! 'Cause on my best day, I know I don't deserve salvation. Aren't you glad that Jesus died for us? So walk away from that sin now." The choir's volume was increasing. "It's not too late."

Pastor continued. "Come on up to the altar. Lay it all down before God. Tell Him you love Him and you're sorry. It's as simple as that." People began to slowly get up and head towards the front. Tears streamed down Tracy's face. "Don't worry about what nobody here thinks. They can't get you into Heaven and they can't keep you outta Hell." More people went to the front. This group walked with more determination. Pastor kept talking. "The Spirit of the Lord is telling me that there is one more person. This person is carrying a heavy burden. The Lord says that you are walking too close to the edge. Won't you come back to Him? Don't let this moment pass you by. Don't walk out of here without getting what God has for you and for you alone."

Tracy was sobbing now. A heat spread through her whole body. She knew that Pastor was speaking of her, but still she could not get up and go to the altar. An usher handed her a fistful of tissue. She gathered her purse and coat. In the aisle, the heat hit her harder. She turned and looked towards the altar before walking the other way. In the bathroom, she blew her nose, and splashed water on her face. Still, there was nothing she could do to remedy the red in her eyes. She took a deep breath and left the bathroom. She was marching steadily towards the door, when someone tapped her on her shoulder. She kept walking. She would break down if she talked to anybody. "Remember me?" It was Thalia.

Tracy turned around to face her. She was stunned to see Thalia in church. Damn, why did this girl keep invading her worlds? She was annoyed and flustered, but she had missed her friend, she needed her now. She wondered if Thalia was still her friend.

Tracy sniffled. Thalia kept talking. "Some service huh? That nigga almost got me. Almost got me up there to bare my soul." She laughed.

Tracy narrowed her eyes. Didn't Thalia take anything seriously? "Oh I thought you were actually here to worship, but I guess you just like popping up on me."

"What are you talking about?"

"You just popped up in Miami. Didn't tell me that you were coming. Didn't tell me that you're working for Derek now."

"Girl, let's not get into this petty sh-," she remembered where she was and caught herself. "I had my reasons for not telling you. But now you know, so what's wrong?"

For the first time ever, Tracy eyed Thalia in suspicion. She had quickly become her best friend and confidant. She had never questioned whether she should trust her or not. She feigned a smile and said, "Nothing."

"Good 'cause I'm starving, let's go get some breakfast."

"Sorry I can't. I have to work on lessons, I'll call you later." She scurried out before Thalia could object.

About half an hour later her doorbell rang. She pulled herself off of the couch and looked through the peep hole. She almost swore. What did she want?

"Since you don't have time for breakfast, I figured I'd bring the breakfast to you," Thalia brushed past her into the dining room.

Tracy watched as she took out Styrofoam packages that contained grilled catfish, grits, wheat toast, and scrambled eggs. She couldn't stop herself from smiling. "Well, it's the least you could do, although it's not in the least environmentally friendly."

"Fuck the environment." Tracy laughed. Sharing a meal with Thalia felt like old times. It wasn't long before they were talking trash and clowning.

"So what in the world were you doing at church? Staking out a deacon?"

"Girl no, you see the potbellied jerry-curl having fools in there. I was staking you out. Figured you wouldn't ignore me in the house of the Lord."

So she had been there to pop up on her. "How have I been ignoring you?"

"Well, we didn't even get up in Miami. Wasn't that shit wild? The people, the beaches, the money. Damn, I'm mad to be back here."

Tracy laughed. "Yeah it was like another world, another life. Why didn't you tell me you were coming?'

Thalia's smile vanished. "Tracy, I've never reported to you."

"I wasn't asking for a report, but you would think something like that would come up in conversation. I'm your best friend right?"

"Miami wasn't about friendship, it was business."

"Oh God, you already sound like them. Okay, so it's business. But it's a business you got introduced to through your best friend. You are working for your best friend's man. And then you crash your best friend's vacation."

"Okay, well I see you're not going to let this go. Crash your vacation? Tracy, please, what part of business, don't you understand? You think X took you down there for a get-away? Girl, everything that he does is about business. Learn how to handle yours."

"And you know how to handle this? Okay O-G. Let me watch and learn from you."

Thalia pushed herself away from the table. "I've never known you to be stupid Trace. You better open your fucking eyes. I'm handling their books not their dicks. I could reinvest and set up off-shore accounts in my sleep. You know what I couldn't do? Get dick-no-tized and forget that my man kills and intimidates for a living."

They shared an icy look for a moment. How many times had X said that it was just business? Was she just business too? She had pushed the specifics of his business to the back of her head. Did he really kill people? Surely he was too high up to do that. But he had to order people to be killed. Wasn't that the same as pulling the trigger?

Thalia was speaking again. "Tracy you're right, I should have told you that I was coming to Miami. I had been hanging out with Derek and just seeing how he doesn't let anything get in the way of what he wants. I mean that man is brilliant. And he was saying how they've been cleaning money through business ventures and I was saying that it would be much easier to invest that money in the market and then he was offering me a job."

"So I took it. Why not? I did everything I was supposed to do, I got the degrees, I got the job, I got the results and those bastards fired me. They shipped me here and fired *me*! Later for that. From now on, I'm making my own rules. I got their severance package and when that runs out I'm going to apply for unemployment and on top of all of that, I still have a job, one that pays a hell of a lot more. Don't gotta pay taxes or nothing." Her laugh was dry.

"Maybe I didn't tell you because I wasn't sure what I was doing or why. But I'm secure in my decision now. You should be too." Thalia had rushed through her words as if she expected Tracy to interrupt her. Now she looked like a child waiting to hear their punishment.

Tracy suddenly felt very tired. The stress and doubts she had been having were threatening to boil over. What had she worried about before she met X? Just work. That was always going to be a mess and now her life was in shambles too. Again. Where would she run to this time?

"Thalia, it's okay. It's just a lot at once, you know? Let's get together later this week." She stood up, making it clear that she was ready for Thalia to leave.

At the door, Thalia eyed her. Never one for affection, she surprised Tracy when she got on her tiptoes and gave her a quick hug. "Make sure you call me," she said and did her signature sashay out of the door.

Tracy stood in the same spot mulling over Thalia's words. Why did the truth always taste so much worse coming out of somebody else's mouth?

X called her that evening. She pushed the ignore button.

12

"No matter where you go, you are what you are player.
And you can try to change, but that's just the top layer."

-Jay-Z

"Public Service Announcement"

SHE FELT A CERTAIN kind of peace as she walked into school. This was her world, one where she knew the rules. She didn't have to ask anyone for admittance.

She spent the first few minutes of each class asking the students about their vacations. A few had actually left the city; mainly to visit relatives. Most complained of being bored and cooped up in the house because of the cold. A few didn't answer. Tracy had learned that breaks from school were far from vacations for some kids. Students who had abusive parents or other undesirable home situations often hated when school was out.

"Well, it's so good to see all of you. I missed y'all a little."

Andre's face lit up when he saw Tracy. Moments like these were the reason why she loved her job. Once the kids were working on their own, Tracy sidled up to his desk. "You know you're a good kid. Incredibly smart. And if you can just avoid certain things for a few more years, you could go so far. As far as you want to really."

He smiled, but kept his eyes on his desk. "I know Miss, thank you."

"You know who else is a good kid?"

"Who?"

She lowered her voice, "LaShonda."

It was the first time that she had ever heard him laugh. "Yeah Miss, she is, but she's a lost cause. Too far gone over her baby daddy."

Tracy hoped that Andre wasn't right. During her free period she got on google and searched for local programs to help teenage mothers. She found a website called "New Beginnings." A few clicks later she was reading about a program that was started by a teenage mother who went on to get her doctorate in psychology. New Beginnings offered workshops on breast feeding, parenting skills, safe sex, self-esteem, healthy relationships, and education. Most of the workshops were taught by teenage mothers who were further ahead in the program. Its mission was to empower teenage mothers to provide a better life for themselves and their children. The motto was "there is life after life."

There was a contact number and she called it. She was told that there was in fact an opening and an informational session in two weeks. She was elated. It wasn't a magic wand, but it did sound promising.

At home she wished she had found a program to help her with her own life. No one had ever told her that love could make you feel so lonely. X had everything that she ever wanted in a man. He was vibrant, intelligent, funny, sweet, and rich. He was the most honest person she had ever known and yet he lived what most would call a dishonest life. He was the quintessential bad guy, but she saw so much good in him.

X's world was black and white. He didn't concern himself with right and wrong. There was only good and bad. If it made money, it was good, money fixed things. If things were good then he was happy.

A man that focused and rational could ruin her. He did not understand emotions; he did not have time for them. He worked to make things good for them and the city, and she in turn was supposed to be happy. It was an equation she could understand, but not feel. Lydia's warning and Thalia's words sounded in her ear.

She was sick of thinking about this. She blasted her "chick jams" playlist Lauren, Aretha, Alicia, and Jazmine were singing her life's story. She dusted, polished, swept, and mopped to her heart's content.

When the playlist ended and her house was spotless, she was still filled with nervous energy. She pulled her hair back, slipped into some sneakers and headed to the gym. She increased the treadmill's incline and speed, and tried to zone out. Now she listened to Beanie Siegel instead of love songs. His raw delivery and throbbing beats propelled her. "Think he a sucka 'cause he don't show it/Paybacks a motherfucka and he won't blow it." She didn't stop until her muscles screamed for release.

Back at home she showered, stretched again, and patted herself on the back for a productive day. She thought of calling X, but got a bowl of ice cream instead. She was licking the spoon and watching *Golden Girls* when her phone rang. Their picture from the banquet popped up. Her head was cocked towards him and she was smiling, he was staring straight ahead. How telling. She didn't pick the phone up.

The next day, she couldn't wait to see LaShonda. The girl shook her head when Tracy approached her in the hallway. "I can't talk now Miss."

"Okay. Well here's a pass. Come see me during your lunch."

"Okay," she didn't match Tracy's eyes.

"I mean it LaShonda."

"Okay."

Tracy was busily grading papers when LaShonda knocked tentatively on the open door. Something about the forlorn look in her eyes put Tracy on notice. She tried to smile brightly enough for the both of them.

"Come in, sit." LaShonda did as she was told with heavy footsteps. She walked like she was headed to her execution. Tracy plunged forward. "You know LaShonda, you're a very bright girl. I see so much potential in you. So often we think nice things about people, but don't take the time to tell them. We always think that they know. Well, I don't take the encouraging word for granted."

She paused. LaShonda was tight-lipped and embarrassed. "Of course, potential isn't enough. You have to have ambition, drive. You have to be willing to do whatever it takes to get to where you want to be." *God, she sounded like X.*

"And you need help. I know you have a baby and so many people want you to believe that you can't reach your dreams after that. That's not true, you just have to work harder. You just have to want more for you and your daughter. There's this program, New Beginnings, they help teenage mothers. Girls a few years older than you and in similar situations will teach you about college, resume writing, networking, nutrition, make sure you don't have another baby—

The sound that emitted from LaShonda's throat was a cross between a cry and a gag. She held a hand to her mouth as if to try to stop it from escaping. Her momentary silence wasn't enough to stop the tears from streaming down her face.

Tracy crossed quickly to the door, closed it, and sat at the desk next to LaShonda. She couldn't suppress the urge to reach over and hold her hand. LaShonda hung her head, her heavy bangs hid her eyes.

Tracy let her cry for a few moments before she asked her what was wrong. LaShonda could barely get the words out between sobs, "Miss, I'm pregnant."

Tracy snatched her hand back. How could LaShonda have been so stupid? You would think that having a baby by a no good, useless nigga would make you use condoms, if not also birth control. This girl seemed to be hell bent on ruining not only her life, but also her daughter's. Before you know it Lashonda's daughter would be sixteen and knocked up. How long would it take before three generations were welfare recipients, bottom feeding off of the system? And of course they would have a sob story. Some pitiful tale about how it wasn't their fault.

Tracy blinked a few times before speaking. "I see and I assume you're keeping it?"

LaShonda recoiled like she had been slapped. "Of course I'm keeping it. I ain't no baby killer."

Again, anger rose to Tracy's face. Why did these girls act like they were too holy for an abortion? They were quick to fight, drink, fuck, and smoke. Did their sharecropping Baptist roots only stop them from one sin?

Tracy shook her head in resignation. "Is it by the same guy? Is he still fooling around with Nicole?"

LaShonda's eyes were glued to the ground as she nodded yes.

"Well, LaShonda, I certainly didn't have all of this in mind when I called you in here. I just wanted to help."

LaShonda rose and met Tracy's gaze. "Did you mean what you said Miss, that I have a lot of potential?" Her words reeked of insecurity. No wonder she was in the situation she was. Girls that weak would always be semen receptacles for useless men.

"Yes. But potential will get you nowhere if you don't start making the right decisions."

*   *   *

Thalia called her at four. "Are you sick?"

"No, why?"

"Um, because the tutoring program that you chair is starting in fifteen minutes. I thought you would be here by now."

"Shit, I completely forgot. I'm leaving the school now."

Their sorority's mission was service. They provided that service through different initiatives including health, developing world leaders, and global poverty. Tracy ran the education committee which threw school supply drives, arranged college tours, and offered tutoring for struggling students. They were expanding to a new rec center today.

She drove as quickly as her Accord would allow. She needed a new radiator, so she couldn't afford to push it too hard. At least she could use some of the money X had given her for that. She shook the thought of X away.

The rec center was lively. The walls were painted in bright shades, chubby faced youth rushed about. The sounds of laughter and bouncing balls and crashing feet filled the air. Thalia and two other sorors had already set up one of the meeting rooms. Tracy gave them all a quick hug.

"I'm so sorry I'm late."

Thalia shrugged. "Don't worry about it. Do you like the way everything is set up?"

"Actually, let's make today less formal. We're just getting to know the kids we're gonna be tutoring. Miss Lewis, the head of the center's education program, says we can expect six to twelve kids each week. Most of them are third graders. So how about we push the tables together? And just do ice breakers today? We can see which personalities match up, what areas the kids need help in."

"Okay Teach, you're the expert."

Miss Lewis led four girls and three boys to the meeting room. "Hi kids. I'm Miss Mitchell, and this is Miss Richards, and Miss Scott, and Miss Williams. We will be here every week to help you with your homework. How about you guys tell us your names and grade?"

The kids were absolutely adorable. Jose, a Puerto-Rican eight-year old, was Tracy's favorite. He told her all about his passion, dinosaurs. "Did you know that arch-i-lows are still finding dinosaurs?"

"Do you mean archeologist?" Tracy corrected.

"Yeah, that's what I said. I'm going to be an arch-i-low when I grow up."

Sonya, a pretty third grader in pigtails, was enamored with Thalia. "Miss Richards, do you think you can help me with my times table next week?"

Thalia beamed down at her. "Sure Sonya."

Tracy excused herself to go to the restroom. Maybe she should recertify and become an elementary teacher. They were so cute and so eager. And little kids didn't get pregnant.

When she left the bathroom she saw X talking to Miss Lewis. He handed her a check. "You know my uncle is always happy to help the kids. He knows that you run a tight program and that his money will go far here."

"Please tell Derek how much we appreciate his continued support and generosity." Miss Lewis rushed off.

X crossed over to Tracy. "You're a hard woman to get in touch with these days."

"You see what I'm up to."

"You volunteering up here?"

"Yes, we're tutoring here every week."

"That's cool. Miss Lewis is good people. She knows what she's doing."

Tracy nodded. She wanted to hug him, but she stayed where she was. "Well let me get back to it." She paused a moment before turning and walking away. "Okay guys how about we start to clean up?" Thalia and Sonya shared a lingering embrace when it was time to go. Tracy elbowed her. "Somebody getting that itch, huh?"

"I would love to have a daughter like her. But knowing my luck, I would end up with a bad ass like that Demetrius."

*   *   *

That night X didn't call, he showed up. She took a deep breath before opening the door. She still didn't know what she wanted, she wasn't sure if she would be able to resist him long enough to make up her mind.

"You've been avoiding me."

"I had a life to get back to." He looked so sexy leaning against the door frame. "You coming in?"

"No, I need you to come out."

She didn't want to go outside in her scarf, robe, and slippers. "Okay let me change real quick."

"No. Come on, I have something to show you." She let him lead her out to the parking lot. She gasped when she saw a steel grey Infiniti G35 coupe with a pink bow on top. She walked to the car and pressed her nose against the window. She took in the leather and wood grain interior, noticed the 5 speed transmission, he had even gone as far as getting her sorority's vanity plates.

"Is this for me?" She squealed the words, jumping up and down before she heard the answer.

"I told you this was just the beginning. And I didn't exactly give you a birthday present."

He looked so pleased to have made her happy. She threw her arms around his neck, pelting his face with kisses.

He told her everything that she wanted to hear. "Baby this new product is killing niggas! We got feens walking over from the east side to get some of this shit. I mean they walking in this cold. This shit is straight up certified. Got the feens stamp of approval." She couldn't help but laugh at that. "We racking it in baby. We've tripled, damn near quadrupled profits. No one else can compete with that. They scrambling, trying to figure out who has the streets flooded." She cast him a worried look. "Don't you get it babe? They all about to be shut down. We're about to own this town, finally be able to clean it up. It's time to step out of the shadows baby. And as long as we're smart, as long as we build the city up and keep the homicides down, businesses will come back here. Everything will be different and everyone is going to be grateful and not ask questions." He placed his hand on her cheek. "I only got two more years, two years tops in the game."

"Really?"

He stepped in closer to her. "Yes, really. You're the woman I knew I would find. I want a family."

She looked away from him. His look was too intense, she felt herself melting. She could still walk away from X. The last few days without him had been hard, but they were doable. She could write all of this off as a fling. Or she could stay and let him build a home for her. She looked back into his eyes. They told her more than words ever could. This was a man she could stay in love with. This was a man she could do some good with. She believed him. God help her, she believed in him. Two years. It would speed by and then they would have the rest of their lives. Two years.

She grabbed a coat, she had to take her new car out for a test drive. She felt such a sense of satisfaction when she eased into the driver's side. She deserved this. They stayed parked for a while as she played with the features of the car. She found a neo-soul station on the satellite radio and finally eased out of the spot.

The car was perfect. There was dual climate control. There were heated seats. The clutch was sensitive to her touch and ready to do her bidding. The car was deceptively fast and handled well. Every curve on the road was an experience. She felt like she could drive forever. She ended up taking them on a tour of their relationship, to the Northside to the Italian Steakhouse, to downtown to the basketball stadium, they went into ghost town past the after-hours spot, and finally to the top of the parking lot.

She thought back to when he had brought her here. She had been intent on blowing him off, but he had been so patient, so persistent. He had done everything that he said he would do.

She took off her seatbelt and straddled him. They just stared into each other's eyes for a while. When he slid into her, his stroke was probing but gentle. His kisses were the sweetest. He stayed the night.

Somewhere in the middle of the night she woke up to him caressing her body. His touch was light, and he left no inch of her untouched. His right hand settled above her heart. His lips rested near her ear. "I love you."

The next day Tracy called Thalia. She was her best friend and there was something comforting about the fact that Tracy hadn't stepped into this new life alone. They had both crossed over into something unchartered. And although their outlooks on the situation were different, there was no denying that they couldn't go back.

For a while it was just like that. Tracy, X, Derek, and Thalia. They were a family. Her other friends, her coworkers, hell even her real family, became outsiders. They couldn't understand the world she was in, they knew nothing of it. They only got pieces of her. They got warm smiles and "I'm doing just fine and you's?"

*   *   *

Tracy and X operated in their own realm, floated between worlds. He went with her to school board meetings, shook his head at the idiocy of their policies. She went with him to Derek's lavish dinners, listened quietly to the cryptic references to the business. He went with her to the faculty party, nodded politely at chit-chit. She went with him to clubs, smiled brightly as his trophy and pretended not to notice the women who threw themselves at him. They both went to political fundraisers, on quiet walks, for long soaks in the hot tub, to the heaven that was their lovemaking.

Saturday nights were an occasion with them. This particular Saturday she sat in front of the vanity he had recently bought her and ran the flat iron over her edges. X walked in and stood behind her. He looked at her reflection appreciatively.

She turned around to face him. "If you don't tell me where we're going, how will I know what to wear?"

"Nice try. No, jeans, but no ball gowns either."

She stuck her tongue out at him before walking into her closet. She chose a snug maroon dress with a scoop neck and silver heels. X nodded his consent.

They arrived to the Auditorium, a theatre style, seated venue that hosted everything from concerts to large church services to sporting events. Tonight, the stage was set up as a boxing ring. X led her through the swell of the crowd. It was a hodgepodge of the city's underworld—hustlers, dealers, gold diggers, and workers. They were greeted by most. She played her position, smiled and kissed cheeks, pretended to be interested in the pleasantries that were exchanged. She laughed on cue, but never strayed more than a foot away from X.

Tyriek and Sean and their girls were seated a few rows from the front. X took them aside. Tracy made small chat with the ladies. "Your shoes are cute."

Sean's date, Tracy had long ago given up on trying to remember their names, raised her foot so the red bottom showed. "They're Louboutins."

Tracy nodded. "I can see that."

The girl bobbed her head. "Yep, Sean takes good care of me. I like your hair. Is that Remy?"

"No." She held in a chuckle.

"Oh, you need to upgrade. All that other shit sheds."

Tracy glanced over at Tyriek's girl. At least Tyriek had better taste in women. Sheila was quiet, but the facial expressions she made let Tracy know she was no dummy. Today, she rolled her eyes.

"Words of wisdom, I'm sure." X motioned to her and she went to him and followed him to their front row seats. The undercard was a welter weight fight that garnered a few dramatic moments, but ended with an anticlimactic split decision. Beads of perspiration formed on the tip of her nose when Jason's name was announced as the challenger for the heavy weight fight.

She hadn't seen him since his confrontation with X in her apartment. So much had changed since then. The fact that she used to deal with him embarrassed her. She glanced over at X. His expression hadn't changed.

She had never seen Jason fight before. Tonight she could see traces of the prize fighter that he used to be. He was quick on his feet, but his punches were anxious. He occasionally dropped his guard to get in a few jabs to the body, but he was hesitant to take a big shot. He put up a good fight until the fourth round.

X whispered to her. "This nigga hurt you right?"

She remembered the shame she felt when Miss Johnson told her Jason was married, his smugness on the phone. Yes, he had hurt her, but her tongue couldn't form a response.

"You know I couldn't let anyone get away with that."

Jason was sluggish in the fifth round. It seemed to take him a great effort to keep his hands up. When the champion pelted his face with a series of combinations, he swayed backwards like a drunk oak tree. She glanced at X. He was grinning.

The sixth round was disastrous. The crowd screamed for blood and it seemed that Jason would be knocked out at any second. The champion was doing everything in his power to send Jason to the canvas, but Jason's stubbornness kept him on his feet. She willed his cut man to throw in the towel. A right cross finally sent him crashing down. He didn't get up.

A murmur ran through the audience, the woman next to her gasped. It took every ounce of willpower in her body to keep her in her seat. Jason had hurt her, but his punishment was far worse than the crime.

Paramedics wheeled him out. Someone later told her that Jason spent seven days in the intensive care unit. She tried to forget the fight, forget that she had ever known him.

13

SPRING CAME AND WITH its budding flowers, something else grew. Tracy could sense it. It was like the menacing sight of storm clouds; something surely was about to rain down.

She dismissed it as unnecessary worrying, everything was perfect. X was great, the school year was wrapping up.

A rainy Wednesday changed everything. As usual, she had fun driving her new car. It handled well on the slick roads and she glided into her usual parking spot. She slung her purse over her shoulder, eased her feet on the asphalt in case of puddles, thrust her umbrella open, and exited into the downpour. At the door, she swiped her badge. She barely got wet.

The chemistry teacher on the first floor smiled at her in the office. She smiled back, checked her mail, and headed to her classroom. A group of girls rounded the landing as she headed up to the third floor. One with braids was speaking. "Yeah, so I told that motherfucka, he better get his shit together." One of her friends saw Tracy and elbowed her. The girl with braids blushed. "Sorry Miss Mitchell."

Tracy smiled "Good morning ladies." She looked directly at the braided girl. "And if you have to talk to him like that, then he's not worth keeping." She continued her trot up the steps. In her room, she opened the blinds while she hummed to herself. She had been doing that a lot lately. She checked her email, entered some grades into the book, put the warm-up on the smart board. The bell rang and the familiar buzz of children thickened in the hallway.

She stood outside of her class to greet students. Miss Hernandez walked down to her. She held her cell phone out in front of Tracy. "Mira, look at my niece. Isn't she the cutest little thing? She has a trail of hair from her back to her tushy." Tracy listened with a smile. She shouted "Good morning!" down to Mr. Thorte, he didn't even uncross his arms. She and Miss Hernandez laughed.

Her classes were working on persuasive essays. They dragged transition words across the smartboard and placed them in paragraphs to add fluency. She told them to sit down and do the same with their writing.

Third period was her free period. She texted X and started planning a new lesson. Then she used the bathroom, washed her hands, blotted the shininess on her face, and headed back to her room.

The hallway was different now. She heard the volume of the crowd before she saw it. Above the students' heads she could see Nicole and LaShonda.

LaShonda had been skipping her class and Tracy hadn't intervened. The girl's fate was pretty much sealed and Tracy was relieved when she stopped coming to class. There was no room for disappointment in her new, happy life.

But there she was now, falling on top of Nicole. Tracy moved towards them, light caught the glare of something silver in Nicole's hand. Suddenly Tracy felt like she was moving in quick sand.

LaShonda was doubling in pain. Nicole was kneeling over her. Tracy hesitated, it wasn't her job to break up fights and oh God, Nicole had a knife. She was still for a second.

The fear in LaShonda's eyes was sharp, she knew what was coming. Nicole's jaw was set with determination. She meant to kill. She was going to kill the girl whose laughter used to brighten Tracy's day. She was going to kill the girl who was so beautifully unaware, the girl who told everyone that would listen about her daughter, the girl who refused to kill the baby in her womb.

LaShonda shifted her gaze from the knife and to Tracy. Their eyes locked and the second passed. Tracy could move now, she had to. Her arms wrapped around Nicole just as the knife was sinking into LaShonda's throat.

The rest passed like a dream. Her movements were all instinct now; the fear had gone from her. She dragged Nicole off of LaShonda and rushed her into the lockers. The crowd fanned out, this carnage was more than it had bargained for. Tracy could hear the screams, but they sounded distant. Nicole wasn't moving. She lay crumbled near the lockers, seemingly in shock from it all.

LaShonda's eyes were still fixed on the spot where Tracy had been. Blood rushed from her neck, it gurgled a bit. All color was drained from her pretty face.

The dream sped up after that. She remembered her wails, her sobs, how she threw herself over LaShonda's body. But there was nothing else to shield her from. The knife had already met its target. The security guards, in their normal fashion, arrived too late. It took three of them to pull her away.

The hallway surged with a demonic chaos. Camera phones were swirled around. The panicked shouts of teachers mingled with the cries from the students and the blood that they were all standing in.

An announcement ordered a lockdown and everyone was shooed into classes. In the confusion, Tracy followed her students into her room. No one thought to stop her. She stared back at twenty-three pupils. Although most of these kids had felt the sting of death before, this was different. Death was not supposed to be in here. No one said a word. She had never been in a classroom so quiet.

Tracy took in gulps of air and struggled to contain herself. A teacher had to always seem like they were in control. A teacher had to be professional and a Black teacher had to be a rock, proof that it was possible to make it out, proof that education did work.

She wanted to say something comforting. She thought of LaShonda's eyes locked on hers. How could she have ever thought that she was enough to save them?

It was too much. It was too fucking much. Why did these kids have to go to this shitty school? Didn't they at least deserve to have a safe place to learn and dream? Wasn't slavery and the blood hounds and the lynchings and the fire hoses and crack and AIDS and Trayvon Martin enough? Couldn't they at least have a good school? Who had decided this for them? Did God decide *this*?

The air was still too thick, too hot. She wanted to rip at her collar. Instead, she ran a blood stained hand through her hair. She looked at her students. They were still looking back at her. She felt like an amoeba under a magnifying glass. What did they want from her? What could she really give them?

She was crying before she knew it. Screaming before she could stop herself, knocking over desks, kicking at chairs.

Andre was the only one who dared to calm her. "Miss, Miss." When his quiet words failed to subdue her, he wrapped her in a hug and dragged her to the floor. A few other kids joined their embrace.

They were huddled together like that until Miss Rosa, the school counselor and two uniformed police men came. They stood awkwardly in the corner as Andre gave her another hug. She hugged him back, clung to him actually. "It's okay Miss."

An announcement came over the PA system. "Today our school has been rocked by tragedy. Today, the senseless violence in this city has claimed the life of one of our own. Our prayers go out to LaShonda and her family and to all of you. The buses are here early, we will begin dismissal with the first floor."

The cops had to spoon feed her their questions. "These two students have had a long feud?" She nodded. "And you saw Nicole stab LaShonda?" She nodded. "Did LaShonda have a weapon?" She shook her head.

Miss Hernandez said she would drive her home. No. Well, wasn't there anyone she could call? Yes. She called X, but when she heard his voice on the line, she couldn't clear the frog in her throat to speak. Miss Hernandez took the phone, "I'm sorry there's been an emergency at the school. Tracy needs you to pick her up."

She insisted in waiting alone in the parking lot for X. So many teachers that normally didn't return Tracy's "Good morning" had come to see her. "What a shame." "I heard you were so brave trying to stop it." "If there's anything you need…"

What she needed was another chance. She needed another chance to do what she said she would do when she took the job. She needed another chance to talk to LaShonda. She needed a chance to tell her that it was never worth it to fight over any man. To tell her that she was so much better than all of that. She needed a chance to grab Nicole earlier. She might as well have plunged the knife in LaShonda's throat herself.

X flew out of the car when he saw her. "Baby, what happened?" His hands were all over her, trying to find the source of the blood. "Baby, what happened?" She collapsed in his arms.

*   *   *

Mrs. Smith called the next day, "As far as I'm concerned you're a goddamn hero. I can't imagine the trauma you've experienced. Take as much time as you need."

Tracy's words came before she could consider them, weigh their meaning. "I won't be coming back."

"Take some time and think it over. You know you're a huge asset to this school." Funny, the principal had never told her that before.

She had never been to a funeral before. X, well-versed in the protocols of death, walked her through each step. He picked her dress and laid out her shoes, held her hand and led her through the packed church. Tracy recognized a lot of kids from the school. They

~ 174 ~

wore colorful airbrushed t-shirts with images of Lashonda plastered on them. She could feel their eyes boring into her. She knew LaShonda's mother the moment she saw her. The grief that cloaked her was unmistakably that of a mother.

Death was no stranger around here and it was greeted warmly. It was in the altars of teddy bears and liquor bottles left at the scenes of homicides, in the airbrushed t-shirts and hats with RIP dates, in the tattoos of the faces of the fallen. Today the choir, preacher, and speakers were enthusiastically somber. They worked the crowd into a mournful frenzy. The level of theatrics was almost offensive. LaShonda was a good, loving girl. Her life didn't need stretched out notes and hollering to be felt.

X whispered to her, "They're just trying to show how much they loved her. That's how it normally goes at these things." The tribute was still hard to stomach.

LaShonda's mother stopped her after the service. "They said it was you who pulled that crazy bitch off my baby." Everyone near them seemed to freeze. X squeezed her hand and she managed to nod.

"Miss Mitchell right?" Again she nodded. "You as pretty as she said. Shonda was always talking about you. 'Miss Mitchell said this and Miss Mitchell doesn't do that.'" She lowered her eyes. "She told me how you was always so nice to her, telling her that she would make it. I guess I never had time to tell her that. I'm glad that she heard it from somebody."

What she didn't know, was that Tracy had given up on LaShonda and faltered when she needed her the most. But she returned the mother's embrace and held on tighter as sobs racked her body. It felt like her insides were bleeding.

X helped her through the door to her apartment. Once inside, she shook off his embrace, stumbled to the bedroom, and managed to collapse on the bed. Everything went dark.

It was pitch black, but she could tell she was in a movie theatre. The screen zapped on with a brightness so sharp, it was almost blinding. Yet she couldn't look away. It was like she was looking through the screen. The movie began to play. It started with the first day of school. LaShonda had smiled at her. "Where should I sit Miss?" To a week later, "Can I take out my phone to show you my daughter?" To a couple of months after that. "Hmmm, Miss, I see you smiling extra hard today." LaShonda's body shook with frustration when Tracy broke up her first fight with Nicole. The movie captured the way her eyes squinted when she smiled, the shame on her face when she told Tracy she was pregnant.

The scene changed. LaShonda's mouth opened with the first stab. Nicole's eyes were stones, the knife was an extension of her hand. Tracy was covered in blood—it was seeping out of her pores. She was drowning in it.

She woke up screaming.

*   *   *

Tracy watched the water sliding down her bedroom window. It came down in thick sheets, covered her world with a slivery sheen. She thought back to the last real words she said to LaShonda. Could she have been any more condescending? Who was she to preach about right decisions? After a few days the rain lessened to a steady drizzle. But when she closed her eyes she could still hear it. Her tears came next. She buried her head in her pillow, gagged on her own sobs, but the tears wouldn't stop. She cried until her eyes were swollen, until her throat was raw and then she cried some more. Everything inside of her hurt. She wanted to pray, but her lips wouldn't form the words.

X checked on her several times a day. Sometimes he sat on the corner of the bed. Sometimes he held spoonfuls of soup to her mouth. Sometimes he kissed her forehead.

Thalia came. She stood over her bed for a moment and watched her. She sat down gingerly and took Tracy's hand. "Honey, we have to get you into the shower. Do you think you could do that"? Tracy didn't respond. Thalia sat quietly for a few moments and then scooted closer to her. She helped ease Tracy into a sitting position. "At least let me wash your hair."

Thalia's hands were gentle as she lathered Tracy's hair. She dipped her slowly back into the basin of water, and then wrapped a towel around her head. She read from Ecclesiastes before she left, "To everything there is a season, a time for every purpose under heaven: A time to be born. A time to die. A time to plant, and a time to pluck what has been planted. A time to kill and a time to heal. A time to break down and a time to build up. A time to weep and a time to laugh. A time to mourn and a time to dance." She kept reading even as Tracy wept.

$$* \quad * \quad *$$

She was bare and sinking very slowly, very painfully, into a portal. She didn't feel panic when the walls closed in. She kind of liked the feel of the pressure, the weight of it, the finality it suggested. Her sleep was draining and intoxicating, she was drunk with it. X often had to shake her awake.

He read her the letters. He said the video of her pulling Nicole off of LaShonda had gone viral and the letters had been pouring in ever since. First they were from her students, her kids. They told her how much they loved her and needed her to come back. They told her how much she had taught them, what an inspiration she was. Tracy strained to hear X's words, she cringed at the poor grammar. Apparently, she hadn't taught them enough.

Her colleagues wrote next. They said they understood that it might be too painful for her to come back, but hopefully she wouldn't turn her back on teaching, it was obvious that she was born to do it. And finally, letters came from all over the country. People telling her what a hero she was, that they could only hope that their children had teachers as dedicated as she.

She got a lot of interesting calls too. Local television stations and journalists from *Essence* to CNN and even Fox News called in hopes of interviewing her. She promptly turned them all down. This was not a story, this was reality. Judging by the current state of things, it was a reality that nobody really gave a fuck about.

Tragic left her a message. "I see you're still knee-deep in it, huh? So am I. We'll see who wins." He didn't identify himself, but Tracy could easily recognize his voice just as she could recognize X's. Anger gnawed at her stomach.

An unmarked envelope with a copy of *The Real* came to her house. Jimmie had written 2,000 words entitled "The Lost Ones—The Plight of Ghetto Youth." In it he discussed how suburban schools were becoming increasingly safer while those in the inner-city had become a breeding ground for gang activity and violence. A few sentences made her sit up in bed. "While bigger cities such as New York and Los Angeles have experienced moderate increases in graduation rates and a decline of violent incidents, smaller cities are becoming more and more dangerous. Rochester, New York, a city with one of the lowest graduation rates in the nation, continues to see a spike in homicides and other violent crimes. This violence, in turn, permeates the schools as evidenced by the murder of LaShonda Terry. I would be remiss, if I didn't mention the brave heroics of Tracy Mitchell, the teacher who tried to save LaShonda's life, and former contributor to *The Real*. Tracy, don't stop fighting the good fight." Tears streamed down her face. She was so proud to see Jimmie back on track, but she didn't even know what the good fight was anymore. What difference could any of them really make?

X didn't comment on any of the correspondence. He just asked her to eat. Fed her when she refused, eased spoonfuls of broth between her lips, like a baby. Sometimes he bathed her. He soaped her up so gently, lifting her arms to reach underneath, dipping her slowly back in the water to rinse off. He oiled every inch of her deeply, thoroughly. It was like he was trying to reach deep inside, to stop her from spilling out from herself.

He was keeping her alive. She could feel him through the fog she had passed into, wiping her brow, kissing her on the forehead, watching her as she slept. He told her the same thing every night. "I love you. Fight." She wondered if his mother had been the same way in her last days.

After three weeks, she was doing better. She had gotten up and into the shower on her own. She dried and was about to get back under the covers when he said, "You have to be stronger than this." She glared at him, but he continued. "Who else could have done what you did? Who else would have tried to save her? You're needed there."

He hadn't been there. He hadn't seen her dismiss LaShonda from her heart, hadn't seen her freeze when she saw the knife. But he was right. Even in her failure, she had done more than most would. She would do even more now.

She began to dress. X watched as she put on charcoal gray slacks and a white short-sleeved blouse. The clothes felt loose on her. Did she really used to worry about such frivolous things as her weight? It seemed like years ago. She tried to brush her hair and finally settled on smoothing it into a bun with her hands. She didn't even think to bother with make-up and jewelry. She kissed X and left in silence.

Her hands shook when she glided the car into the parking lot. She thought she was going to puke on her way up the stairs. She had to place a hand on the wall to steady herself; she could feel the squeeze again, feel herself slipping into somewhere dark, some-where inescapable. Luckily, class was in session and the hallways were virtuously empty. It looked like they had finally managed to crack down on things. Why did it take a tragedy for that to happen?

She made it to the third floor, saw herself hurling Nicole into the lockers, saw the blood gushing from LaShonda's throat. The squeeze tightened. She was sweating, the taste of bile rose in her throat. She clasped a hand to her chest and took deep breaths. She stopped just before her classroom. She heard Andre's voice trying to settle the class, "Come on, y'all know y'all wouldn't be acting like this if Miss Mitchell was here." She smiled for the first time since that day.

She opened the door and stepped back into the best part of herself. She threw herself into her work, into making amends. Her lips formed smiles that her heart didn't feel. She still listened and she still cared. Sometimes she thought that the caring was the worst part.

X's steadfastness was incredible. He moved her in with him. He worked long days, but he still held her every night and told her how much he loved her. And he still told her to fight.

The rains relented and the sunshine made a glorious entrance. Little by little, Tracy's grief lifted; the walls began to retreat. She found herself genuinely smiling, even laughing.

14

"Grand mama hit me with three words, 'Son keep prayin'
This shorty hit me with three more, 'Son keep blazin'
They both deep statements, from two unique places.
Real, forever real, I just love to hear the streets say it."

-Mos Def

"The Corner Remix"

THE SPRING ERUPTED INTO beautiful long days. The smell of lilac hung in the air as fresh buds clung to the tree branches. Traffic moved at a slow pace, not because of treacherous roads, but because of the swell of people in the streets. Everyone was awake from the hibernation that winter and the rains had imposed upon them. It was now time to rejoice.

The smiles and laughs she had gave way to bigger ones. The weather restored her. Sometimes she felt guilty for that. Her life had managed to march on while LaShonda's would forever be stunted by that fateful day in the hall. There were moments when the walls of grief closed in on her, but in the end, Spring prevailed.

The city was alive. There was a late night walk down the cobblestone streets of High Falls. Early mornings spent at the public market. The open stalls offered everything from salmon to peaches to fresh flowers to toothpaste. Grubby faced vendors shouted to each other and joked with shoppers who in turn strolled at a leisurely pace. The saxophonists played to their own delight, only bending forward slightly to recognize the dollars passerby dropped in their open instrument cases. They spent afternoons having lunch and people watching at sidewalk cafes along Park Avenue. At dusk, they ventured down the foot path to Lower Falls. Small animals scurried by as they descended down towards the waterfall. It loomed in majesty, they were restored by its mist. There was the warm night spent at Frontier Field, they licked the pretzel salt off of their fingers, rooted for the home team.

One day X insisted on dropping her off and picking her up from work. Windows down, they whizzed down the freeway.

"How was your day?"

Tracy thought back to bored expressions and complaints she received when she introduced the research project. She had thought the students would be excited to work in groups to learn about the Black Panthers, slave rebellions, apartheid, and historically Black Colleges and Universities. Their lack of interest in their own history was infuriating. "Long."

"What you need is something to clear your head." He turned the radio up and "Feel Some Type of Way" played.

Tracy laughed. "This dumb shit will empty my head."

Still they sung along with the ad libs. "Don't look like that!" Though this simple hip-hop was undoubtedly lowering people's IQs, Tracy could understand its place. It certainly was hard to stay mad when she heard it.

He switched from the radio to his iPod and laughed. "That's enough of that shit. Have you heard Big Krit's mixtape?"

She shook her head. "He was in the cypher at the hip-hop awards, right?"

"Yeah, I think you'll like his stuff. He's from Mississippi, but he got a New York flow."

She bobbed to the music and wondered what adventure lay ahead. They exited and followed a smaller route into Canandaigua, a beautifully quaint village. She marveled at the architecture, read the signs of shops that they passed. After a mile or so, they parked and walked along the canal. There were other couples along the gravel path. Mothers jogged behind strollers, toddlers trotted alongside their dads. She looked over at X. He could be so patient, so still. He would make a great father.

A canoe jutted out of the water. He stopped and walked towards it. "Wait, is that for us?" His response was a smile. He helped her in and then took his spot, used the oar to push off. He fumbled a bit and she laughed. He smiled back at her sheepishly and shrugged. "It looks easy in the movies."

They rocked along at a relaxed pace. The bank gave way to weeping willows. Here the birds chirped louder, the squirrels crashed around in the brush. She closed her eyes and inhaled. She was enveloped by the warmth of the sun.

When they were back on land, she grabbed his hand and led him a few feet inward from the path. They made quick, easy love against a tree.

They had uninterrupted peace until the next day. They were sitting on the couch, she was turned towards him and her legs draped his. She glanced up from her book and noticed his furrowed brow. He folded the paper. "What's wrong?"

"One of ours got dropped on Cedar."

She never really knew how to respond when he talked to her about work. He was normally so nonchalant about it, so factual. He used terms like losses and revenue; he could have been talking about anything.

Today was different. He was rattled. She needed to speak delicately. "Is that a big problem?"

"Yeah."

"What does the paper say?"

"It says that 'an unidentified black male was gunned down on the corner of Cedar and Wilcox. No witnesses have come forward and the police have no leads.' Cops gon be all over this shit. Everything is manageable if it remains local. But if bodies keep dropping out here, then the feds gon show up."

"So what comes next?"

His hands were clasped under his chin. He didn't answer for a while. "I don't know. They dropped Malik. He should have been untouchable. Niggas getting real bold right now, desperate."

There were two more shootings that weekend. Five, the following week. Some of the killings happened in broad daylight. Some in front of crowds. But no one saw anything. The streets thinned out instead. Though the sun was still glorious, few were daring enough to go outside to enjoy it. The air felt heavy. Young mothers watched their children with a new attentiveness, grandmothers looked on out of the corners of windows.

It wasn't that spring violence was a new phenomenon. Good weather brought fights, Rochester knew and understood this. It was only logical that folks who had been pent up all winter would be eager to stay outdoors and would run into friends and foes. And it was only natural that some of these reunions got bloody. Most of it was harmless enough. The kids, mainly girls, fought in clumps in the middle of the street. It was normally downtown or a block away from a school, so the inconvenience of it was pretty avoidable. It only got serious when bricks and socks filled with combination locks were used. The late teens, early twenty crowd fought outside of clubs and bars. These alcohol induced brawls seldom resulted in murders. There was the normal bout of domestic violence and rapes, a dozen or so drug relateds.

But these killings were totally different. They had no use of logic or nature, they were unsettling. Community activists called for a cease fire. The victims' families begged witnesses to come forward. The mayor and police chief vowed to arrest and prosecute the perpetuators. No one saw anything.

"Tyrell Stevens, was gunned down on Filmore Street. He, and two other men, who have yet to be identified, were standing in front of his house at five o'clock last night. All three men died on the scene. Police have no further information."

That kid was only seventeen. Was X behind it? Or was the twenty-three year old that was killed in Ghost town one of his? It was like she could hear all of the wailing mothers. She thought of LaShonda's mom at the funeral.

She couldn't sleep. The first night she laid with her eyes closed, willed her mind to submit to the fatigue her body felt. Light filled the room and she went through that day on edge. She was exhausted the next time they went to bed. Surely, sleep would find her now. It didn't, and she spent the night tossing and turning. The next night was the same, she got up and drank a glass of wine, took a hot bath. She was tipsy and drowsy, but still her mind refused to surrender to sleep. She sighed and turned over, facing X. His chest rose and fell slowly, his face was relaxed. She ran her index finger over the bridge of his nose. He couldn't be responsible for all of these killings, all of this pain.

He spoke without opening his eyes. "What's on your mind baby?"

She hesitated. How could she tell him what was on her mind? She didn't want to speak these things out loud; she had been trying not to think them.

He pulled her to his chest. "Come on, baby talk to me. You can ask or tell me anything."

"I thought that the way you and Derek did business was different."

"Different how?"

"Different than all of the people who have been dying." Her voice shook. "How can you be okay with this?"

"I'm more than okay with it."

"What?" She tried to pull away from him, he held her tighter.

"You know I didn't want a war, but it couldn't be avoided. Don't you understand? The street is being cleaned up. We are getting rid of everybody that wants to hold on to the old way of doing things. Everybody. There's two different types of niggas in the game. There are those that need the game. They use it as a tool, as a way to survive. Shit, the best ones use it to get out. Then there are those that hide behind the game. They use it as a cover for all of the evil that runs through their veins."

"You don't even know, you don't even know what these niggas are like. Their families get on the news crying like they don't know how sick these motherfuckas are. That one that got killed on Fillmore? This nigga gave rock to little girls, I'm talking kindergarteners, and fuck 'em. Everybody was afraid to touch him because he's some kin to Big Irv."

She got a chill. "But they can't all be like that—"

"Why can't they? Why would anybody turn down an opportunity to link up with us, make more money, live peaceful, and limit their chances of going to jail? Ask yourself what type of nigga turns that down?"

"What if they want to remain independent? Not everyone wants to be a franchise. How do you know it's not that?"

"I just know, I always know. It's a gift."

"A gift? What kind of gift covers your hands in blood?"

"Tracy," his voice deepened, "We don't always want to do the things we are called for. I know you don't want to walk into that school every day. But what we do is necessary. What we do is destined. Everything had to come together perfectly for us to get to this point. I'm in a position to clean this city up because Derek controls the dope. Derek is in a position to control the dope because of you. Amir wouldn't have dealt with us if it wasn't for you. You were the missing key to all of this. This is God's work. Our lives are more than our own." He kissed the top of her head. "Baby, this isn't meant for you to understand. I don't always understand it."

Though his words quickened her heart, she still couldn't sleep. She just needed to understand what was happening. She went to see Thalia the next day. She found her breaking up weed at her dinner table. Thalia slid the crumbs into a rolling paper and glanced up at her. "Competition is unavoidable in any business. This time less fortunate factions have teamed up to regain their territories. Hitting Malik was a statement."

"So anybody working for Derek has a target on their heads?"

"Stupid people. Malik was parked a block up from the wrong corner in a Porsche truck. Anybody could tell he was made." She licked the edges of the paper and rolled them into place. She lit the end and took a long pull. She exhaled, the smoke billowed out in a gush. "Derek and X have squeezed this town for every dime. Somebody was bound to stand up. But this war was over before it even started."

War. Now that was the right word to describe what was happening. The way X talked about it, he made it sound poetic, romantic even. He didn't leave room for the fact that people were terrified to come outside. They were living in a war zone. Tracy shook her head when Thalia extended the joint towards her. "What do you mean?"

"We anticipated all of this. Niggas don't know who exactly is flooding the town. They just see Tru City spreading out with the best dope. So there's been some banging on the corners, but it won't go up much further than that."

"Derek could have easily put everybody else out of business. But he can't afford the heat of having an operation that large. Bin Laden is dead, all of these gun rampage cats keep offing themselves, people need a new villain. Scary, Black guys always fit that bill. But that's everything Derek is not. He's charming, discreet. He cuts a check to every charity and to every winning campaign. He has an image to uphold. So he kept it small, broke down into independent states. Everyone buys the same shit from him, and runs it out of their hoods, peacefully, quietly. No more standing on corners and all of that shit. In a couple of weeks all of this will die down."

Thalia took a long drag and held the joint out to Tracy again. "Girl, you'd be surprised to see how this town is ran. And don't think that people don't remember you either. Everyone knows you tried to save that girl and you came back to work to save the others. You couldn't make up that shit. You on X's arm says something. Y'all are like the dynamic duo, real live super heroes. Ghetto superheroes."

Tracy took the joint from Thalia and inhaled lightly to Thalia's applause. She held the smoke in her lungs for a while and exhaled.

She used to love this feeling of watching her worries dissolve into smoke. Smoking always cleared her head.

Thalia stood up and stretched. "Enough talk about business. Let's go out."

Going out now was a completely different experience than it had been a few months before. Now it was like they were a part of a secret society. She never waited in line or paid to get in. She was always taken to a table and bottles were always delivered. And when she was with X, things went to another level. The whole night revolved around them.

She and Thalia walked past the line and headed straight towards the door. Tyriek was walking towards them. He kissed them both on the cheek. Thalia swatted him on the ass. "Where you going?"

"Smoke break ma."

Thalia sucked her teeth. "Fuck 'em, smoke in there."

He shook his head. "I don't like to be all out in the open with my shit. See y'all inside."

The club was packed. Tracy surveyed the dance floor. Like church, there was an 80 to 20 ratio of women to men. The women danced in clumps, hoping that their flowers were the brightest, their scent the most intoxicating, their mating call the most attractive. It was like watching the nature channel.

They walked to the back room that hosted the VIP section. Sean, a few dudes from the crew, and about a dozen damn near naked women were sitting behind the velvet rope. Tracy laughed. She forgot that it was Sean's going away party. Sean was cool, 'a stand up dude' as X called it. And though she normally scoffed at his affinity for bird bitches, tonight she was happy to see him surrounded by so many eager women. She gave him a big hug. "You know the time will whiz by. Let us know if you need anything."

Sean laughed. "Okay gangsta mommy, you know I got it." Tracy elbowed him playfully and walked away when she felt a lump in her throat. She hated goodbyes. Thalia followed her to the dance floor. The music blasted, and Tracy did an obligatory two-step. She hadn't smoked in a long time and her mind was somewhere else. In the crowd, she noticed a man walking towards them. He wore all black and a grave expression that she had seen somewhere else before.

She couldn't stop staring at him. His walk was a steadied march and his eyes had a single focused hardness. Tracy remembered what he reminded her of. Nicole had the same look before she stabbed LaShonda. Tracy grabbed Thalia just as he reached for his hip. "What the—" Shots rang out before Thalia could finish. Tracy pushed her towards the emergency exit. The crowd fanned out in panic as they barreled towards the door.

They exited into an alley and Tracy took off running. She stumbled, and her right shoe came off. She kept running. Thalia panted behind her. "Wait girl, we're out of there, slow down."

But Tracy couldn't slow down. She wanted to be as far away from anymore death as possible.

"We gotta tell X."

Thalia was lagging behind her, "Tell X what?"

"I saw him."

X could barely make out her words. He always made it a practice to never discuss business on any phone. "Come to the spot." He hung up.

Inside, X and Derek were sitting at the bar. This felt entirely different than the first time she and Thalia had joined them there. X stood when he saw her, "What happened?"

"We were at Flex. Sean and all of them were in VIP. I saw this dude and I could tell that he was going to start shooting. He just opened up on the VIP, right there, in front of everybody, no mask or anything. Thalia and I barely made it out of there."

This time Derek stood up. "Did he hit 'em?"

"I don't know. I don't see how he could have missed." She was suddenly very tired.

X was watching her. He put his arms on her shoulders. "You saw him?" She nodded. "What did he look like?"

"My height, well, when I'm in heels. Thin, dark skin, dreads, scar across his face." She traced the place on her face where the scar was. X and Derek exchanged glances. They knew who she was talking about.

X kissed her on the forehead. "Okay, we'll handle this. Don't worry. You hear me? Just go straight home."

She went home with Thalia. Thalia rolled another joint and watched her.

"Go ahead and say it." Tracy said.

Thalia shook her head. "I'm not saying shit. Maybe you should try it some time."

She held her gaze. Tracy didn't look away. She had gone to X. She had given the description. She had pointed the finger. She hadn't hesitated this time.

X's call woke her a few hours later. "You okay?"

"Yeah. Why wouldn't I be? You at Thalia's? I'll pick you up."

*   *   *

It was a lazy, Saturday morning. X rarely slept past six and she had grown accustomed to rising with him. Sometimes she went to the gym, and other times she couldn't peel herself away from him. He was a creature of habit. He woke up, kissed her awake, had a cup of coffee and read through three newspapers. He said that was how his father had done it. Hopefully, he wouldn't do things exactly like his dad, lest he get the same result.

This Saturday she had joined him at his breakfast nook. She jabbed her spoon into a grapefruit when the headline on one of the newspapers caught her attention. "Drug Captain Captured." Heat rose to her face. She snatched the paper up and hurriedly scanned through the words. "Eighteen members of one of the most ruthless gangs in the region, Fight Club, were indicted on Friday afternoon on twenty-one counts of drug trafficking, eight counts of witness intimidation, seventeen counts of gun possession.... The gang is known for its undying devotion to each other. Three members are believed to have been executed for cooperating with federal agents. The mayor is calling this prosecution one of many steps in returning the city to those who actually care for her."

Fight Club was one of Tru City's rivals. X was watching her, "Impressed?"

"That's one word for it. How did y'all pull this off?"

"Do you remember our first date?"

Tracy thought back to the dinner at the steakhouse. "Yes."

"Remember the magic trick?" She nodded. "Wanna see it up close?" This time when he did the trick he showed her how he had contoured the napkin to look like there was still a salt shaker underneath it. In reality the salt shaker was already under the table.

"Everyone has their eyes on the napkin, thinking the salt shaker is still in there, but the magician is way past that. That's us. These niggas think we're going to continue dropping bodies, keep a war going that's costing us money and bringing us heat. We're past that. It doesn't matter to me if it's Fight Club or Tru City. They throwing up gang signs and dying in the street, but all of 'em are afraid to live."

"So this is a win-win-win. The people are happy; the streets are safe again, better than anybody can remember. The mayor is happy; and we'll make sure she knows that we're the reason she was able to deliver on everything that she promised. Tru City is further in our pocket. Shit, Fight Club should even be grateful. A cell is better than a grave. A couple of them are actually going to learn something when they go upstate." He shook his head. "Some dudes need to go to jail. Our construction sites are booming. We spread enough money around that every rec is open and ran by effective people. I'm talking, we got the president of Rochester Bank to step down and take over Campbell Street Rec. Now the little niggas got something to do. You wait and see. Next school year, every school will have a chorus, a step team, debate team. Baby this is it. We're bringing Rochester back." He reached over and kissed her.

Tracy ran a hand through her hair. "So what are you going to do when you walk away from all of this? Can you walk away from all of this?"

He smiled, "Only if you're beside me."

15

"Instead of war on poverty,
they got a war on drugs so the police can bother me."

-Tupac

"Changes"

THALIA MANAGED TO REMAIN perpetually in search of an elusive item for her condo so they spent many afternoons rummaging through yard sales, antique shops, and thrift stores.

Thalia set a vase back down. "So what are you going to do for X's birthday?"

"His birthday?"

"What kind of dysfunctional ass relationship do y'all have where you discuss the intricacies of drug empires, but not birthdays?"

Tracy laughed, "It just never came up. What can I get him? He already has everything."

"You could go always do a threesome." She winked at Tracy suggestively.

Tracy threw a pillow at her. "Be real."

"Well, if you insist on being a prude, throw a party. A party is the gift that keeps on giving. Everyone will be there kissing his ass. Let them bring the gifts. All you gotta do is put it together. It'll be fun! He's turning thirty, right? You have to go all out. We just went through hell. Now it's time to celebrate."

Big parties weren't exactly X's style, but it was the perfect time for him to have one. This party would be a statement. She could imagine them all dressed up, everyone toasting X, his brilliance finally acknowledged.

She called Derek to solicit his help with inviting guests. As usual, he was eager to be in the spotlight. He urged her to make the party as grandiose as possible. "Really do this shit. Top of the line all of the way. Have Thalia give you some money." She gritted her teeth. Derek really could be obnoxious. Sometimes Tracy wondered how X truly felt about his uncle. X rarely spoke around him so their interactions were hard to read.

She did as she was told though and reserved the biggest ballroom of the city's biggest hotel. She commissioned a florist, light designer, and the hottest DJ. Costume furniture was brought in. She went over the guest list herself, she organized the hotel security and arranged to have some of X's people at the door as well. The menu was full of X's favorites. The DJ was instructed to play everything from A Tribe Called Quest to Future. In honor of his favorite color she had a strapless, navy blue, mini dress made. It fit her like a glove.

On the day of his birthday she woke him up with kisses. He smiled and pulled her to his chest. "Happy birthday baby."

He cleared the sleep out of his voice, "How'd you know?"

"The better question is why didn't you tell me?"

He shrugged, "Same reason why you didn't tell me."

She smacked him playfully. "We have reservations at Pluto's tonight."

* * *

He looked like old Hollywood in navy slacks, patterned vest and shirt, and wingtip shoes. A navy Fedora completed the look. Tracy walked around him appraisingly. "Oh shit, I see you."

He posed for an invisible camera. "Yeah, you know. I'm on my grown and sexy shit." He pulled her into him and cupped her ass. The dress hugged it perfectly. "Maybe we should stay in." He licked at her earlobe.

"No, you turned thirty. This is a big one, we have to go out. Don't worry. I have a special outfit planned for later."

When she pulled her Infiniti into the parking lot of the hotel, he raised an eyebrow. "How about we stop here and have a drink?" She had never lied to him before and she found it to be exhilarating.

When they entered the ballroom they were greeted with a standing ovation and thunderous applause. Tracy looked over at X. He looked uncharacteristically rattled. He whispered to her, "You shouldn't have done this."

"Sometimes you gotta outdo the Joneses baby."

It was the perfect night. Thalia, Derek, Tyriek, Sheila, and Councilman Brooks sat at their table. Laughter and loud chatter rang out throughout the room. After the food, drinks, and toasts, X began to relax. Leaning back in his chair, his hand on Tracy's lap, he received his well wishers. It was like a Black version of the Godfather. The people stopping at their table ranged from his street family, to politicians, to barbers, to obvious women throwing themselves at him. He joked graciously with everyone, but never ventured more than a few feet from Tracy. She liked the attention but something about it unnerved her.

They were on the dance floor when she brought it up, "You having fun baby?"

"Yes. Thank you. This is the best birthday I've had since Pops died."

"It's that why you're a little tense?"

"I know you wanted to do something special for me and I appreciate it. But something doesn't feel right. I'm keeping my eyes open, can't let anything happen to you."

"We got people stationed all over the room. The hotel security is on alert. We only invited fam. I can't let anything happen to you either."

The festivities began to wind down after three am. It was a warm spring evening and people milled around in front of the hotel. X stood behind her with his arms wrapped around her waist as they waited for the valet. He whispered in her ear. "You are so fucking sexy." His manhood rose against her ass. She leaned into it and raised his hands to her breasts. She couldn't wait for him to see what she had on under her dress.

The valet was handing her the keys when they heard the first shot. Then they were rushing towards the car, screeching out of the parking loop as the shots continued.

Time became suspended, everything about the ticking seconds seemed warped. It was like being in slow motion and fast forward at the same time. Her hands shook on the steering wheel. What the hell had just happened? She looked over at X, he retrieved a chrome plated gun from his waist band. "Go back around."

She knew better than to object. She downshifted to third and pulled back into the parking loop. The crowd from the party had dispersed. Hotel security was hovering over two people. Tracy couldn't tell whether they were moving or not. "Keep going."

They rode the rest of the way back to her place in silence. Were those people dead and where were the shooters? Did they hit who they were aiming for? Were they after X? Who would be after X? She replayed the night in her mind. Nothing seemed out of place.

When they entered her house, he began to talk fast, "Did you register the ballroom under your name?"

"Yes."

"Okay, the cops are going to be here soon then." He took out his cell. "Levy, meet us at the station. Probably downtown." He hung up. "Go change. Sweats, sneakers, put your hair up."

"What?"

"Go fucking change." She scurried towards the bedroom. He followed after her. "Babe, I don't know how these motherfuckas are gonna come up in here, but I do know that they're coming. I need you to do exactly as I say. You hear me? Do exactly as I say."

She stepped into her sweat pants. "Okay."

They might ask us to come in for questioning, they might arrest us. Either way, they will split us up. They come down harder if you don't say a word. Might beat us, might keep us in there for hours. Might not get any food."

Tears welled in her eyes. He grabbed her hands. "I'm not gonna let that happen to you so, we are both going to talk. Our stories have to be the same."

She found herself nodding calmly, but fear had twisted her stomach into knots. She cleared her throat. "Our story is the same. We didn't see the shooter and we have no idea why the shooting took place."

"Right, but they're going to ask you more than that. They'll ask when and how did we meet, go ahead and tell them the truth. They'll start telling you all types of wild shit about me. Act indignant, do your boogie bitch shit, but keep it short. Tell them that I live off an inheritance. That's it. Don't answer any more questions. They'll tell you that I said this and said that, you'll know that's not true. Don't answer any more questions. Don't say anything else."

He kissed her. "Tracy, baby, we got this." He held her face in his hands. "Cops don't know shit. They get all of their information from interrogations. They either beat a nigga's ass on the spot or set 'em up--put a dirty gun or some drugs on 'em. They start talking about years and niggas start talking. Some chicks are tough enough to handle it; but I don't want to be with someone with balls that size. I chose you because I know that you're smart enough not to break."

A blinding light flashed and a deafening explosion roared in her ears. She fell to her knees and put her hands over her ears. X wrapped his arms around her. She blinked rapidly, the darkness lifted and she could see a swarm of black uniforms. Then there was the thumping of boots and hands that pried them apart. Three officers kicked at X before dragging him off. Tracy screamed. An officer jammed his knee in Tracy's back, forcing her torso towards the ground. He yanked her hands behind her back, the handcuffs snapped at her skin. She cried out and was pulled to her feet. An officer pushed her towards the front door. His masked colleagues tore knives into her sofa, ripped paintings off of the wall.

She was pushed into the back of a paddy wagon. The doors were slammed and she sat in darkness. Tears streamed down her face. She rocked back and forth and whispered softly to herself, "Don't break, don't break." The car stopped. Doors were opened and one of the SWAT pulled her out. They were in front of the station and the cop pushed her before him into the building. A uniformed officer manned the bullet proof enclosed desk of the station's reception area. He buzzed them through an unmarked door and they entered a fluorescent lit hallway. The doors back here were dirty and scarred. Tracy whispered to herself, "Don't break. Don't break."

She was pushed into the room and into a metal folding chair. The cop left and the door slammed. She closed her eyes again. Time passed. The door opened and two detectives walked in.

"Miss Mitchell?" It was the Black one who spoke first. His skin was a deep chestnut brown and marked with acne scars. He had slow, roaming eyes.

"Yes?"

The white one stepped further into the room. He looked like the detectives on the cop shows—rumpled suit, medium height, heavy around the middle, thinning hair, and a prominent nose. Tracy felt a hot rage building in her. "I'm Detective Nikols and this is Detective Jamison. We already know more than enough so let's not waste any fucking time. Tell me everything you know about X and you can walk outta here."

Tracy's nostrils flared. She had never felt like this in her entire life. She wanted to see this man bleed. She wanted to hear him cry out and beg for his life. She took several breaths before speaking. "Detective Nikols, I assure you that whatever it is that you think you know it doesn't justify your men storming into my house and ripping it apart. Is this how you treat people? Throw a woman into the back of a pitch black paddy wagon, kick a man that's not resisting? That's how you get your rocks off? Let me tell you something, it's going to take more than that. I'm a citizen of the Unites States and I know what my rights are." Her eyes darted to the Black one. "And you stand for this? I understand that you're probably trying to serve the community, but there are better ways to do it." She stared at him and took another breath. "Now, what can I clear up for you gentlemen?"

Detective Jamison spoke. "I apologize for the way you were treated Miss Mitchell, but you gotta understand the severity of what you're involved in. One person was killed tonight and the other is critically injured. We have very reliable information that points to X. Now you don't need to get mixed up in any of this. We don't even have to record this arrest. Let me help you."

Were they serious? Were they working their good cop, bad cop bullshit already? She stared straight ahead. Nikols interrupted. "So Miss United States Citizen, why don't you start off by telling me how you know X, one of the most ruthless and notorious drug dealers in Rochester?"

"Pardon?"

He laughed and leaned over the table. "Cut the bullshit."

She narrowed her eyes. "There's no need for profanity. I don't know what you're talking about."

He laughed again. "And what should I do, curtsy. Who the fuck do you think you are, the Queen of England?"

"Not at all." *Short answers. Stay calm. Don't offer any information.*

"So, how do you know him?"

"If you're referring to Oxford, I met him at the gym."

"How did a little priss bitch like you get caught up with him? What is this some socio, psychological shit you're studying? What, you making a fucking documentary? Ok, great, tell them to zoom in then. The man you're fucking is a drug dealer. He kills people. Or does that not matter to you because he doesn't use profanity?"

"You're mistaken."

"No, you're the one who's mistaken. He has been linked to half a dozen murders. How do you think he makes his money?"

"He lives off of an inheritance."

"He lives off of the profit he makes by addicting half of the fucking city to heroin."

"Again, you must be confusing him with someone."

At that he leapt from his seat and reached over the table towards her. He brought both of his fists down with a bang. He roared into her face, "Do you have any fucking idea how many orphans that man creates, how many little girls he turns out? We're living in the dawn of the dead and that motherfucker is at the center of it."

"So, I'm not confusing him with any fucking body. I know all about him. Now I wanna know what you know about the motherfucker who is dropping bodies like flies. Tell me about the dope. Tell me about his friends. I wanna hear about tonight's shooting and I wanna hear it now. Don't think your pretty little ass can't end up in a box too. If you don't start talking, you're an accessory to murder. Translation, twenty fucking years."

Her heart felt like it was going to beat through her throat. She blinked several times to keep the tears at bay. She had never been this angry in her entire life. Detective Jamison shoved Nikols away. "What the hell is wrong with you? Go talk to X. Get out of here." Nikols stared at him for a moment before turning and storming out. Detective Jamison looked at her sympathetically. She almost smiled before she realized that he was the good cop.

"I thought you looked familiar."

She exhaled slowly. "Excuse me?"

"They showed your picture on the news when LaShonda Terry got killed. Everyone said such wonderful things about you. When I saw the story, I thought that's what this city needs. More people who care. More people who are trying to do the right thing." He paused. How stupid did he think she was? She sat in defiant silence. "To meet you like this is crazy. Especially since you don't have any idea what you're mixed up in. Sister, let me help you get out of here. Just tell me what you saw tonight."

Sister. She sighed. "Well, if your partner had let me get a word in, you would know that I didn't see anything. Oxford and I were standing in the parking loop when we heard shots. We ran like everybody else, didn't see anything."

"Are you sure, why don't you walk me through the whole thing--" The door opened. Nikols and a well-built man in a tailored suit walked in.

"The warrant you received was to search my client's apartment only. Since you boys didn't find anything illegal her presence here constitutes an unlawful arrest. I suggest you uncuff her now."

X was waiting for her in the corridor. His eyes searched her face. She looked away. He took her hand and led her back outside into the warm night air. He whispered into her ear. "You know I'ma take care of that motherfucka. He will die for putting his hands on you."

A man stepped out of a white Lincoln Navigator and opened the back door. X turned and spoke to the lawyer. "Good lookin' Levy, I will get with you soon." He helped Tracy into the car. Inside, her body shook with the sobs she had been holding in. X pulled her to him. "Baby, I'm sorry, I'm sorry."

The navigator stopped in front of her apartment. Her front door was split and hung off the frame. Tracy started to cry again. "I don't want to go in."

X put his arm around her. He spoke to the driver. "Zeke, get somebody over here to put a new door up." He led Tracy towards her car. "You want me to drive?"

"And strip my gears? No thanks."

"Ok, let's go to my place." She hoped he didn't notice how her hands were shaking when she put the car into gear.

He lifted her up when they entered his loft and carried her up to his bedroom. He laid her gently on the bed and took off her sneakers and sweats. He kneaded the balls of her feet and rubbed out the tension in her toes. He kissed his way up her legs and unzipped her sweatshirt. He noticed the teddy she still had on underneath. "Baby, I'm so sorry. I'm going to make it better. I'm going to take care of you. Please don't leave me."

They had already been through so much and he had always taken care of her. She thought back to the way he had fed and bathed her when LaShonda had died. How patient he had been. If it wasn't for him... But then she thought of the flash grenade going off, the hands on her body, being pushed to the ground. He said he would never let anything happen to her, but what could he really do?

He took off his clothes and made love to her. She faked it for the first time. Maybe she had been faking all along. Two years had seemed like nothing. But two years like this one could kill their love; it could literally kill them both. There was no more hiding from that fact.

*   *   *

The next week she and Thalia attended a chapter meeting for their sorority. It was pretty standard fare. They went over the minutes from the previous meeting, talked about the community service that the chapter was doing, went over the finances.

Tracy was waiting for Thalia outside of the bathroom when Soror Eileen, a lieutenant with the police department, approached her. Eileen wasn't the most active member and Tracy didn't know her that well. Still she smiled as the older, stout woman walked up to her. She spoke in a whisper that made Tracy bend slightly to hear her.

"You know I came up here just to talk to you right?"

Tracy's smile faded slightly. "Okay."

"I heard that you were picked up for questioning about that hotel shooting."

"Picked up for questioning? Is that what you call SWAT kicking down my door and setting off a flash grenade. And then Detective Nikols, seemed hell bent on being--"

Eileen cut her off. "Do you really not know what you're involved in? That man is the heir to the biggest drug ring in 500 miles. That man is responsible for half of the murders in this city. I'm sure that he was the target of that shooting and if you continue to see him you are putting yourself directly in the line of fire."

Tracy took a second to calm herself before she responded. This was the most she and Eileen had ever spoken. Tracy had found the woman to be a bit gruff, not to mention unpolished. She had excused these things and attributed them to Eileen's profession. Now she could see the cop written all over the woman. "Soror Eileen, I appreciate your concern, but this is a sorority meeting not a police station. This isn't the proper time or venue for this discussion."

"When would be the proper time? When they bring you in a body bag?"

Tracy laughed. "Yes, then I'll actually have time to entertain bullshit."

Thalia had exited the bathroom and had been watching the exchange a few feet away. She began talking a mile a minute the moment Tracy approached her. "What the hell was that about?"

"What did it look like?"

"It looked like Soror Detective Sergeant Captain Eileen is in your shit. When did she start showing up at meetings?"

"When she had someone to interrogate about a shooting."

Thalia flipped her hair and picked up her Michael Kors bag. She waved at an elderly soror and moved closer to Tracy. "What did she say?"

"The usual. That he's a horrible, gangster monster and I'm going to *die* if I continue to see him."

"Does it seem like she knows anything?"

Tracy shrugged. "I don't think so, but I bet we start seeing her around a lot more. Maybe she'll join my committee."

"Be serious. This shit is getting too close to home. What if she's right? Somebody is dead and the other person is still in the hospital. What if that had been you?"

"It wasn't me. Are you forgetting that the party was your idea?"

"I'm not forgetting anything. Tracy, I don't know. This whole thing has snowballed. I know it sounds stupid and naïve, but I thought it would be more fun than this."

Tracy looked at her friend. She had never noticed the lines around her eyes before. "I know what you mean. But hey, it's just another day at the office, right?" Thalia didn't answer.

16

"Go!"

"Amir's coming." X delivered the news with his trademark matter of factness. Tracy put her fork down.

They were all at Pluto's. Derek wiped his mouth, "For what? You approved this?"

X shrugged. "He says that he's coming to sweeten the pot a bit."

Thalia cleared her throat. "I don't like it. There's no reason for him to come here. We paid him. That's it. Any additional contact is an unnecessary risk."

"Right. His ass probably caught a federal charge and is trying to haggle his way down to some country club. Feds probably got him meeting with his connects. He'll do fag time and niggas like us catch a buck in Greenhaven, Attica.

X shrugged again. "Scared money don't make money. We'll play it the same way we did in Miami. Risk paid off then."

Derek stared at him. "This is how motherfuckas crap out. You got to know when to walk away from the table. 'Scared money don't make money.' Fed cases don't make money either. We're in the best position we've ever been in and now you wanna get loose? We just went through a fucking war and now you wanna double down? Sean and Malik are dead. You forget about that? The only thing that's keeping us in control of this shit is our product. And you wanna let the motherfucking connect come here when our shit is just restabilizing? Why would that slick back motherfucka bring any good our way?"

X shrugged again. Derek glared at him. Thalia threw her napkin on her plate. "Well, I have to be going."

X stood up. "Yeah, we out too." He and Derek slapped hands. In the car, he asked her thoughts about Amir's arrival.

"I don't know what it means. But I would agree that the less contact we have with him the better."

X shook his head. "The less contact Uncle D has with him, the better. We have to always be ready to make a move. Can't leave any opportunities uncovered."

She didn't know what he meant and she didn't ask. She went with him to see Amir and Lydia at the Hyatt. They had home field advantage, but the ball wasn't in their court yet. She remembered the instructions that X had given her in Miami. She knew so much more now. At the hotel, the sound of her clicking Jimmy Choos fell in line with X's long stride.

Lydia was waiting in the parking lot alone. Her silk pantsuit hung elegantly against her frame. She was brazenly looking at Tracy. X didn't notice. He shook Lydia's hand and stepped away so Tracy could offer her greeting. Lydia hugged her tightly and held both of her hands as she surveyed her. "Gorgeous."

"Thank you. You too."

X interrupted the female appraisal ritual, "Where's Amir?"

"He's not coming."

Tracy turned to see his reaction. He clenched his jaw, but remained silent. Tracy expressed his annoyance, "What is this?"

Lydia waved a hand, "Amir has been detained. His father, my uncle, is very displeased with him. His playboy ways are accepted here, but it's an entirely different manner when he does those things back home."

X was disgusted. "Amir is your cousin?"

Tracy interjected, "It's a cultural thing. I still don't understand. Why did Amir call X to say that he was coming?"

"That was before his misdeeds, but don't worry I can be of assistance."

Tracy and X exchanged glances. He took a deep breath before speaking. "Assistance with what?"

"It's my father's poppy fields that are making you a rich man. Amir has been caught with his hand in the proverbial cookie jar. Overcharging and pocketing the profits. My father wants me to conduct an audit and resettle accounts with a few trustworthy buyers. Amir's ways were too brash and risky. We prefer fewer, but heavier investments."

"And what stops you from pulling the same trick as your cousin?"

Lydia shrugged. The gesture was sexily feminine on her. "We didn't have to renegotiate. You wouldn't have known about any of this. I'm here as a good faith gesture. My family is looking forward to a long and profitable relationship with you."

X continued to study Lydia. "And you would come all the way up here for that?"

She shrugged again. "We want to remain in business with a few stable buyers. I need to see for myself that you have control over things. Besides, I needed a reason to see Tracy."

"I can understand that." He kissed Tracy on the lips. "Ok so I will leave you two to it. Babe, call me when you're ready." He was gone before she could protest.

Lydia's grin was sinister. Tracy didn't have time for games. "Let's get a drink." She led the way inside, past the lobby and to the bar. Once seated, she stared unabashedly at Lydia. She let a long moment pass before she spoke. "What did he do?"

"Pardon?"

"To get grounded, what did he do?"

"I know he asked you to stay on and work for him, take my job. But in the end, I'm still here and he's not." She plopped her olive into her mouth. "Amir never was one for discretion. It seems my darling cousin and estranged lover has a penchant for both sexes. I guess it runs in the family."

Tracy eased closer to her. "Look, I can appreciate the magnitude of a woman scorned and I am flattered by your not so subtle advances. But don't get it twisted, I'm not for sale and I have no time for bullshit. So you tell me exactly what you can do for X and exactly what it's going to cost."

"Do for X? Aren't you concerned about what I can do for you?" Lydia swirled her drink around playfully.

"Didn't I say cut the bullshit?"

"Each key for 25."

Tracy grabbed her iPhone and texted "25" to X. "And?"

"I don't understand your hostility. Here I am offering you a killer deal. You think your competition would be this indignant?"

"My competition isn't nearly as reliable or discreet as we are. You said it yourself. You're not doing us any favors."

"No? What favors are you doing for Oxford? Here you are doing his dirty work. What do you owe him?"

Tracy took a dainty sip of her drink. She was determined to remain in control. How could Tracy ever have envied this woman? "I owe him nothing, and it's a wonderful feeling. I hope you have it one day."

"There are other things in my future, other conquests, including you. So yes, 25 for each key, but you already know what that's contingent upon."

Tracy had stepped into a new life and left her former self behind. There were no more inhibitions. No more fears. She had wanted Lydia since the first time she saw her. She would have her now. And X would have his deal and they would cut Derek out. His time was over.

She gulped the rest of her drink. "So you have a room right?"

It happened quickly. Once the door of the suite closed it was a flurry of hair and clothes. Designer garments were quickly discarded in their frenzy to get to each other. Lydia's lips were soft and her agile tongue quickly darted into Tracy's mouth. Her hands were like painters, swirling around on the canvas of Tracy's body. She pushed her towards the bed.

Lydia's weight on top of her was much lighter than X's. Still the magnetism of her lithe body sent shivers through Tracy. Her tongue devoured her flesh as she inched her way down to her center. The build up was too much for Tracy. She interrupted Lydia's leisurely stroll and pushed her head down.

Lydia's tongue on her clit set off a climatic wave through her body. It was better than she had allowed herself to imagine. The swirls of her probing tongue and the pressure that she applied quickly sent Tracy over the edge and back again.

Lydia watched her get dressed with a self-assured smirk. "Maybe next time you'll come to visit me."

Tracy smoothed her hair and returned the stare. "Maybe."

*   *   *

"I'm done," she told X. He was there in five minutes.

"Yo, she must love you. 25? How'd you pull that off?"

Images of Lydia's head between her legs flashed before her. "Just worked out that way."

"I wanna show you something."

When they pulled up in front of his loft he handed her the key. "This is yours. Everything is yours." He waited for her to open the door. Inside, he showed her the code to the alarm system. "Its 5-21-76, my parents anniversary. When is your lease up?"

She stared at him. Here he was offering her, she didn't know exactly what he was offering her, but it seemed like the golden ticket, and she had just... Well, what exactly had she done? She had made a business deal. She had bartered her sex for an advantage that would set them for life and allow them to do a world of good. They had two years left in this business and this town would be a better place once they were done. There was no room for guilt.

She cleared her throat and answered, "July."

"Perfect. We'll sell your things, no, we'll give them away to charity, I know you'd like that. Then you can move in here."

"And then what?"

"What else is there? Baby, do you have any idea what you just did today and what it means for us?" That was a question she should be asking him. She nodded. "We're doing it, we're doing us. I want you around all of the time. I love waking up to you and seeing your smiling face. I love watching you sleep. So then what? I don't know, but I know I need you with me."

He closed the distance between them. One hand rested on the curve of her hip while the other slid into her hair. He tilted her head towards his as his fingers massaged her scalp. His gaze was intense, searching. The electricity was building between them but it wasn't the flash of lightning that she had shared with Lydia earlier. This was like the converging power of a windmill; unassuming, but vigorous. When he spread her legs and thrust himself inside of her she felt like she was flying.

17

Days are shorter, nights are colder.
Feelin' like life is over, these snakes strike like a cobra.
The world's hot, my son got knocked.
Evidently, it's elementary, they
want us all gone eventually.

-Nas

"If I Ruled the World"

JUNE, END OF THE school year. Every morning during her climb up the stairs she thought about LaShonda. She could still see her smile, hear her laugh, feel the girl's admiration. When Tracy's feet touched the third floor she automatically chose a route that never intercepted the exact spot where LaShonda had died, where a new part of her had been born.

In her classroom, she walked around—straightening desks, smoothing the display board, running her hands over the walls. This had been her space. And her professors and everyone had been right when they said there was no way to prepare for the first year of teaching. Still, she was proud of herself and of her students. They had all learned. Some lessons can't be learned from a textbook, but some are still isolated to a classroom.

Just a week of review, finals, and then she was done. She didn't know if she was coming back next year or not. At twenty-five she was already disillusioned with two careers. Still, her heart was filled with the hopes she had for this place, with the love that she felt for students, with the knowledge that she wanted to impart.

So in the mornings, in her empty classroom, in that dirty, over-crowded, and failing high school, she began to pack away memories. She tried to brand the faces of her favorite students into her memory. She tried to remember every insightful thing they said. She tried to forget her own failures. She tried to bottle up their laughter, the raw honesty of their words.

She met Thalia one night at the after-hours spot. She worried about her friend sometimes. Thalia had become more and more engrossed with Derek's enterprise. She traveled with him to the Caymen Islands, supervised the cash flow of the fronts, and managed to clean up millions of dirty cash. She rarely talked to outsiders or frequented establishments that weren't part of the business. There was a seriousness to her that hadn't been there before.

Tracy was wearing skinny jeans, a long, fitted graphic tee, and Giuseppe pumps. Thalia made her look like a bum in a black Zach Posen dress, pearls, and stilettos. Tracy bent down to hug her, "Is there a high fashion accounting convention in town?"

A smile barely curled Thalia's lips. "Been in court all day. One of our spots got raided. Wasn't much product there, but the niggas inside had enough guns and ammo to start a militia."

"When did any of that become a part of your job description?"

"Gotta make sure the Jew lawyer is earning his pay. You're right though, I gotta fall back. Soror Detective All-In-Our-Shit was there too."

Tracy gave Thalia a look and signaled for the bartender. She took a long gulp of her Hennessy and apple juice before speaking. "So now she knows that both of us are tied to this. Great. How did a spot get raided? They must have had some concrete evidence in order to get a warrant. Great. We don't know what was said when they interrogated the fools that were in there. For all we know, they told every fucking thing they know. And then Eileen sees the current president of our chapter in court, sitting with the defense. Great. This place is probably under surveillance, and now they have us both on film. Why didn't you tell me about this court shit before I came?"

"Don't get paranoid on me, smart ass. You think she didn't know about you before today?"

"What the fuck are you thinking? You have just publicly associated yourself with a criminal enterprise. I thought your job was to cook the books not supervise lawyers and do drive bys and work in the drug factories and shit. Jesus Thalia, are you trying to get locked up?"

Thalia closed her eyes and ran her hand through the roots of her hair to the ends. She began talking the minute her eyes opened. "I don't need a fucking lecture. You think I'm unaware of the danger I am in? Yes, it's my job to make your boyfriend look like a CEO as opposed to the greedy animal that he is. You get to stand back and be pretty and act like you don't know what the fuck is going on. Meanwhile, everyone else is scrambling to minimize the damage that he causes. So if it takes court visits, or target practice, or creative book keeping to do my job well, that's what the fuck I'm going to do."

"Thal, you're digging a hole for yourself that even you might not be able to get out of."

Thalia downed her martini. "It's not like I have anything to lose."

Tracy swallowed her next words. She was really lashing out at Thalia out of fear. She didn't want any more cops running into her shit.

Derek approached them before the exchange could get more heated.

"Hey ladies." He kissed them both and signaled the bartender. He picked up on the tension once he sat down. "Did I miss something?"

"Thalia has been putting in overtime. She went to court today about that raid. Ran into that lieutenant X told you about."

Derek sat up straighter. "I want y'all to stay the fuck from around here. Light being shined up our ass now and we gotta control what these motherfuckas see."

Thalia laughed. "This isn't anything that we can't handle. It's not anything that we haven't prepared for."

"Little girl, how would you know what we're prepared for?"

Thalia didn't reply. She bit her lip like a child that had just been chastised. Tracy stood to go, when X walked in with a young man. Something about the kid drew her attention. Heat raced to her face as the two approached.

X kissed her. "Someone's got to be snitching. This little nigga here been holding it down for us on Wilcox, he has something to tell you D."

The boy, although 5'9, still looked like a little kid. He was just as reluctant to speak here as he was in Tracy's classroom. Instead of looking at Derek, his eyes were fixated on her. Derek noticed and cleared his throat. "Speak Youngin."

"Not with Miss Mitchell here." Andre lowered his eyes, but not before Tracy caught the disappointment in them. She wanted to crawl under the bar. X looked to her for an explanation. "He's in my class and I was just leaving." She damn near sprinted out of there.

She managed to make it to her car before the first tears fell. The look on Andre's face was all too similar to LaShonda's when the knife sunk in. How could she explain being at the Spot and with X? How could he explain being there?

Andre had changed so much. In the last few weeks he had asserted himself as a leader and was no longer embarrassed by his intelligence. He was obviously using that to move up in X's operation. She couldn't really knock that after all that she had learned. Still, she was worried about Andre. He was more likely to be the next nigga to get locked up or killed than the next X. How could she reach him now?

Andre wasn't in school the next day. At home, she wanted to ask X about it, but thought better of it. He had been uncharacteristically frazzled, inattentive and moody. Having already met his evil twin in Miami, Tracy was careful not to do anything to bring out that dormant part of him. She found herself missing her own space. Even though X's loft was spacious, she hated feeling like an unwelcomed guest, hated walking on egg shells.

X was in the kitchen when she went in there to peel a mango. She decided not to break the silence. "What's wrong with you?"

There was an edge in his voice that she wanted to avoid. She smiled cheerfully and said, "Nothing."

"Come on Trace, I don't have time for this shit. What's wrong with you?"

Saying nothing again would exasperate the situation. "Andre missed school, which is rare for him, I'm worried."

"Who?"

"The youngin' who was at the Spot, Wilcox."

"Oh, he's good. Just putting in work. Some things can't wait until 3. Small world."

Small world. It didn't matter to him that her being at the Spot had jeopardized her professional reputation. It didn't matter to him what happened to Andre.

"Why you worried about him anyway?"

This time she couldn't keep her temper from flaring up. "Because it's my job to worry about him. He's a good kid."

X looked at her and smirked. "I thought you were done with all of that *Lean on Me*, goodie two shoe bullshit?"

"No illusions over here, but why shouldn't I try to help him? He's smart, he's loyal, a hard worker. He actually reminds me of you. Chances are though he'll end up dead or in jail. What are your chances?" The last question ran out of her mouth before she could close the gate.

He closed the space between them and grabbed her arm. "Why would you say some shit like that to me? Do you think this is a fucking game? A fucking movie?" Tracy was more frightened by his volume than the force he was applying to her upper arm. "We got cops raiding our shit. A war. Disloyal, fool ass, bitch made niggas and I gotta come home to *my* shit and hear *my* woman wishing me into the grave or a cell."

She could be quiet and wait for his tirade to end. She could always tiptoe around him and be subjected to his tantrums and emotional whims. But she wasn't the kind of woman who would be content with being seen and not heard. She wasn't the kind of woman who would tolerate a man telling her what to say and think. And she wasn't the kind of woman whose arm you could twist.

She was too far in now to walk away. She was here and she needed to let that be known.

She snatched her arm back and began the patented black girl point and neck roll routine. "Your shit? Aren't you the same mother-fucka who said all of this was mine? You think you're in this alone? You think you've been doing all of this by yourself? You wouldn't have made it this far without me. You think there's a bitch alive who could walk in my shoes?" She jabbed his forehead with her index finger, pushing his head back.

His face was contorted in rage. She was waiting for him to say something, but instead he swung. And just like the girls on the playground who liked to mimic her proper speech and pull her hair, he underestimated her speed. Tracy leaned back and avoided the hit. But she was enraged at the sight of his open hand speeding towards her.

The one area X had left untapped was her temper. She had managed to stifle it before, but the thought of her wooing connects in Miami, damn near getting killed, having her house raided, losing the respect of her favorite student, and always putting his needs first unleashed the beast. He had the nerve to raise a hand to her? She would make sure that he wouldn't do it again.

Though quick, she wasn't deluded into thinking she could win a fight against a man who had forty pounds on her. She picked up the porcelain vase from the counter and threw it at him. His duck was a nano second too slow and the vase grazed his head. She slapped the shit out of him before he had time to stand completely upright. He rushed her, lifted her up in one swift movement, and slammed her WWF style onto the floor.

She heard her body crash, but didn't feel it. She was too busy repositioning herself to kick him in the balls. She didn't miss. He doubled over in pain. She kicked him again, this time in the face. He recovered, and swung at her, this time with a closed fist. He missed again.

He reached down and wrapped his hands around her neck. She clawed at his hands, but was unable to loosen his grip. She managed to kick him again as her lungs were screaming for air. She lost strength and the rage seeped out of her. He didn't stop choking until she stopped struggling. Spent, she laid in the fetal position gasping for air.

He was gone before she was able to get up. With the departure of the adrenaline from her system, her body ached. She crawled to her feet and went to a mirror. Even on her dark skin, X's fingerprints were quite visible. She didn't cry; this fight was necessary. She was a part of his world now and he needed to respect that.

He didn't come home or call for two days. She scoured the newspaper for word of arrest or death, but didn't call him.

Andre was missing too. Maybe he and X were off trying to take over the world. It was for the best, she wasn't mentally prepared for an exchange with either one of them. But she did hope that Andre would show for the final.

At her annual review with Mrs. Smith, the older lady matter-of-factly went over Tracy's attributes, reading from the observation forms. "You have a great rapport with the students. Your use of technology in the classroom was a bit lacking."

"Really? I use the smart board every day."

"Yes, but your use is more like a projector. It's not exactly interactive." Tracy sighed and waved her hand. This final meeting with Mrs. Smith really didn't matter anyway. She continued. "You did find meaningful and authentic forms of assessment. You broke your class into groups and had them teach lessons on Black history topics. I heard they all handled themselves quite well. I couldn't believe it."

Tracy nodded. There were only three more days left of work and she looked forward to never having to talk to Mrs. Smith again.

"So there's still this little business about you not coming back next year."

Tracy recrossed her legs. "No business. I'm not coming back."

"Like I told you before, you're an asset to this school, but I understand your decision. Maybe now you can be an asset to this school district."

"I don't follow."

"It's no secret that our district suffers from a lack of diversity among the teachers." She paused, as if waiting for Tracy to respond.

This woman had politely informed Tracy and Miss Hernandez and Miss Campbell and Miss Wilkins that they had all been placed there, against her wishes, solely for the purpose of increasing minority representation at the school. This woman had seemed hell bent on ruining Tracy's first year, seemed to be offended by her very presence. What the hell was she talking about?

She continued, "Now I've had no qualms about saying that I'm not a fan of quota filling, but I'm no bigot." She paused again. "We need highly qualified, effective teachers from all ethnic groups. We need a recruiter to go after them, screen, and prepare them."

"And you think that's me?"

"It could be. I understand you've had a bad run of it here. Many veteran teachers would have buckled under what you went through. You're shook up, I get it. But you're a good teacher and we need more like you. If you can't do the job, at least help us find somebody that will."

Tracy had heard enough. "You're speaking as if I'm obligated. I know I'm a good teacher, thank you for finally recognizing that. But I've already given all that I am going to give to this district."

"To the district yes, but not the students. I was hard on you because I always knew you were good. I just didn't think that the color of your skin made you more qualified than the applicants you beat out. You must see now that education is not black and white. There is no cookie cutter solution to the problems these students walk in here with. Tough decisions have to be made. Feelings have to be hurt. I do that. Our athletic department is one of the few things that get this school positive press and money. So do I make sure the best players make it on that court? Damn straight. The money that those games bring in paid for twenty students' college application fees. So I may not be the most liked person, but I do all that I can for the students who actually make good use of opportunities."

Tracy stood up. "You do what you think is best, and I'll do the same"

* * *

She was surprised to find Andre waiting in her classroom. "Hey Miss."

"Hey, the final isn't until Thursday. What are you doing here?"

"I wanted to talk to you." His words were deliberate, his eye contact direct. The shy boy had disappeared and this man stood in his place. A wall had been lifted between them.

"About?"

"I was just wondering whether or not I should take this test."

"Why wouldn't you? You're an A student. There's no way that you wouldn't pass."

"I know that."

"Then I don't understand your question."

"I don't understand you. You know Miss Mitchell, you're the best teacher that I ever had. You're smart, you're real, you know how to break things down so that everyone understands. You really care."

"Thanks Andre, I really appreciate that."

"And you're so pretty. I don't understand what you're doing with him."

His tone was so stern that she had to blink several times before she spoke. "What am I doing with whom?"

He gave her a pointed look. "Come on, Miss. I mean, do you know what he does? Like what he really does? Do you know what it takes to do what he do? You're not stupid. You gotta know. How could somebody like you be with him?"

"Somebody like what?"

"The day first time I walked into this class, yo, it was crazy. That proper way you talk, the perfume you wear, the way you squint when you're mad. I loved coming here every day. I know you're the teacher and all, but I felt a connection—"

"Andre—"

He stepped closer to her desk. "When that nigga Ryan spazzed on you, I took care of that. When LaShonda got killed, I held the classroom down. Come to find out you're with X. What type of shit is that?"

"I don't owe you an explanation."

"How can you feed me all that shit about college and changing my life and be with him?"

She ran a hand through her hair. "Look Andre, I never lied to you. Who I'm with doesn't change the fact that college is your best bet to making it out." Her voice shook and she took a second to gather herself before continuing. "I knew you were special that first day you walked in here. I wanted more for you than all of this. How can you blame me for that?"

He scoffed. "Making it out? Why would I wanna do that? You made it out?"

"This is temporary. This is a means to an end."

"Miss me with all of that. I know who you are now."

She narrowed her eyes. "No, you don't. Because if you did, you would be watching your tone right now."

He stepped closer to her. "You should be with me."

"You need to think before you say another word. I'm with X. That is never going to change. You're my student—"

"I'm a man."

"Okay, man, how far are you really prepared to take this? You think there's a future for you in all of this? You know the game. You're a pawn. You know what happens to them right?"

"Yeah, a pawn can become king."

"Most don't."

"Watch me." He left.

X called out to her when she got home. She followed the sound of his voice into his office. He sat behind his desk, examining photos. He got up and kissed her on the lips as if he hadn't choked her out the last time he saw her, as if he hadn't been missing for days. She thought about what Andre said. Did she *really* know exactly what it took for X to do what he did? She hadn't wanted to, hadn't let her mind go down that path. But now the realities of his profession were all around them.

She used to think that X could control the uglier parts of his personality that he used for his work. That he could compartmentalize all of his goodness and care and keep it just for her. To her there were two X's. The one that set her soul on fire and the one that ran his business. But now she knew that he was one in the same. He was a force of nature, a black hole engulfing everything around him. She was no exception. She couldn't escape his totality, even if she wanted to. He had changed her so much, that only he would be able to fulfill her. There surely couldn't be another man like him.

"So, you don't have anything that you want to say?"

He sighed. "Trace, I don't have time for this. There's a lot of shit going on."

"I don't give a fuck about what's going on. I only care about what goes on between me and you. I only care about these four walls. You leave all the rest of that shit out there."

"What needs to be established out there and in here is respect. You had your neck rollin', hands all in my face and shit. I don't deal with that chicken head bullshit. That's why I'm with you. I've always been very clear about that."

"Let me be clear. I'm not the kind of woman that you can put your hands on."

X smiled. "Yeah, I definitely learned that the hard way. I had to ice my nuts." She was stone faced. "Ah, come on baby. I got it. I will never put my hands on you again. And you will never talk to me like that. You wanna know something else?"

"What's that?"

"You make a hell of a centerfold." He spread out the pictures that he had been looking at when she came in. She saw images of herself exiting the school, she and Thalia in a parking lot after a sorority meeting, her and a smiling X at a concert, a picture of her walking away from the Spot, her eyebrows furrowed. That was the night she saw Andre there.

Her stomach tightened. "What is this?'"

"Just some of the surveillance the cops have been collecting."

"How did you get it?"

"There's a good man in the department. He sees what I'm really doing, he does what he can to help. And you know something? He's never asked me for a dime. What did I tell you babe? All of this is going to be over soon."

18

*"Boy, I'm ready for whatever, somebody better tell 'em
I'll be here when the smoke clear and
everything settle, for real."*

T.I.

"Ready for Whatever"

2:36 AM. X'S PHONE woke them both up. She cuddled up closer to him. He listened for a few seconds and then sat up abruptly. He hung the phone up. "What's wrong?"

"Uncle Derek is dead."

She sat up too. Derek was dead? She hugged him. He shrugged off her embrace and stood up, his eyebrows burrowed in thought.

"That was one of my police sources on the phone. They're still on the scene. Body just got picked up. His wife will take care of everything."

"His wife?"

He waved her question away and continued to pace. "I gotta get with the lawyer's dirty ass. I gotta tighten shit up. Was supposed to be a delivery in two days. I don't even wanna fuck with that right now."

"Was he shot? Where?"

"They found him in an alley off of Chestnut. How could anyone get that close to him? Shit was hot, been hot. How could someone get close enough to clap him? How could he have been that stupid? How could he let this happen?" He stopped walking abruptly and knocked everything off of the nightstand.

It all landed with a crash. She held her breathe. She didn't try to comfort him again, he would think that she thought he was weak. She didn't ask any more questions that would exasperate him. This was a crisis and she had no idea what to do. She had no idea of what this even meant. Derek was dead? X had simultaneously gotten a promotion and a bull's eye on his head.

But he was asking the right questions. Derek never moved alone. He always had muscle with him. His routine was tight, his house was impenetrable. He wasn't a small man and he was always armed. Who besides X could have ever gotten close enough to kill him? She looked at him again. Andre had asked if she knew what it really took to do X's job. She didn't. But one thing she did know was that there was only one way to get a promotion in his line of work.

"We gotta go to Aunt Evelyn's." She dressed and accompanied X to an elegant Victorian home in Brighton. Tracy had been to what she thought was Derek's home at the time, and it was half an hour west of this place. Even at four in the morning the place seemed bright and cheery, too Middle American for Derek's tastes. She tried to steel herself as the doorbell chimed. A curvy, light-skinned woman with green almond shaped eyes, and a deep scar that ran along her collarbone opened the door. She wore the look of grief and resignation. "X."

He moved towards her and enveloped her in a bear hug, "Aunty Evey."

A few seconds after the embrace, Evelyn stepped away from him and eyed Tracy. Her appraisal was studied, she wasn't new to this. "Can we talk in front of her?"

"Yes. You know I wouldn't have brought her otherwise. This is my lady, Tracy."

She nodded. "Come in."

The home was tastefully decorated. She led them into the parlor and eased herself into a wing backed chair. "Three shots they said. Point blank. He knew the shooter." X nodded. "How did this happen? He was careful, you were supposed to be there." Again, X nodded. "Well, answer me goddamnit. We moved here because it was supposed to be different, safer. You were supposed to be his right hand man and in charge of operations. So how did you let this happen?"

X ran his hand over his head. He wasn't accustomed to answering to anybody but Derek. Even then he had always done so grudgingly. "I can't answer that right now, Aunty. But I promise you this, I will give you somebody's head on a fucking platter."

"You're two hours too late."

*　　*　　*

"I'm going to the Spot, you take the car."

"I'm coming with you. It was someone Derek knew, right? So most likely it was somebody in the crew. You need an extra set of eyes."

He didn't argue with her. The inside of the place looked like a war convention. The muscle was there in full force, loading automatic weapons and muttering to themselves. Andre was present too, but he barely looked at Tracy. Still, she felt relieved to see him there. She wasn't quite sure why. She whispered to X, "Didn't a spot just get raided? Cops would be smart to run up in here today."

He nodded. "We're going to breakfast. Leave all of this shit here. Dre, you riding with us."

In the car, X was uncharacteristically talkative. "Your star pupil here has been rising up the ranks. I had to straighten him out once when he let some niggas rob a spot, but after that, he's been delivering nothing but high caliber work. It's like the kid has eyes on the back of his head. Smart as a bitch too. Knows when to talk, how to follow instructions, good ideas…"

She interrupted him, "A future CEO." She caught Andre's eye in the rearview mirror and held it.

The caravan arrived at Unkl Moe's, a family owned, soul food restaurant. Everyone ate at Moes, dealers, politicians, cops, white collars, blue collars… These groups tolerated each other long enough to dine because the catfish melted in your mouth and the service reminded you of down home. It was also a good place to find out what was going on.

One of the older waitresses, Vera, began to fawn over X the moment she saw him. "Oh X, I haven't seen you in so long." She took in the entourage of hardened men that accompanied him and lowered her voice. "What brings all of y'all out so early?"

X kissed her on the cheek. "Business, always business."

Four tables were hurriedly pushed together. After the drink orders, everyone seemed to squirm. There were no distractions here. No bar to hide behind, no juke box, no weapons to load. Derek's killer was sitting among them. Tracy watched.

"So what's the word?" X stared them all down.

Throats were nervously cleared, but no words were offered.

"All y'all motherfuckas on the payroll, but nobody knows shit? My uncle is on a motherfuckin' slab and y'all bitches was supposed to be protecting him. Now y'all wanna squad up and load up, four hours too motherfucking late. Somebody better know something."

Big Zeek, a man aptly named, was the first to venture a hypothesis. "Had to be one of them Fight Club niggas."

"Had to be? How you know? Which one of them niggas?"

There was an audible sigh of relief when Vera came back to take the food orders. She turned her cheery nature up a notch, picking up on the tension and trying to diffuse it.

X resumed his grilling as soon as she walked away, "Tyriek, tell me something."

Just as Zeek was the muscle, Tyriek was the brains. "Can't say anything for sure yet. I say we grab one of them Fight Club bitches up, put the pliers to his nuts, and see what he has to say. I doubt its one of them though. No one knows where D was dropped at right? But somebody had to see who ever dumped him on Chestnut. Let's ask some feens, some of them hos, somebody saw something."

Tyriek was smart, maybe too smart. Maybe he wasn't satisfied with his current position. She thought back to the night Sean was killed. Tyriek had left the club minutes before the shooting.

Tracy continued to survey the scene. Again, she caught Andre's eye. *"A pawn can become king."* X and Tyriek weren't the only ones who would get promoted in the event of Derek's demise. Andre was being honed; it was clear that he was a valued member of the crew now. She remembered the night she saw him at the Spot. Derek said that Andre knew who the snitch was. Since Andre had been on the scene, a spot had got raided and Derek was dead.

Andre's whole appearance changed to Tracy as she watched him. Gone was the blameless boy that she had once fretted over. In front of her was a cold blooded murderer. The truth struck her like lightning. Andre held her gaze. No words were spoken, but the world seemed to shift.

What would X do when she told him? That was a stupid question. She knew exactly what X would do. She couldn't let that happen. She couldn't lose another student.

Her catfish had just been placed in front of her when Nikols and his sidekick approached their table. Tracy wanted to smack the shit-eating grin off of his face. "My condolences gentlemen." He leered at Tracy, "And lady."

"We're not interested in your condolences. If you came to gloat, you're dumber than I thought." The men at the table seemed to notice her for the first time. There wasn't much that she could do in this situation to help X, but she could shield him from Nikols and his idiot partner. X put his arm around Tracy's chair.

"What, she does all of the talking for you X?"

Again, Tracy interceded. "Don't you have a homicide to investigate?" She looked at his partner. "Don't you have more sense than this Murdoch?"

He cleared his throat. "Miss Mitchell, if you let us get a word in, you would know that we're here investigating Mr. Quinn's murder. We were hoping--"

"You were hoping that we would cooperate with you all. Do your job? Well, you're mistaken."

Nikols spoke. "X, why don't you control this bitch? If I start searching you all, I could probably fill a fucking paddy wagon."

Her voice trembled slightly when she spoke again, "In a public establishment with no probable cause? If you don't like being a dick sucking pig anymore, just retire."

Something in his smirk changed. He stared at her a moment longer before turning on his heels. He almost ran into his partner. Tyriek rose his glass to her. X whispered in her ear, "I see you baby." She squeezed his leg under the table.

Her cell phone buzzed. She retrieved it from her purse and saw that it was Thalia. Tracy hadn't talked to her since the last time she saw her at the Spot and with the craziness of the morning, hadn't thought to call her. "Tracy, everything is fucked."

"I know T, I'm sorry about Derek, but don't worry--"

"I'm not talking about him. He doesn't have any worries where he is now."

"What are you talking about?" Tracy tried to keep the alarm out of her voice.

"Our financial records have been subpoenaed."

Tracy looked at X, who in turn was watching her intently. "Okay, what does that mean? You're prepared for this right?"

"Yeah, I'm a beast with these numbers, but I just think the timing is interesting. Y'all be careful on your end."

X stood up. "Alright, everybody gotta be on point. Riek, you and Zeek make that thing happen. The rest of y'all motherfuckas keep your mouths shut and your eyes open. Dre you stay with me."

Tracy moved closer to X. "That was Thalia. They're subpoena-ing the finances. He's coming with us?"

"Yeah, that's my little soldier. We got work to put in. You're going to work right?"

She checked her watch. It was a quarter to eight and she had to proctor an exam in fifteen minutes. She needed to talk to X alone. What could she tell him about Andre? She knew all too well what the outcome would be if he knew the truth. But what was Andre up to? Was he working alone? Her chest tightened. Was he working for X? Still, she felt uneasy leaving X with Andre. "Yes, you'll pick me up too?"

"Somebody will pick you up. I'll get with Thalia and see what is really going on. You never know with Derek, we might all be fucked."

She wasn't ready to find out exactly what he meant by that.

She was preoccupied during the test. She couldn't shake the realization that she had at breakfast. Andre had killed Derek or at least had something to do with it. Would he be satisfied with that? Was he orchestrating a coup?

After the exam, Tyriek was waiting for her in the staff parking lot. She was glad that he was the one who picked her up. She was interested in his perspective on what was going on. She waited for him to bring it up. They had been driving for ten minutes before he did. "I don't understand why anybody would be stupid enough to hit Derek, especially now."

"I guess it's as good a time as any."

"Naw, Derek was getting out. Said so himself, he wanted to go completely legit. He was even talking about running for office. He was just going to hand everything over to X. That would be the person to hit."

All of this was news to her. "Who knew that?"

"Everybody. You know Derek liked to run his mouth. Nobody ever did it like him. He was a king in this shit." Tyriek's words were a befitting eulogy. Tracy had never particularly cared for Derek and in his death hadn't even thought to mourn. But she had to admit that she had never met anyone like him and he was a great businessman. He had outlived and outwitted so many of his opponents and had managed to have fun while doing so. There was something to be said for that.

Tyriek was still talking, "Everyone's having a meeting at Scout's, police ain't gon raid them."

Scout's was a low budget, titty bar that one of X's distant cousins ran. X often had meetings there, but she never felt jealous about it. The broads that graced the stage in there had stretch marks and an assortment of other scars. They were hardly anything to worry about.

X, Andre, and four of the crew were sitting away from the stage. She was still taken aback every time she saw Andre with X. This was something that she didn't want to get used to. Even though she was damn near married to the game, there was a code of ethics that she was determined to keep. It just wasn't right for him to be there. His future could still hold something else. Andre flinched when he saw her approaching. He wasn't used to their new association either.

X kissed her. "This isn't the type of establishment that I want my lady to frequent, but you know desperate times. Don't have to worry about bugs or cops in here. And it won't hurt for Youngin' to get a peek at some pussy."

Andre laughed, "I've had more than just a peek. Ain't nobody checking for these dusty hoes." Tracy bit her tongue to stop from reprimanding him about his language. She stared at the floor instead.

"That's right. A man ain't shit if he doesn't have the right woman behind him. I got mine." He kissed Tracy's hand and turned his attention to her. "You good baby, did you eat?"

"Yeah I'm fine."

A new girl, Star, was on stage. With a body like Trina and a face like Ashanti, she was sure to get paid. What was she doing in a place like Scout's? She stood in place for a few seconds; her mere presence was enough to captivate her audience. There was a lull in the conversation as all of the men turned to watch her. She flourished under their attention, dropped down into a Chinese split, and began to crawl up the stage.

The music was slow at first as she writhed and grinded her body against the floor, building the anticipation. Then the song changed to an up-tempo stripper jam that the South was known for, and she began to really work the stage. She gyrated to the beat, her ass cheeks even moved in synchronization. She crawled to the edge of the stage, taking care to deliver quick lap dances to the men who sat there. She ended her routine by climbing the pole, twisting her body upside down, and making her ass clap as she slowly slid down. By this time, the stage was littered with bills.

Star's performance put Tracy in a trance too. This girl had rendered every man in there speechless, just by the way she moved her body. She had even captivated X. What would she be capable of if she knew how to work her mind? Tracy respected that power.

X was talking to his team again and Tracy was lost in her thoughts. She watched the way Star worked the room—throwing her head back and laughing, innocently brushing against the men, making arrangements for later. She was a modern day geisha. Men were damn near waiting in line to spend their money on her.

She had Tracy's admiration until she cozied up to X. "Hey Big Man, I'm sorry to hear about D."

He looked her up and down. "We all are."

"Anything I can do to comfort you?" She turned slightly, offering him a view of her ample ass.

"No, I'm good."

"But, if you ever--"

"Bitch can't you hear? He's good." Tracy grabbed a hundred dollar bill out of her Fendi bag, held it up to her, crumpled it, and threw it across the room. "Go fetch."

X jumped in before Star could retort. He gestured towards Andre. "Why don't you take Little Man to the back and give him whatever he wants. And get that hundred before another one of you skank bitches grabs it up."

Star looked deflated for a split second. But she mustered a smile and motioned for Andre. "Come on baby. Big Man, you let me know if you change your mind."

Tracy jolted, but X held her in her seat. "You know you have nothing to worry about. Let me get you out of here. I can't have you all stressed, you need your rest."

She threw him a quizzical glance, but waited quietly as he said his goodbyes. "Aight y'all. Remember what I said."

In the car, he began to explain the situation. "I got with Thalia. My uncle was doing his thing. Investments in political campaigns, charitable donations, riverfront property, office buildings, barber-shops, boutiques. He did a good job of spreading it all around. The money is clean, but this motherfucka didn't pay taxes on all of his revenue. I mean after all of this, he was trying to fool the IRS."

"Is that what the subpoena is about?"

"Yep, federal shit. Tax evasion. They would have got him for some years. Good thing he got popped when he did."

Tracy was surprised to hear him speak so callously.

"You know, I loved Uncle D. He was there for me when my whole world crumbled. He took me under his wing, like a son. He was old school in this game. He taught me the fundamentals to staying above ground and out of a cell. I know we ain't supposed to speak ill of the dead, but a man is just a man, and Uncle Derek wasn't an exception to that. Goddamn, was he flashy and he never knew when to shut the fuck up. He set up Aunt Evelyn even with them being separated for so long, so I give him credit for that. But he wasn't above getting grimy. That nigga would slap his own mama for a fast buck. I always wondered if he had something to do with Pops getting killed. Maybe he got sick of being second in line, you know?"

She nodded. Maybe X had gotten tired of that too. Or maybe he had been biding his time for all of these years. Maybe he had finally found a moment for his vengeance and used Andre to enact it. It would explain why the two were suddenly so chummy. She looked over at him. There were so many things that she would never know. So many things that she didn't want to know.

X showed her the new security code when they got home. There was a new panel of televisions in the living room. They displayed the images from the surveillance cameras that were stationed around the premises. "What's all of this?"

"Security. I gotta protect my family. I want you to apply for a gun permit, only legal shit where we rest our heads. We're going to the range tomorrow. You can shoot mine until we get you squared away."

"Do you think all of this is necessary?"

"Hell yeah. You got something you want to tell me?"

Her heart quickened. Was he on to Andre? "No."

His smile made her even more anxious. "I haven't seen any tampons in the garbage for a while."

With all that had been happening, she couldn't remember the last time she took her birth control. There had been quite a few instances after LaShonda died when only the feel of X inside of her could comfort her. She grabbed the counter to steady herself. "Shit, I haven't been--"

"I mean, I wanted to marry you first, but I guess this will work too."

His happiness was so infectious that she felt guilty about being worried. She hadn't even realized that she was late, hadn't even had time to process the possibility of pregnancy, consider her options. What options did she have? An abortion? She thought back to her last conversation with LaShonda. "*I ain't no baby killer.*" Was she? What did this mean for their lives if she had the baby? She wanted to be a wife, not a baby mother and with everything crashing around them the thought of new life in the midst of so much death was terrifying. "Babe, let's not get ahead of ourselves. Let me find out for sure first."

He walked over to her and held her hand. "There are some things that I already know for sure. You're the one and you were so right, I couldn't have done this without you. Even now everyone's looking to me for answers and I'm looking to you. I need you with me. I've wanted to do this for a while. I was just trying to plan a proposal that's worthy for you. But the truth is, we don't need all of that. Everything we need is right here. I will never hurt you and I will always take care of you."

He slowly lowered himself to one knee. She held her breath when he removed the black velvet box from his pocket. "I should have asked you this a while ago, will you be my wife?"

The earth stood still. This was the moment that women waited their entire lives for. This was the moment she had dreamed about. This was the moment where the man of her dreams showed her that he felt the same about her. She now knew who would father her children, who she would grow old with. This was her moment of stability.

The race was finally over. The race to be fine enough, tidy enough, freaky enough, cool enough. She had crossed the finish line. She knew for months that she utterly and completely was in love with X, but had never truly let herself imagine or even hope for this moment with him.

He wasn't perfect and she continued to learn how much so. But she respected and trusted him. He was sincere and sexy, and she still got chills when they touched. He laughed with her and made her feel safe. With him, she could be herself. His way of life was wrong, but somehow he was right in it. Tears clouded her eyes. She loved him with every breath in her body. There was only one thing she could possibly say, "Yes."

He looked so relieved that she laughed. When he opened the ring box the tears that she had been holding in escaped down her cheeks. Staring up at her was a two carat, princess cut diamond set in a platinum band. When he slid the ring on her finger, everything felt right.

Her husband to be picked her up off of her feet and twirled her around. "I love you and I'm going to make you so happy, you'll see." When he kissed her, it was like she was floating. They never made love so sweet.

Derek's memorial interrupted their celebratory mood. X said Evelyn wanted to finally move on with her life and sending Derek off was the first step in doing that. Of course the coroner wouldn't release the body yet. Still, Evelyn insisted and the memorial was being held today. She would have Derek lowered into the ground privately.

Tracy was surprised when X pulled up in front of her church. "The memorial service is here?"

"Yeah, you always talk about how much you love this church, so a few months back I gave an anonymous offering. Plus, half of the pastors in the city were afraid to have the memorial at their church. Derek lined all of their pockets and now they scared that somebody is going to shoot the service up."

They pulled into the newly repaved parking lot. Tracy guessed they had put X's money to good use. The lot was full, but someone had marked off a space for X. Inside, there wasn't an empty seat. Everybody wanted to say farewell to the illegitimate king of the city. Thalia was noticeably missing. It made sense, death and grief and wives that pop out of thin air weren't her scene. Tracy had wondered what Thalia's relationship with Derek really was. Guess there was no telling now.

The mixture of attendees was a reflection of Derek's various layers and associations. There were politicians who Tracy recognized from their campaign ads, realtors, crooks, and not so plain clothed cops. People turned around in their seats to check each other out.

Tracy and X sat next to Evelyn in the first row. Several of Derek's women were behind them, but Evelyn seemed unaware. What a strange kind of grief she wore. The man she loved and probably hated herself for loving was dead. Her eyes were blood shot and she wrung her silk handkerchief, but she did not drop one tear inside of that place. Hers was a defiant grief.

Pastor opened the service up. "I know some of you are surprised to see me here. I was thankful when Oxford Quinn asked me to officiate this memorial. I knew Derek Quinn and I saw some of the good that he did in the community. Too bad it wasn't enough to wash away all of the harm that he caused. What a man does in the dark, will come to the light." The audience murmured. "Oh, that's not what y'all expected to hear? You thought you were going to come to the house of the Lord and not hear the truth? Well, I'm happy to disappoint you then." Tracy looked down at her ring.

"Don't get me wrong, I am not here to speak ill of Derek Quinn. His life can be a lesson to us all. He was a conflicted man. He knew that the life he was leading was not what God wanted for him and he tried to make amends by doing community work. I acknowledge his contributions. He tried. But ultimately, it wasn't enough. The Lord recognizes faith before works. You can't buy your way into God's favor, you can't haggle, and you can't bribe him. Nothing we can do will please Him unless we first accept Jesus Christ as our Savior. And that's not as easy as it sounds. Truly believing and submitting to Jesus is a lifelong commitment and battle."

"It's about balance. The Lord will spit you out if you don't believe in Him but try to do the right thing. He will also spit you out if you claim that you believe in Him yet there's no difference between your actions and those of the worst sinner. When you're truly a child of God, you don't need to tell anybody so. People will recognize your faith by the good you speak and do. Jesus said, 'If you love Me, keep My commandments.' It's not enough to love and believe in Jesus, you need to do the right thing."

"Some of y'all out here walking a fine line. You know the Truth, the Way, and the Life, but you choose to ignore Him. You choose to do your own thing. Your justifications are so elaborate that you almost believe them. 'What good will it be for a man if he gains the whole world, yet forfeits his soul', Matthew 16:26. Did you hear that Word? Don't be so consumed with the here and now that you forget about the eternal. What could be worth eternal damnation? Money, cars, power, women? That man? Don't be foolish." Again, Tracy twisted her ring around her finger.

"I got a unique bunch of people here. I don't live in the pulpit, I know a few things. I know what some of y'all are into. This may be my one opportunity to minister to you and I won't waste it. I thank God for placing me here right now. Derek Quinn's presence was huge. He was able to touch so many different people, look at all who are here. Derek was a good man who went the wrong way. I thank him for a chance to get to speak with y'all and I pray that the Holy Spirit will make my words come alive in your hearts."

"There is a time to mourn and I would be foolhardy to tell you not to. But let us celebrate Derek's life and the good that it still could bring."

There was a smattering of applause when Pastor left the pulpit, but knowing him, he probably didn't mind. His words had hit their mark. Had she really put X before God? She couldn't remember the last time she had gone to church or had even prayed. She used to reason that the Lord knew her heart, but now she had filled that to the brim with X.

There were a dozen of other speakers—women wailing about how good of a man Derek was and how he didn't deserve to die, activists applauding his charitable donations, business partners reminiscing about his savvy and flair, but Tracy barely heard a word. She was relieved when it was time to go.

Evelyn yanked her aside. "Don't be like me."

"Excuse me?"

She grabbed Tracy's left hand. "You'll be marrying more than just him."

She barely had time to process the words before X grabbed her right hand and led her out. She did look back at Evelyn, she was standing alone, an island in a sea of people.

Everyone else was chatting in the aisles and slowly making their way out of the church. Several people seemed to be waiting for an opportunity to talk to X. "Don't you need to meet and greet some folks?"

"Nah, we have an appointment."

"We do?"

"Yes, at your gynecologist."

The car ride was excruciatingly long. She kept playing back Pastor's and Evelyn's words. If she was pregnant there truly was no turning back. She would forever be closing the door on the life she used to lead and she now knew that also meant closing the door on God. She was ready to be X's wife, but she wasn't ready to have his child. It wouldn't be fair to bring anyone else into this deliciously dangerous life they lived.

How could she have been so careless? What kind of life could they provide for a child? What morals could they really instill? X had grown up with a dad like him and look how he turned out. What about its safety? There were people who wanted to kill or lock X up, what would they want to do to his child?

She felt like she was going to hyperventilate by the time they got to her doctor. How did he even know who her doctor was? Why couldn't they have done a home pregnancy test or why couldn't he have asked her to set up the appointment like a regular person? She shook her head at that thought; there was nothing regular about X.

The waiting room was empty. Dr. Abed was a middle-aged, Egyptian man who didn't overbook. He was thorough and pleasant and today, he seemed even happier than usual. "Tracy, dear, what brings you here today?"

She looked over at X before answering. "We think we're expecting."

Dr. Abed spied her ring, "And congratulations to you both on your engagement. You'll make a beautiful bride. Why don't you go ahead and change into the gown. I will be right back." He closed the door behind him.

"I like that dude." X planted a lingering peck on her lips. "We gotta meet with a wedding planner tomorrow. You probably wanna do this before you start to show right?"

"*If* I start to show, we're here to find out for sure remember?" She pulled the gown over her head.

"I already know for sure."

Dr. Abed returned and guided her feet into the stirrups. "When was your last period?"

X answered for her, "Two months ago."

"Okay, so we're going to do an ultrasound. Most doctors don't start off that way, but I like for everybody to see what's going on. This may feel a bit uncomfortable." He inserted an instrument inside her. She tensed a bit and X smoothed her hair. All three of them turned their attention to the screen. "Okay, so here we can see that the lining of the uterus is thick. That normally indicates a pregnancy." With his free hand the doctor highlighted and clicked on the area. "Oh yes, it is three times the regular width." He moved the instrument around in her. "Ah yes, here is our little bundle of joy." He pointed to a dot on the screen.

This was real, this was really happening. "That little dot?"

"Your last period was two months ago?" He consulted his chart. "Okay, so that would make your due date February 12th."

They all shook hands and the doctor started rambling about precautionary blood work, prenatal vitamins, her next appointment. X eagerly soaked up all of the information as she nodded like a puppet.

There was roaring in her ears. It wasn't that she wasn't happy. It was just so sudden, so permanent. She had never considered being a mother. A wife sure. But a kid? Where was the fun in that? And there was so much going on. She needed time to figure this all out. Figure out how to be with X and not lose herself. They needed to figure out what their next move was going to be, she needed to figure out what was next for her after teaching.

But that little dot had taken all of that away. There would be no more second guessing, no more temporary repentance. She could no longer stick one foot in and take it out. This wasn't the hokey pokey, it was her life. And this life she chose demanded absolute allegiance as did the life she left behind. Her Pastor was right, God had spit her out.

X opened her car door. "I've done some reading on this and you may feel fatigued during the first trimester. Once we get through this week, you'll be able to get all of the rest that you need."

He jinxed her. She dozed off as soon as they got on the thruway and woke up as they pulled up to what looked to be an abandoned farm house. "Where are we?"

"Honeoye."

She followed him along a dirt path that led to the back of the building and a small pond. Twelve dummies were lined up across the field, each three feet part apart from each other. She was incredulous, "You set this up?"

"Not this time. We use this spot a lot though. Niggas always bragging about how much they bust their guns. I'm more concerned with how many times they hit the target. My squad not trying to catch any unnecessary heat for hitting an innocent and when we bust at a nigga, he won't live to testify." He removed a gun from his waistband. "This here is a .25. Hold it."

The gun was slight, but its weight was not lost on her. She ran her hand over it, taking in the sleek design, tracing the grooves that hinted at the weapon's power. What she held in her hands won wars, settled lands, and issued supremacy. Not even the Zulu nation was strong enough to defeat it.

"That's good, don't be afraid of it."

She grinned wickedly, "I'm not." She was in love at first touch. What should she fear as long as she held it? Who would even expect her to know how to use one, to be able to pull the trigger? She knew for certain that she would do so if the time ever came. She was a woman now, a mother, about to be a wife. Nobody would take anything from her ever again.

X nodded. "I didn't think that you would be. The safety is that small latch on the left. First thing you always have to do is push it up. Don't forget that. Remember you're in control, it's a tool in your hands." He eased behind her. "Never pull it out if you're not ready to use it, if you're not ready to kill." He stiffened her arms. "No wobbly indecisive movie shit. Clear head, straight arms." He put his foot in between hers, forcing her to widen her stance. "Stand strong, if you're even at this point the decision has already been made for you." He paused to let her take in the meaning of his words. "Look at where you're shooting, where you want the bullet to go, but you gotta look past that too. It's like chess, you gotta think three moves ahead. Pulling the trigger is just one move." He paused again. "Shoot."

She pulled the trigger, felt the surge of energy as the bullet was propelled forward, heard the shot rang out, saw the impact on the dummy. She had aimed for its head and she didn't miss. She worked her way down the line, considering X's words, determining them to be true. She took her time. She aimed for the heads, for the hearts. She was strengthened by each shot.

19

"I done came up, put my life on the line
Soaked the game up, now it's my time to shine
Time to change up, no more second in line"

-Memphis Bleek

"Coming of Age Da Sequel"

SUMMER. SHE ONLY HAD to proctor her own final and then she was closing the door on the best and worst part of her life. She smiled at her kids. Andre was seated in the first row, twirling a pencil, looking completely at ease. He had morphed in front of her. As she moved about the room, distributing materials, and reassuring students, she watched him.

Tracy knew the truth she saw in Andre's eyes at Unkl Moe's, but she hadn't dealt with it. There are just some things that are so inconceivable that the human mind blocks it out, stores it away for as long as it can. And though Tracy was being hardened, she wasn't immune from that. But the truth was sitting right in front of her now, an unrepressed memory, demanding to be addressed. She couldn't afford to underestimate Andre, and she couldn't afford to avoid the truth.

It was terrifying to speculate about the reason behind his actions. Had he always been this ruthless and in her initial naivety she missed it? How could his sixteen year old ambition be that strong that he would kill Derek? There would be no dissuading him now. He was clearly committed to the path that he was on. Was he working alone? The next thought stole her breath, was he targeting X next? When she looked in his direction again he was staring at her, she didn't look away.

She read the directions and gave a few more encouraging words. She steeled herself, busied her thoughts with the internet, researching pregnancy tips, and thinking about the colors and theme of her ensuing wedding. Periodically, she got up, walked around, and answered questions. She was trying to keep moving, trying to keep thinking about anything other than Andre, other than what she had to do.

The two hours finally passed. "Okay, have a wonderful summer. I will really miss you all. Please be careful."

One by one they hugged her while Andre patiently waited. Even though he finished his test first he was the last student to leave. "What, I don't get a hug?"

She obliged him with a one-armed, church hug. He let his hand linger on her hip before she broke the embrace. She remembered how she had clung to him the day LaShonda had died. Oh, how she had loved that girl. She had loved Andre too. This death would be far worse.

She was engaged to X and carrying his child, she had to love her family first. She had to be smart here. "Do you know what you're doing?" Her voice cracked.

He gestured to her ring hand. "Do you?"

She couldn't let this moment slip away. She owed him enough to try one more time. "Andre, you know I know and that I won't say anything." Had her pregnancy hormones already kicked in? Tears welled up in her eyes. "Call me a hypocrite, but I wanted more for you than this."

He nodded. "I know and I appreciate that *Tracy*, I really do. But this is what I want."

Stalemate. This was it. His youthful hastiness would prove to be deadly. Though he had taken the bishop, he forgot that the queen was still on the board. Her time with X had taught her that patience was what won matches. Andre had shed his too early.

He didn't know that he was dealing with a lioness protecting her cub. He was trying to take away her world, a world that she had sacrificed so much for. He was sixteen, a man as he had told her. He was old enough to know better.

She straightened herself and smiled. "Well, I guess I'll be seeing you then."

She called X, he had to know about Andre right away, but his phone kept going straight to voicemail. She called Thalia, but she didn't answer either. She damn near ran out of the building and sped the entire way towards the Spot. Heads turned as she entered. She ran a hand through her hair and willed herself to calm down. *Think three moves ahead.*

Tyriek stood up as she approached. "It's the first lady."

She waved a hand to dismiss his joking. "Where's X?"

He shrugged. "I thought he was with you. Y'all have a big day to plan right?" He motioned towards her ring.

She smiled weakly. If they even made it to the big day. Oh God, what if X had picked Andre up? Could she trust Tyriek? How much longer could he be content with just being a lieutenant? He might be in on things with Andre. She stalled, "What happened with Fight Club?"

"Uh, I'm not sure if I should be talking to you about this."

Again, she waved a hand to dismiss him. "I'm the first lady, remember?"

He nodded, "Well, this isn't the place."

"You're right, ride with me."

He looked around indecisively. "Maybe we should wait for X."

She stared him down, "Maybe that'll be too late." He begrudgingly followed her. "Give me your keys." She hopped into the driver side of his tinted Maxima. He hesitated for a moment before getting in beside her. She pulled off without saying anything.

She stopped at a corner store. She knew what she had to do, what she would do. "Can you go in there and get me a bottle of water?" He nodded and exited the car.

She took the .25 out of her purse, ran her hands over the cold metal, recalling the lessons that it had already taught her. Tyriek returned shortly. When he slid into the car he was greeted by a pointed gun.

He put his hands up, "What the fuck?"

"Where is Andre?"

"I don't fucking know."

"Where should he be?"

Tyriek looked at her like she had two heads. "Look Tracy, this isn't exactly your scene. You don't know what the fuck you're doing."

She slid the safety up. "You don't know me. Now you can tell me where Andre is or I can kill you right here. You're supposed to be the smart one, what is it going to be?"

"He's off of Jefferson."

She remembered when she had taken X to "work." How he had said he had to straighten someone out and Andre came to school beat up the next day. She hadn't pieced that together before now. Andre hadn't forgotten that beating. Her heart lurched. "I know the place."

When they pulled up in front of the trap she had very specific instructions for Tyriek. "Give me your gun." The weapon he reluctantly handed over was heavier than hers, presumably deadlier. Good. "Tell him one of those Fight Club niggas confessed and it's time for him to put in some work. Have him meet you out back."

Tyriek was skeptical, "And then what?"

Did he always ask these many fucking questions? "And then have him meet you out back." He gave her a disapproving look, but finally got out of the car.

She watched him wait for entrance and then she slid out too. All sins are equal she reminded herself. Killing somebody was no different than lying to Nikols and his idiot partner. The decision had already been made for her. She thought of the Ecclesiastes verse; this was her time to kill.

She wasn't worried about the law. In their town bodies came a dime a dozen and most of them went unsolved. She wouldn't get caught. Their broken down police department wouldn't be dispatching a forensics team over some nobody tatted up kid. The hood might tie the body to X. There might be retaliations, but all of them would be brainless, the responsible party never touched, but somehow the shedding of new blood would ease the ache. And then somebody else would die and the whole process would start again.

Tracy's hands were sweating as she jogged into the vacant lot. There were broken bottles, dirty diapers, condoms, even an entire commode littered about. She waited around the corner of the house with the gun extended. She would start shooting the moment she saw Andre. A long minute passed. There was no slowing down the pace of her heart and no turning back. Tracy's knot twisted stomach reminding her of the life that was growing inside of her. That life needed two parents, would have two parents.

More agonizing seconds passed before finally Tyriek emerged, alone. Fuming, she stepped away from her hiding place and pointed the gun at him. "Are you fucking stupid?"

He shook his head. "He's not in there."

She didn't lower the gun. "Where is he?"

"With X."

She put the gun down, turned, and threw up.

Back in the car, she couldn't stop her hands from shaking or the sweat or the visions that were running through her head. Andre would blindside X. Hopefully, the kill would be quick, the casket could be open.

Her hands stopped shaking, the muscles in her face hardened. How dare she be hurt? How dare she pretend to be shocked? She had known that this very thing could happen the whole time; she had known that it was actually likely to happen. Somehow X's smile and his hands on her body, and his voice in her ear, made her forget that, had made her believe in his invincibility. It had made her a fool.

She had allowed this to happen. She should have told X what she knew about Andre. She hadn't said anything because she couldn't explain it, how could she make such an indictment off of a feeling? But what had X told her? Hadn't he said that he just knew? That he always knew? X had called it a gift. Tracy had saw the killer in Nicole, she had spotted Sean's murderer, and she saw the killer in Andre. How had she known these things? She shared X's gift.

Her nostrils flared, but she stared straight ahead and forced herself to imagine her mornings waking up without X and imagine herself eating alone and going to sleep alone and doing it all over again and again. She did, however, not imagine her belly getting bigger. She would not go through with that. She could not have and raise a child of his. She would get it taken care of.

How could she have thought *they* could have a happy ending? That they could get married, have a child, and walk away? Those endings were for civilians--nice people who cocooned themselves from the world and left the fighting to somebody else. Her sweat began to dry, her skin goosed under the air conditioning. She could feel Tyriek watching her.

"You really think Youngin' is gonna try to kill X?"

She could barely nod.

"So you was gonna merk him?" She nodded again. "Yo, I need a girl like you."

They didn't say another word. She pulled up in front of her car and got out. She tried X again, straight to voice mail. She called Thalia, no answer. End of the road. She tried to think optimistically. Maybe X would detect something, maybe he would kill Andre. Or maybe X was already dead. Where the fuck was Thalia? The walls were back and finally closing in on her. Everything she feared was upon her.

There wasn't anything else to do. Her hands went to her stomach. Oh God. She was hysterically screaming, beating the steering wheel, calling out to God. "Please Lord let him be okay. Oh God."

She screamed and cried until her throat was sore, until her body was weak and she couldn't stand to be in the car anymore. Her mind was reeling with thoughts of X, with prayers for X, with longing for him. She drove to Thalia's, her car was there, but no one answered the door. Out of options, she headed home.

Entering their home was almost too much to bear. It was part of the world that X had given her. The entire place smelled like him, felt like him, pulsated with memories of him. She couldn't sit still so she paced. When she couldn't pace anymore, she cleaned. When she couldn't clean, she paced and finally, she sat down at the kitchen table.

20

"Now I move with aggression,
use my mind as a weapon.
Chances are never given, they're tooken like interceptions"

-Meek Millz

"Ambition"

TRACY WOKE UP TO the sounds of a key in the lock. Her heart raced. The gun was in the other room. She couldn't unfreeze herself from the table, this was it. Someone was punching in the code into the alarm system. Their footsteps were getting closer.

She closed her eyes. She would be with X. They would be a family, just not in this world. Her lips instinctively mouthed a prayer. When she opened her eyes she saw him, X. She leapt from the table and ran to him, almost knocked him over when she jumped into his arms.

"Damn babe, I missed you too. You're hormonal already?"

She held his face in her hands. Kissed him all over, squeezed the life out of him. She hadn't known until today how much she loved him. She hadn't known how much she would do for him. "Where's Andre?"

X laughed. "Yeah, I talked to Tyriek." He raised her hand to his lips and kissed it. "You're a queen. You have my respect, you got my niggas respect. That's not an easy thing for a woman to obtain. Love comes easy. I loved you the first time I saw you. It's different now. We're one. I took care of Youngin', I got eyes too." He kissed her and lowered himself to one knee. He put his head to her belly. "Did you know that your Mommy is a gangster?"

She swatted him. "Get up. I wanna know everything."

"Not here. Let's take a drive."

Tracy reached to grab her purse. Her cell phone rang. It was an automated message. "You have a collect call from the Monroe County jail system. Next, it was a live person, "Thalia Richards." Again, the automation, "In order to accept this call you have to enter your credit or debit card number. You may pay $25, $50, or $100." She hurried for her purse and punched in the numbers. Thalia was frantically talking, "Oh my God, Tracy. Tax evasion, can you fucking believe this shit?"

"I'm putting you on speaker. Okay, go ahead."

"Some faggot feds picked me up at the bank. That asshole cop was with them. X, this shit isn't looking good."

"Be cool, T. You called Levy yet?"

"No, this is the first time they let me use the phone."

"They had you in interrogation this whole time? Did you demand counsel?"

"I'm not a fucking idiot. *Tracy*, I told them I wanted a lawyer. They said okay, they wouldn't ask me anymore questions. But believe they kept me in that cold ass room for hours. That fucking cop kept coming in, said it wasn't an interrogation because he was doing the talking, said they have surveillance of the whole operation, under covers, people in the crew ready to testify--"

X interrupted, "Thalia, you know that's bullshit."

"Didn't I just tell you that I'm not a fucking idiot! You think I don't know this fucking call is being recorded? Tracy, I called you. Take me off of speaker."

Tracy looked to X for his permission. His nod was curt. "Okay T, it's just me and you talking."

"Okay, call Levy, get him on this."

"Of course. You need anything else?"

Her voice quivered, "Tell your fucking fiancé to let it be known who I am. I might be here for a while."

"Thalia, everyone knows who you are, no one will touch you. We're gonna get you home."

"Hurry up." The line went dead.

Nikols was on her heels as she walked to the parking lot from the lawyer's office. His leer was even more oppressive than normal. "How's your friend holding up? You'll be joining her shortly. It'll be like old times, like a sorority meeting. But instead of helping the kiddies, it'll just be a bunch of burly bitches munching on each other. Don't worry, they'll love you. You ever been fucked with a pipe?" Tracy didn't lose stride. *Three moves ahead.*

She was extremely worried about Thalia though. They never knew who or what they would lose to the game. Just yesterday, she thought her fiancé and father of her child was dead. Instead, she lost someone who used to be like a son to her, a little brother. She couldn't lose Thalia too. She had already been in jail for thirty-six hours and Levy said bail wasn't a sure thing. Even the mighty Thalia couldn't withstand this kind of pressure. When they spoke on the phone last, she sounded exhausted; like she had finally been tamed.

Tracy was tired too. All she wanted was time to plan her wedding and sleep. That would happen soon enough though. She was going to make it happen. She pulled into the back of Scouts and entered through the employee entrance.

Tyrone, X's cousin, was talking to two dancers when she entered. He stopped in mid conversation. "X with you?"

"No, where's Star."

He pointed her to the makeshift dressing room. Foot lockers marked stations that divided up the counter space and mirrored walls. Each station was a reflection of the occupant's taste. Some had flowers and balloons, others perfume and liquor bottles, others still with small Bibles and pictures of children. Five dancers milled around the room. They chatted with each other while they did their lashes, stuck bobby pins into weave ponytails, and smattered make up on their faces.

Star sat alone at her station in front of a bouquet of wilted roses. She sipped Hennessy from the bottle and watched Tracy in the mirror. There was a hostile recognition on her face.

Tracy pulled her wallet out as she walked into the center of the room. She used her teacher's voice when she spoke, "Ladies, Star and I need to speak privately."

A girl with a jaguar tattooed along the length of her arm turned around in her station. "I don't give a fuck. I'm not done getting dressed."

Tracy nodded and walked up to the girl. She placed a hundred dollar bill in front of her and leaned so only she would hear her words. "Get the fuck out."

The girl whirled around in her seat. Tracy stared back at her. She got up, brushed past Tracy and sashayed out. Tracy addressed the other women. "Now ladies if you will be so kind to follow your colleague, you'll receive the same compensation."

She was met with blank stares. Star sighed. "If y'all leave she will pay you too." The room cleared out quickly. Tracy handed each girl a bill when they filed past her. Star continued to stare at Tracy's reflection. "So you think you can buy everyone, huh?"

"I just know that everyone has a price."

Star nodded as she beat her pack of Newports. She selected one, eased it seductively into her mouth, lit it, and took a long drag. Her eyes were closed as she exhaled. "You liked what you saw last time."

"Most of it."

"Hmm. Got a jealous streak?"

"No, just an intolerance for disrespect."

Star nodded again. "But tossing money at someone isn't disrespectful?"

"Money makes a point."

Star turned around and blew smoke in her face. "Who's making the point now?"

Tracy took a breath before she spoke. "You're good at what you do, but not because of your body or the way you shake your ass. You're good because you know men and you know how to work them."

Star nodded. "What, you need help working yours?"

She used her ring hand to flip her hair. "Obviously not. But I do need help with something else."

*   *   *

Tracy watched Star appraise herself in the Macy's fitting room mirror. The low cut, peach colored dress she wore hugged her curves, but stopped modestly above her knees. She looked at herself from all angles. "I don't like it."

"It looks good on you."

"I look like an old lady."

"You don't look like a stripper."

Star spun around. "I don't have a problem with looking like or being a stripper."

"Is that all that you want?"

"What else is there?"

"More."

They found six dresses that Star liked, three pairs of jeans, eight tops, and four pairs of shoes. Tracy picked out tasteful accessories for her and a subtle perfume. She took her to a Black owned make up salon. The make-up artist did phenomenal work, revealing Star's innocent beauty. She couldn't have been more than nineteen.

Star's eyes darted around in Pluto. "I'm supposed to be impressed?"

"No, you're supposed to enjoy." Tracy held Star's gaze. She needed this girl's help, but Star needed to realize that she needed Tracy. She remembered what X told her when he took her to Jefferson—an employee had to see value in their work. "So Star, what do you want out of life?"

"I already have it."

"That's bullshit."

She clenched her jaw. "Okay, I want to act. Like I want to be a big time actress."

"What's stopping you?"

Star faltered. That wasn't the question she was expecting. "It's not that easy."

Tracy sipped her water. It was crucial that she control the pace of this conversation. She had to reel Star in slowly, but she also didn't have a lot of time. "How so?"

"Because I have a fucking daughter, and a life here, but somebody like you wouldn't understand that."

Tracy leaned in closer. "Lower your voice."

"Why? Am I embarrassing you?" She snorted.

"No, you embarrass yourself. A woman, a lady, is in control of the attention she gets. When people look at her, they see what she wants them to see. That's lesson one Miss Actress."

"Whatever."

She was like one of Tracy's students, defiant with no purpose, angry with no target, too indignant to seize an opportunity. Tracy knew how to handle that. "So, explain to me exactly how your daughter stops you from being an actress?"

Star bit her lip. "Movies are made in California. I gotta make sure that there is always a roof over my daughter's head, food in her stomach, a safe place for her to sleep. I can't just be trekking across the country."

"You're practical. That's good. I could help you with all of that."

"Why?"

"Look at your menu."

A cheery, tanned, blonde waiter came to take their order. Tracy smiled up at him. "I will take the snapper."

Star's tone was dismissive. "Give me the chicken."

"Thank you." Tracy smiled and handed him their menus. She waited until he wasn't in earshot. "Why did you talk to him like that?"

"Why wouldn't I?"

"It's not lady like for starters."

"I don't give a fuck about being no lady."

"How many ignorant, Black stripper bitches do you see in movies? Haven't you ever learned something other than how to get a dick hard? Excuse me."

Star looked remorseful when Tracy returned from the restroom. "So when are you going to tell me why we're here?"

"I will tell you why when you're ready to hear."

*　　*　　*

Later that evening, she barely touched her dinner. X reached across the table to hold her hand. "Baby, you have to eat."

"I haven't had an appetite."

"You need to keep your strength up."

"I know, the next crisis might be right around the corner." She brushed away tears. She felt responsible for Thalia being in jail. She had introduced her to this lifestyle. She should have known that Thalia would jump right in; her friend never did anything halfway.

"You're right. There will always be a crisis. There will always be somebody dead, or in jail, or stealing, or trying to take my spot, or snitching. But there will always be us and we will always handle it. Don't you feel His hedge of protection?"

"This is protected? Derek is dead. You were about to be next. Thalia is in jail. Thalia! This isn't some fucking pawn, she's my best friend!" She exhaled. "She's supposed to be my maid of honor and our child's godmother."

He leaned back in his seat and watched her for a while. "So, we'll do whatever we can to help her."

*　　*　　*

Tracy sat behind the defendant's table at the bail hearing next to Irv Levy. Since the raid, Tracy had learned that he was the best criminal defense attorney in the area. Levy, though in his forties, had a well maintained body and a thick mane of hair which men decades his junior envied. His grey eyes were sharp and probing, his clothes impeccable. He was a shark who built a fortune on handling high profile drug cases and murders. X had always made it very clear that he was not to be trusted.

"Don't get your hopes up. There's a strong likelihood that bail will be denied." His lips barely moved when he spoke.

Tracy studied him before speaking. "She has no criminal record. This should just be some white collar misdemeanor crime. Shouldn't she get a slap on the wrist?"

"Only she's being charged with conspiracy to defraud the government, not shareholders, and she doesn't have a resemblance to any Wall Street bandits. This is really about the federal attorney trying to get a high level drug bust. But Derek died and she doesn't know when to pull her pants up."

A bailiff led Thalia into the courtroom. She wore a pinstriped blouse, a black, high-waisted pencil skirt, and red pumps. She looked composed and collected. She looked like herself. She nodded in Tracy's direction and whispered to Levy.

The federal attorney, a disheveled red head, was speaking. "Your honor the state requests that the defendant, Thalia Richards, be held with no bail. Miss Richards is just one suspect in a sprawling criminal enterprise and her connections make her a flight risk. The state believes that Miss Richard's detainment will lead to the arrest and conviction of several refuted drug dealers."

Levy was adamant. "Your honor, Miss Richards has no criminal or arrest record nor does she have any connections to whatever fictitious criminal enterprise the state is referring to. What Miss Richards does in fact have are connections to this community, and has served it through charitable work and donations for years. She is not a flight risk because the state does not have a case. This is nothing more than a fishing expedition, witch hunt, and classic example of unlawful arrest and false imprisonment."

The judge, raspy voiced and white haired, banged his gavel. "That's enough, Mr. Levy. I'm sure your office will file a complaint with the proper authorities. As far as bail is concerned, this pretty, little lady doesn't look like she's going anywhere--"

"Your honor, Miss Richard's detainment is paramount in our case--"

The judge laughed. "I suggest you build a stronger one then. Bail is set at forty thousand dollars."

Tracy could hear Levy's smirk. "We will post today."

Thalia broke Tracy's embrace. There was something different about her, something forlorn. Tracy tried to smile big enough for the both of them. "Okay, so you're a free woman. I'm sure you're dying for a good meal."

"I'm not free, I'm just home for now."

"You're not free yet", Levy interjected. "Their case is paper thin."

Thalia turned to him "Yeah? And how many billable hours is it going to take for you to shred it?"

Levy laughed. "Thalia, always so distrustful. I'm actually going to refer you to a tax attorney for this one. I'm sure X will provide me with plenty of billable hours." He exited the courtroom.

Tracy and Thalia shared a moment of uncomfortable silence. What had initially seemed like a victory, now looked like a momentary cease fire. Tracy studied her friend. "What aren't you telling me?"

Thalia's smile was sad. "Nothing that you need to know." She left Tracy standing there.

*   *   *

At Scout's, Star worked the stage with a fine tuned showmanship that Tracy hoped would prove to be handy. This girl loved an audience. On stage she wasn't ashamed or tawdry, she was alive. Her eye contact was direct and seductive. The command she had over her body was impressive. There wasn't a soul in there that didn't want her.

She sat down with Tracy after her set. "Do you enjoy dancing?"

Star picked up Tracy's drink and downed it. She scrunched her face up once she realized it was just cranberry juice. "What are you a Mormon?"

"Answer the question."

"Do I enjoy it? I mean, every bitch in here got some horror story about dancing. It can be dangerous, but so far so good for me. But do I like ugly, funky, old men touching on me? Of course not. But I do like the feeling dancing gives me. On this stage, I'm the star. When I dance, all eyes are on me, all eyes. And the money's not bad."

"Has a man ever turned you down?"

Star looked down. "Just yours." Her smile was genuine when she looked back at Tracy, "And I wondered why, but then I met you. X is no dummy."

*   *   *

Thalia had been home for a week, but Tracy hadn't seen her since the bail hearing. X mused that she probably wanted to distance herself from the 'criminal enterprise'. But Tracy knew Thalia and she knew there was something else going on.

Thalia had developed a highly sophisticated money laundering system. The cash was filtered through legitimate businesses, campaign contributions, charitable donations, and transferred to offshore accounts. What couldn't be cleaned immediately was buried. On the books, X was a successful entrepreneur who owned real estate, hair salons, day cares, dry cleaners, printers, and restaurants. He paid taxes on all of his declared income. Derek hadn't.

Thalia must have advised him to give Uncle Sam his cut. She was nothing if not thorough. How could she have been sloppy enough to get herself tangled up in Derek's shit? Something wasn't right.

Though her supposed best friend hadn't answered or returned her calls, she doubted she would leave her standing on her steps. Thalia answered the door wearing a beautiful ankle length hunter green dress. Her long hair was spiral curled, her make-up impeccable. She didn't look like a woman who was waiting for the other shoe to drop.

"I don't want to hear it. Grab your keys, you're coming with me."

"Tracy--"

"I don't want to fucking hear it. Get your shit and come on." Thalia didn't issue another protest.

Tracy sped down the parkway. The two lane road took them away from the city and into a wooded area, but the surroundings weren't enough to quell the anger building in her. She didn't quite understand it, couldn't touch it yet. She needed to figure out what she was missing. Fortunately, Thalia was silent until they reached the beach.

"Wow, this is romantic." Thalia said.

"It's secluded."

Tracy led the way along a path that meandered through the oak trees before finally ending at the shore. The ground was riddled with logs and pebbles. Gulls cried above them, the surf crashed into the sand. In the distance, families laughed as they chased after naughty dogs. Lovers strolled past them, hand and hand. It was really a beautiful place and she hoped that its serenity would guide the conversation. She missed talking to her friend. They stopped and sat at a boulder, facing out to the lake.

Tracy broke the silence. "Levy said you haven't contacted the lawyer he referred you to."

"I contacted my own."

"So how much did you take?"

Thalia visibly flinched. She turned and faced her. "It's not too late for both of us to just walk away from all of this. I know you love him and he loves you, but Trace, is it worth it? We didn't really know what we were getting into."

Tracy shook her head sadly. "I can't leave him and I never will, godmommy."

"You're--"

"Yep. Now tell me, how much did you steal?"

"Does X know about this?"

"Do you think you would still be breathing if he knew?"

Thalia bit her lip. "Tracy, you have no idea how much they're bringing in. It's at least a million a week. Cash. Derek didn't know what the fuck to do with all of that. He wouldn't ask X, always had to keep Junior at bay. You know, he was really scared of him. He said there was no telling what a nigga that smart would do. Why do you think he brought me in so quickly? He hired me that night at the banquet. He was desperate. So while I was setting up accounts, I set up a little one for myself. I deserved it and it wasn't like he would ever miss it."

"Why didn't you pay the back taxes?"

"I loved him." She shrugged and tried to look away before Tracy noticed the tears in her eyes.

"And?"

"And he's not like X. He rather run around with whores than be with me."

"So you set him up?"

"He gave me herpes." Thalia wiped the tears that had spilled down her cheeks. "I have to live with that for the rest of my life. I figured he could live with five to seven years."

Tracy sighed. "So what happens now? Did you figure that part out?"

"I will take a plea bargain. I can't have anyone taking too close of a look at the financial records. At least I'll be rich when I get out. I'm never working for another man again."

Tracy picked up a rock; it was light in her hand, smooth and cool to the touch. She tossed it up and down, considering its weight, considering Thalia's words. She stood up and hurled it into the lake. It barely made a splash. She turned away and walked back towards her car.

* * *

She met Star at Shooters. The younger woman looked effortlessly pretty in a lavender-colored maxi dress. Unfortunately, she had returned to her stage make up and weave. Tracy didn't return her smile. She wasn't too keen on female interaction at the moment. Star searched her face, "What's wrong?"

"What's right?"

Star looked worried. "Do you still need my help?"

"I still want your help." She looked around the bar. There was an older man dressed in his bus driver uniform. He looked like he had the weight of the world on his shoulders. "I'm going to the ladies room. Have that bus driver over there buy you a drink."

When she returned, Star was sulking. The glass in front of her remained empty. "What happened?"

"I went over there and asked that fat fuck to buy me a drink. He said I should be doing the buying."

Tracy chuckled. "Star, why would a woman like you have to ask a man like that to buy her a drink?"

"But you said…"

"I said to have him buy you a drink, not to ask for one. Don't you know by now that most men are scared of beautiful women? So a young, good looking woman comes up to him and asks for a drink, he immediately thinks you're a prostitute, lost a bet, or trying to empty his pockets."

"In order to get anything out of a man you have to make him think it's his idea. He has to feel like he can't take the risk of never seeing you again. You have to touch something in him."

"How do you do all of that?"

"Just get him to look at you." Tracy made a sweeping gesture with her arm that sent Star's glass crashing to the floor. She put her hands to her mouth.

Joe was smiling when he approached them. "Is my favorite little lady having a temper tantrum?"

She lowered her hands and smiled apologetically. "Joe, I'm so sorry about the mess."

"Don't worry about it." He winked.

The bus driver had been watching the exchange. "Next round's on me," he mumbled.

Tracy nudged Star and whispered to her, "Say thank you."

Star smiled over at him, "Thank you." His lips almost formed a smile in response.

Star turned towards her with a newfound respect. "How do you know how to do that?"

"What kind of men do you date?"

She shrugged, "You know, the typical guys around here. Party promoters, wanna be rappers, hustlers."

"Do they treat you right?"

"One of 'em, the party promoter, brought me roses to the club," she smiled.

Tracy thought of Jason. "That's a simple trick. You could get more. You want a man, a real one, one that takes the time to determine that you're right for him. One that is just as concerned with how you act as he is with how you look. Weed the little boys out quickly."

"So how do I get a real man?"

"All you have to do is get him to look at you. But when he does, you want him to see somebody he can build a life with, someone who will help him reach his goals." She studied her. "Less make-up, classier clothes. A real man wants a woman that looks good, but he doesn't want everybody to wanna fuck her. That only causes problems." She reached out and touched Star's hair. "Decent weave, but you gotta get rid of it. We need you to look like the girl next door. Why did you put those lashes back on?"

"Umm, hello, it's like a part of my uniform."

"Right, you have to look like a porn star." Tracy discretely placed a stack in Star's purse. "Take the next two weeks off, Tyrone won't mind. Get your real hair cut in a cute style. I will see you tomorrow."

Tracy crossed the bus driver on her way out. Star beamed when he sat down next to her.

*　　*　　*

X was waiting for her in the living room when she got home. He looked displeased. "Tracy, you're supposed to be resting."

She dropped to her knees in front of him. He didn't stop her when she unzipped his pants. She looked up at him, "Is that the only thing I'm supposed to do?"

21

"The love is unconditional.
Even when the condition is critical,
and the livin' is miserable
Your position is pivotal, I ain't bullshittin' you."

Talib Kweli

"Get By"

STAR DAMN NEAR BOUNCED over to Tracy's table after she finished her set. "So I went in there, to that bar and sat down. My heart was beating so fast, I don't even get nervous when I dance. So I'm racking my mind, trying to figure out a way to get him to look at me. Of course, they all looked at me when I walked in, wasn't no other Black people in there, but I needed him to *really* look at me. So I went to the jukebox and put on Destiny's Child." She laughed. "Everybody looked at me then."

"So he comes over and asks me what I'm drinking. I ordered a beer and he started talking to me about the game, Yankees and Cubs. I did like you said, asked him questions to get him to talk more. I asked about the players, if there was a rivalry, if he ever caught a fly ball." She smiled, "I had him thinking I know about baseball."

"I noticed that he wasn't drinking. He said he doesn't anymore, it always got him in trouble. So then I told him men always get me in trouble. He asked how so. I told him about how my daughter's father used to smack me around in front of his friends; now that's somebody who loved to put on a show. Of course it was curtains for him the day I stabbed him and barely missed his lung. Dude looked at me strange, but said he could respect it."

She lowered her voice and glanced around. The jaguar girl was on stage. A few men watched her, some were engrossed in a game of pool, and others solicited girls in the crowd. Jaguar just didn't have Star's presence. Even as she talked, several men anxiously waited for her to get up from the table. Oblivious or relishing the attention, Star pushed her new auburn weave off of her face and downed her drink before she continued. "So we went to the grocery store..." She saw the alarm on Tracy's face. "Don't worry, we were in his car and he went in alone. He bought some sparkling grape juice so we could toast each other, you know because he doesn't drink. We went to the hotel and I put that stuff in his glass when he went to the bathroom."

Her face clouded and she looked down, played with her bracelets while she finished the rest of the story. "But it didn't take right away. And he kept telling me how pretty I am and how he couldn't wait to touch me. I didn't know what to do, I had to kill time, and it wasn't like I could leave. We were in the middle of it when he passed out."

Tracy interrupted. "Why didn't you just dance for him?"

"That's the one thing I didn't think to do."

Tracy digested Star's words. She had changed since the day she first saw her. Her outward appearance was the same, but there was something new burning inside of her. She reminded Tracy of herself, of the quick transformation her time with X had inspired. So everything else went as planned?"

Star met Tracy's gaze. When she smiled, for a split second, Tracy saw LaShonda. So young, so vibrant, so eager to please. "Yes ma'am."

*   *   *

X shook her awake. "Baby, baby, you gotta hear this."

She needed sleep. The bed was her addiction these days. It took more of his urging before she sat up. "What?"

He pointed to the television. The news was on. Half a dozen reporters hurled questions at a handcuffed Nikols. His head was down as two other cops walked him through the crowd.

"Detective Nikols, how much money was found inside?"

"How long have you been addicted to methamphetamine?"

"Where did all of the cash come from?"

"Is it true that you've been robbing low level drug dealers?"

Tracy rolled over. X rubbed her back. "Can you believe that shit?"

"Yeah I can believe it. Someone had to put him down."

"You--"

She laughed. "I'm all in baby. Just one year and eight months left, right?"

Epilogue

ANYBODY ENTERING WINSFIELD FEDERAL Prison, for any reason, was made to feel like an inmate. The guards had no knowledge of or use for pleasantries. If you weren't one of them, you were a threat. In order to see your loved ones, you too had to go behind bars and be subjected to the same treatment as them. You were guilty by association.

The guards' speech was punctuated with curse words and accented by the spit that flew out of their mouths. Tracy spied a few visitors in front of her discretely wiping the places where it landed. The visitors were searched, warned, and degraded. Once through the visitor's gauntlet, the correction officers breathed down on them like a prison breakout was imminent. Maybe once upon a time she would have tried to bust Thalia out, she had loved her that much.

Six months had passed since their conversation on the beach. Thalia's theft wasn't the troubling thing, it was the secrets that she kept. How could Tracy trust her?

A Latina officer pointed her towards the third visiting booth. Seeing Thalia, even through the plexi glass, induced a flood of emotions. She looked young and vulnerable in the standard orange jumpsuit. Her hair was pulled back into a ponytail; she wore no make-up or earrings. Tracy cleared her throat to settle the emotions that threatened to spill over. She stared at her one-time friend for a long time before she was able to pick up the phone.

Thalia spoke first, "You're the first visitor I've gotten."

"Your family doesn't know you're here?"

"Which family should I invite?"

"What?"

A solitary tear ran down Thalia's cheek. She didn't bother to wipe it away. "My dad was killed when I was two, the state took me from my mother a couple of years after that. Bounced around foster homes until I was eight. By then I learned how to play the game, smile real pretty, say the right things. I got adopted by some good people. Huxtable type niggas—rich, educated, well meaning. They gave me everything, but they never really understood me, no one really knew the real me. Something about Derek felt like home."

Tracy nodded. No wonder Thalia was always so secretive, guarded. Looking at her, Tracy remembered the old days, the days of the sorority meetings, the banquets, all of the times they spent laughing and encouraging each other. Their trip to New York, Miami, the dinners with X and Derek. They had been like sisters and family loves unconditionally. Things were different, they were different. Still, they shared a bond that they would not, could not find in another person.

"You will be home before you know it."

Thalia smiled. "So how's the new mommy?"

Tracy faltered. How was she? It was like one day she blinked and her entire life was different. She had everything. She had nothing. And soon, she would have a child. "I think it's a boy."

Disclaimer

ALWAYS WANT MORE is fiction. All events and occurrences are a reflection of my imagination which is colored by the way I've experienced the world. Any resemblance to actual people and events is coincidental and is not meant to inflame or disrespect. The inclusion of Cam'ron, Common, Busta Rhymes, Ashton Kutcher, Just Blaze, Drake, Nas, Nicki Minaj, Kanye West, and 2 Chainz was an artistic decision to help readers accept Tracy as an authority on hip-hop. None of the events regarding Cam'ron, Common, Busta Rhymes, Ashton Kutcher, Just Blaze, Drake, Nas, Nicki Minaj, Kanye West, and 2 Chainz actually took place. If you sue me, you must be broke. Or you're the Illuminati.

Acknowledgments

THANK YOU LORD FOR protecting my dream and keeping me steadfast. Thank You for all that is to come and I ask that You keep Your hand on me all the days of my life. Above all else, I thank you for Jesus Christ and my salvation and all of the things that are possible because great is He that is in me. Being this passionate about my people is a double-edged sword. Thank You Lord for the man that handles all of those emotions.

Thank you baby for inspiring this story, thank you for giving me the push to start. Thank you for being there throughout the tears and tantrums and moments of doubt.

God thank You for the family that made me a writer. Thanks Ma and Aunt Vera for never censoring what I read. Thanks Dad for never accepting mediocrity. Thank You Erica and Annah for being the best sisters anyone could ever ask for, y'all have been a part of this since day one. Keith, thank you for showing me what it means to surrender a dream to God's will. Thank you to the McCullough&Edwards family, we support like no other, with a special thanks to Antoine for giving me that fresh young perspective.

Thank you to the beautiful women who read the rough, rough, rough draft of this book. Your enthusiasm is what got me here. Erica, Annah, Kanika, Kate, Candace, Mommy, Brandi, Idonia, Jeanine, Charisse, Little Vera, Aunt Tynise, Komeika, and Tonya.

Thank you to my editors Jen Howard and Kate Gilmore. Your input was crucial.

Thank you to my circles that put me in this position. Thank you to my Church of Love Family, past and present. Thank you to the University of Virginia. Thank you to the Theta Kappa Chapter of Alpha Kappa Alpha Sorority, Incorporated. A special thanks to Manifest Destiny. I wouldn't be who I am without you.

Thank you to everyone who prays for this project, shared the link, contributed money. I am SO grateful to have all of you in agreement for the success of this book. WE are going to be a New York Times bestseller. Thank you to Kickstarter and to every single one of my donors: Harry Roldan, Kecia McCullough, Grandma Barbara Edwards, Uncle Deji Awopetu, Sharon Taylor, Jeanine Flournoy, Ivo& Donetta Tchoroleev, Erica Jackson, Julieannah Awopetu, Keith Booker, Ciandress Jackson, Seyi Oseni, Robert Rodgers, Kofi O. Boakye, Brandi Collins, Justin Bray, Vera Graham, Brian M, Domari Dickinson Lewis, Kanika Wright, Lauren Haskin, Lauren Morelle, Theresa Cunningham, Mia Worth, LaVon Dyer, Martin W. Smith, Janelle Armstrong-Brown, Janet Osho, Ebony Callands, Kamaria Burns, Nyibe Smith, Vera Richardson, Victoria Lynch, Faith Jones, Leigh-Ann Webb, Ewunike Aminata, Traci Branch, Alicia Lewis, Stephanie Nicole. Amanda Whitfield, Tamika Griffin, Angelique Lynch, Ashley Owens, Danielle Buford, Jasmine Adams, Gatumbi Gathuka, Jessica Calloway, Olivia West, Sharisse Barksdale, Joyelle Proctor, Raina Bouphavong.

Thank you to the city of Rochester, New York. You made me and I am going to do everything in my power to bring attention to what's happening here. Thank you to the students of the Rochester City School District, being in your presence made me a better person. You deserve a quality education; I'm fighting to bring that home.

Thank you to all of the writers whose work has colored my world—way too many to name. But I must single out Pearl Cleage, BeBe Moore Campbell, Chimamanda Ngozi Adichie, Isabel Wilkerson, Sistah Souljah, and Michelle Alexander whose recent work deepened my perspective.

About the Author

ALWAYS WANT MORE IS my first novel. Like Tracy, I was an English teacher in the Rochester City School District before moving on to Monroe Community College. I have often found the line between my classroom and the streets to be nonexistent. I obtained my Bachelors of Arts in Drama and African-American Studies from the University of Virginia and Masters of Education from Roberts Wesleyan. My literary style has most been influenced by hip-hop music and classic Black literature. I live in Rochester, New York with my husband.

CPSIA information can be obtained
at www.ICGtesting.com
Printed in the USA
FFOW04n1950290515
13803FF